Team Tomás

A Saints team novel

By Ally Adams

Atlas Productions

For the WAGs

And to Jenny, the best, best friend ever.

Books by Ally Adams

The Saints Team series:

Team Lucas

Team Tomás

Team Niklas

Team Alex

'I want to open my eyes to see Tomás's dark chocolate eyes looking at me and if it is just the one night, then I'll live with that too.'

Chapter 1

Open your eyes... no, no wait. Okay, deep breath, ready... almost. I might have had a bit too much to drink last night, fine then I was drunk, but so was Tomás, I think. Actually, I can't be sure about that either because Tomás Carrera – the gorgeous goalkeeper for the Santa Ana Saints soccer team – has a lot more experience than me at having a drink or ten. And now I was lying in a room that definitely wasn't mine; in a bed with someone next to me; and, it was time to turn and face the music. On the upside, at least I was still wearing my underwear.

God, please let it be Tomás next to me – I'll go to church every Sunday for a month, honest. Good grief, now I was attempting to bribe God... I had sunk to a whole new low. It was the hangover or at least I think I had a hangover... can you get a hangover from four or five margaritas? I wasn't a big drinker and I had never really been shit-faced drunk so a hangover would be a first.

I consoled myself that it had been a night of firsts, but I kept one of the firsts for another time. Damn it. I took a shallow breath so I didn't wake the person next to me. *Just get it over with.*

I rolled over slowly and... *what the hell?*

Beside me were three pillows propped up to run the length of the bed. Was that supposed to be like one of those fake pillow guys? I quickly glanced at the first pillow, nope, no face printed on it. I'd been spooned by a pillow! It actually wasn't bad, I made a mental note to get one.

So, I was in a room, which was definitely a guy's room – no self-respecting girl would mix stripes with a pattern. The bed was huge, king-size with a big four-poster bed frame around it. I saw my red dress hanging over a chair. Did I take it off? Seriously, that's it, I'm never drinking cocktails again, ever, I decided. Not more than two anyway.

I rose, quickly dressed, turned to the mirror and patted down my hair. The good thing about having wavy hair is that you can't always see my cowlick that sticks up in the morning. It was now on some weird angle protruding perpendicular to my head. *Whatever.* Bag... I saw it beside the bed and grabbed it. I reached in for my phone. There was a message from my best friend Mia; sent about thirty minutes ago.

'Going for a run, call me when you can. Was a great night! Mx'

Huh, I scoffed. Clearly she didn't help finish the pitcher of margaritas. I brightened – *I'm glad we had a good night.* I started my deep breathing, motivational talk again and elected to face the music. I picked up my strappy sandals, opened the bedroom door and peered out. Wow, nice place, really nice. I hadn't been to Tomás's place before but I was guessing that's where I was – Mia wouldn't have let me go home with anyone else and this place definitely had a South American influence: exposed timber ceiling, wrought iron railings, lots of earthy tones, white-colored walls and terracotta tile flooring. *Looks like a woman had a hand in the choice of rugs and cushions in bright red and yellow... hmm.*

I wandered down the hallway, listening carefully, but the place was pretty quiet. I found the living area and then the kitchen.

'Hi... you must be Alice?'

I jumped a foot high in fright as a woman's voice greeted me. She stepped out from behind the cupboard with a spoon in her hand and an apron on.

'Sorry, did I scare you?' she asked, with a smile.

I clutched my heart. 'Only a little.'

She laughed a big wholesome laugh.

'I'm Valentina, Tomás's sister. I live downstairs but we share the kitchen.' Even though she looked younger than me, she was all woman; tall, full-bodied with dark flowing hair and deep brown eyes. I stood about a foot shorter and maybe three cup sizes smaller – I felt like a kid next to her.

She continued, 'Tomás has gone to training, but he said for you to stay as long as you like. Tea?'

'Yes please,' I said, feeling only a little embarrassed that I was the morning leftover.

She studied me and smiled. 'Sit, please.' Valentina motioned to a chair beside the kitchen island. 'I heard it was an enjoyable night.'

'Did you hear anything about me?' I asked hesitantly.

She smiled. 'No, but Tomás mentioned this morning that you were sleeping in. He slept in the guest room,' she added.

I closed my eyes for a second and breathed a sigh of relief. When I opened them, Valentina gave me a smile that said 'been there, done that'. *The guest room.* Right, so I didn't spend the night with Tomás, just the night in Tomás's bed. I shook my head as she raised a spoonful of sugar above a teacup.

'Don't worry, nothing happened and I tucked you in with the pillows just to make sure you were warm enough,' she said, reading my mind.

I think I went three shades of red. 'Thank you,' I said. 'I don't usually get drunk.'

She put up her hand to silence me. 'I'm no saint in that department; you don't owe me an explanation.' She filled the teapot with boiling water.

I grinned. 'I appreciate that,' I said, 'but I really am a two-glass screamer. I don't know what came over me – a pitcher of margaritas I think.' I sighed.

Valentina laughed again.

I was secretly relieved that Tomás and I didn't do *it*. If and when I slept with Tomás Carrera, I wanted to be completely sober and remember every single glorious moment of it.

Chapter 2

The day before... and how I ended up in Tomás's bed

The *Shaken Not Stirred* bar was crowded with Saints' players, WAGS (the wives and girlfriends), playing staff and its usual crowd. My best friend Mia was officially a WAG now that she was going out with the Saints' captain, Lucas Ainswright – the very same Lucas who was on the other side of the room from us and watching her like a stalker. So intense that guy, and so cute.

I had a foot in both camps tonight... my college friends were here, plus I was sort of with the team if being a WAG equals one kiss, two dances and a major crush on goalie Tomás Carrera. Mia calls it a WRAG – a wife, girlfriend and ring-ins.

The Saints' post-game parties were always pumping especially when they won and the object of my desire, lust and dreams, Tomás, played a major part in this week's win. All the social media was tweeting that he was going to be the name to watch. Oh, and I was watching my potential Latin-lover with the warm golden skin, dark bedroom eyes

5

and full lips as though I was his biggest fan, who just so happened to want to tear his clothes off and kiss every inch of that golden skin.

Where was I? Oh yeah, he had a great game... that boot of his and the foot in it worked some magic. He prevented the opposition from scoring with great style. Being just short of six-foot, he covered a lot of ground with his athletic, nimble body. I fanned myself thinking of him. And given most professional goalkeepers don't hit their prime until they are into their thirties – according to my dad – the media was pumping Tomás up for a big future.

Mia arrived back at our table with a jug of margaritas – bad news. She filled my glass, then Cassie and Melissa's. Caleb, the thorn amongst us roses, held up his beer, opting out.

'Lucas is watching you like a lion watching his prey,' I said to her over the loud music.

She glanced towards him, their eyes locked and his face softened. They had it bad. I looked for Tomás and had lost sight of him. I heard a loud cheer and turned to see the game being replayed on the screen. Lucas and Tomás were heroes at different ends of the ground… Lucas kicked them in, Tomás kept the opposition from doing the same. It would be kind of weird if Mia and I were dating them – like dating two bookends, weird in a good way that is.

'Where's Tomás?' Mia asked bringing me back to earth.

I shrugged.

'What's the story with you two?' she asked.

I noticed Melissa and Cassie moved in closer to hear my answer.

'I hate to say it but… I just don't think he's that into me.'

Mia bit her lip and didn't respond. I wonder if she knew something I didn't, but wasn't telling me to protect me. Why did I have to fall for someone who every girl wants to be with? Why couldn't I fall for the barman or D.J., which only every second girl wants to score with?

Cassie sighed. 'Story of my life. I'm always in love with someone who is not into me, and never in love with the ones who want me. Seriously, what's wrong with me?'

'The same thing that's wrong with Alice, clearly,' Melissa contributed. *Big help.*

I looked at Cassie with her beautiful glossy red hair and ice pale blue eyes and doubted that any guy would fail to notice her; then again, Cassie, Melissa and I were all single.

'Right then, tell us the story from the top,' Cassie said. 'We need to be the judge of this for ourselves.'

I took a deep breath. 'I met him at the pre-season party at Lucas's place and he danced with me a few times and said we should hang together sometime.'

'Then,' Mia interrupted, 'at training a week later he asked after Alice again.'

'But didn't ask for my phone number,' I reminded her. 'Then he saw me again here after their last game, got my number, and said the same thing again…'

'We should hang together sometime,' Cassie said, finishing the sentence for me.

I nodded. 'Then he messaged me to go out and have a coffee.'

'That's good, isn't it?' Melissa asked.

'Absolutely,' Mia agreed.

'Except it is coffee,' I said. 'Not dinner, or a drink. You know coffee says 'I'm not taking a big gamble on you… not putting in much time… not sure you are worth more… I'm just sucking and seeing', so to speak.'

'I'd love to be sucked.' Cassie sighed. We all giggled – I blame the margaritas.

'Coffee might just mean he's a bit short of money this week,' Melissa offered.

We all looked at her, frowning. Melissa was a real, genuine blonde. No streaks, no bleach and sometimes we had to allow for that.

'This is Tomás Carrera,' Mia reminded her. 'His contract for one year is probably more than we'll earn in ten years.'

'He can afford coffee,' I agreed.

'So…' Cassie pushed on, '… did you have coffee?' Two guys came over to our table and Cassie moved them on. 'I need to hear this story,' she said, reading our surprised expressions.

'We went out for coffee last week and it was great. I spent four hours getting ready; he came in jeans and a T-shirt and looked like he'd just stepped off a billboard. We talked, like really talked and he was so hot. He played with my hand on the top of the table and he said I was cute at least three times. We stayed for nearly two hours – we had two rounds of coffee – then he kissed me on the cheek and said we should do this again. I didn't hear from him all weekend and then he messaged me yesterday to ask if I'd be here tonight and I said yes and that's it.'

Cassie and Melissa sat back and looked at each other.

'What?' I asked looking from one to the other. 'What does that look mean?'

Caleb leaned forward. 'It means he's just not that into you.'

'Shut up.' I hit his arm.

Caleb laughed and rose. 'Got to go, a cheerleader needs a drink,' he said and made his way towards a couple of the Saints' cheerleaders standing at the bar. Caleb was a bit of a hottie himself if the cheerleaders decided they were tired of sporting guys and wanted a college student who couldn't kick a ball. Speaking of sporting guys, Melissa nodded towards the door.

'Don't look now but half of the college football team just entered. Didn't you have a crush on Finn Lalor last season? He's here,' Melissa said.

I tried to look without doing an obvious turn. Yep, it was Finn. Until Mia met Lucas through her part-time job and opened a world of Saints to her friends, securing a date with Finn – the hero of the college football team – was aiming high for a college girl like me. But now thanks to Mia, soccer star Tomás Carrera – with his handsome Latin ways, beautiful face, long legs and toned torso – was on my radar.

Finn noticed me and waved, and I waved back. Oh, the injustice of the world... last semester I would have wet myself because he noticed me. Now, comparing Finn and Tomás – hmm, we're talking the difference between handsome and godlike. If only Tomás would either totally ignore me or totally like me! He was doing my head in.

I sighed. 'My round,' I told the girls.

I grabbed the empty margarita jug and headed to the bar, leaving them to talk about my sad and sorry situation. I drew up at the bar next to three gorgeous models; well I'm guessing they were models by the manes of hair and long legs. The Saints always had a collection of beautiful women hanging around. I ordered another pitcher and then my ears pricked up at their conversation.

'He's gorgeous and that accent is adorable, but he's a caveman,' Blondie One said. 'Twice he has taken me from behind, did the hair-pulling thing and even smacked my ass. Turned me right on,' she said, and giggled.

Blondie Two laughed. 'He does like it rough. I don't mind a bit of rough but I want sweet too.'

'Sweet and sour,' Blondie One agreed.

Eeww, had they both slept with the same guy? I guess they looked alike and maybe they just wanted casual sex. Lighten up Ms. Judgmental, I told myself.

'Tomás hit on me too, but I had to work that night... hostess job at the jewelry launch,' the brunette said, and the other girls nodded knowingly. 'But I'm still open to it,' she said, suggestively.

OMG, they were talking about Tomás, *my Tomás*. The caveman, apparently.

Blondie One said, 'he's a wham, bam and thank you ma'am, guy. I was still sore two days later.'

'He told me that he didn't want to look after anyone,' Blondie Two said, 'so he didn't want a relationship.'

'Maybe that's why he doesn't do sweet talk and tenderness,' Brunette suggested. 'He's worried someone will fall for him and get all clingy. He gives great gifts though; I got a beautiful necklace with a drop diamond. Maybe it's his way of softening the blow when he fobs you off.'

'He bought me a watch I was admiring as we window shopped on our date. Seriously though, would it kill him to not be so agro? Nik is so much better, such a sensitive lover,' Blondie One said.

The waiter pushed the pitcher of margaritas in front of me and I thanked him. I gave the models one last look – so they were doing German Nik too – the midfielder. Mia really liked Nik, said he was very sweet, but I didn't know him that well.

So my Tomás is a man-whore, I mused; a caveman man-whore who justifies his actions by buying off the girls afterward with gifts – kind of like prostitution but no money changes hands. I sighed. I was so barking up the wrong tree. Maybe he knew that after coffee... maybe he smelled that I was a virgin and not worth the effort required. Maybe he just liked them long, tall and glamorous.

I arrived at the table, put the pitcher down, and then I felt a hand on my shoulder.

I turned to see Tomás standing there in all his Latin glory.

Chapter 3

'Hello *Bella*,' Tomás Carrera said and leaned down to kiss me on the cheek. He was breathtakingly beautiful – a chiseled jaw, the darkest of chocolate-colored eyes, a radiant smile with white teeth that belonged in a toothpaste commercial, and he rocked a pair of jeans and a T-shirt. He was strong, but not over-built.

I think I lost the power of speech and my memory was wiped clean of everything the ladies at the bar just said.

'You look cute,' he said, running his eyes over my legs and red dress. Even sitting down, I think I had just appeared naked in his eyes – an amazing skill. I stood up.

'Hey Tomás,' I began to introduce him to my friends but he gave them a charming smile, grabbed me around my waist and we were gone.

'Dance floor, come dance with me, *Bella*,' he said holding me so close that I don't think I walked there. He shuffled into the packed floor and we swayed together. I didn't get to show off any of my great dance moves because I was pressed against him, but it was a small price to pay. I'm a girl who knows when to make sacrifices.

'Al...iss, Al...iss, Al...iss,' he said my name with that sexy Spanish accent, smiled and shook his head.

'T... oooo... mmmm…ass...' I dragged his name out and looked at him suspiciously.

'You haven't called me,' he said, with surprise in his voice.

I pulled back the few inches I could to study and frown at him. He had this teasing, sexy, dejected look on his face that I just wanted to kiss off.

'Um, I think you're meant to do that calling thing,' I said.

He grimaced, as if that was way too hard. He left one arm around my waist and with the other, removed my hand from his shoulder and closed his fingers around it. He rocked me against him. I'm not sure what music was playing, as I was too distracted to notice.

'That's cute, Al...iss. So very old fashioned, but it is the twenty-first century,' he said with a small grin.

I loved the way he said Alice – like the A was so important and it softened off to this sexy 'lis' sound at the end. Ah yeah, focus.

'I'm not old-fashioned,' I protested.

'You just like to be hunted and you want me to be the hunter?' he asked, with one eyebrow raised.

I got jostled by some over the top dancer behind me – hmm, I think it was a ploy by Melissa to push me closer to Tomás's chest. Tomás didn't move to straighten me up but I pulled away slightly; I didn't want to look like one of his groupie fans. This conversation with Tomás wasn't going well. I tried again.

'Do other girls call you?'

He shrugged. 'Of course.'

'So you give them your number?' I put him on the spot.

Tomás grinned and taking his hand off my waist, he ran it through the shaggy, brown layers of his hair. He exhaled while he thought of a response. Then that hand found its way to my butt and rested there. Good response.

I let him off the hook. 'Well I guess I could call, but...'

'Not even a one-line message...' he started again with the hard-done-by look.

I smiled and rolled my eyes. 'I messaged you back last time.'

'You're just not that into me Alice,' he teased and put his forehead on mine.

I pulled back to look into his eyes. 'No Tomás, you're just spoilt for choice and I'm just...' I tried to find a good analogy that wouldn't spoil the mood. 'I'm just another cookie in your cookie jar.'

Tomás's head shot back and he looked at me with a huge grin. He burst out laughing. Even with all the music on the dance floor, people turned to look at him. I joined in the joke, but I think I went three shades of red and just wanted to crawl under the D.J.'s desk. He laughed so much that he had to lead me off the dance floor.

One of the players came up and hit him on the back. 'We're going on a crawl, coming?'

Tomás shook his head. 'Nuh, Cookie and I are going to hang here,' he said.

I cringed. *Great, that's going to be how he remembers me from the rest – not cute, sexy, funny, pretty, great in bed, nope none of those – he's going to remember me as a cookie.*

*****

Tomás sat with me and my friends and Lucas came over to join us. We had a hot table – I kept pinching myself, looking around at Tomás, Lucas, Mia and my college friends and thinking is this for real? But then I'd get the cold glares from some of the girls at the party and I knew it was for real and we had two of the team's best players and cutest guys at our table. I wished I could get a photo but I didn't want to look like a groupie. I wondered if I could get Melissa to sneak to the bar and take one without anyone noticing, but then she'd want to be in the photo... it's tricky managing your own social media, I pondered. I could learn a lot from the Kardashians.

I glanced to the bar and saw Finn Lalor looking my way. Yeah Finn, do you know how many times I tried to get you to look my way last semester? I did everything but become the football team mascot... and I would have done that too but I was too small for the horse costume!

Tomás and Lucas picked up the drinks tab for the next hour or maybe it was two and I moved off the alcohol onto diet soda. I would have killed for a coffee... killed one of the girls pawing Tomás. Yeah, seriously, women were coming to the table to talk with him while he sat with me.

Mia nudged me. 'We're going, do you want a lift?'

I watched as Lucas kept his hand always on her... on her arm, her neck, somewhere. He was sober and driving. 'Lucas is happy to drive you home.'

Lucas looked over on hearing his name. 'No problem, Alice,' he said. 'We're taking Cassie and Melissa too.'

'We've got my car,' Mia explained. Only two would fit in

Lucas's Lamborghini. I began to wonder what Tomás drove and then he spoke up.

'No, I'm going to get Al...iss home,' Tomás said. He was sober too. I guess they don't drink much during the season – ah, the life of a professional athlete, and a definite bonus for the drinking girlfriend, even if two was usually about all I could handle.

Lucas gave him a warning look and Tomás nodded. Nothing was said but obviously, the look covered it. That was sweet of Lucas. Mia always says he protects people in his orbit, I guess being Mia's best friend, that's me now. Things were looking up.

'Are you ready to go, Cookie?' Tomás lowered his gorgeous head next to mine and whispered the words in my ear.

I tried to look angry but ended up giggling. Even Cookie sounded so cute when he said it. Ah, this man was going to be the end of me. I nodded and we rose, Tomás helping me up. He pulled my jacket off the back of the chair and helped me put it on; so cute the way he joined it at the front as if he was protecting me from the cold – such a gentleman.

I said goodbye to everyone and we jostled our way out of the club but not before two women passed Tomás their phone numbers – seriously – and he posed for three photos with fans. He gave a wave to some of the other players still there and collected me as I waited by the exit saying hi to Finn – tall, blond, athletic, green-eyed Finn – who was the subject of many of my erotic dreams last semester and it had nothing to do with his ball skills.

Tomás took my hand and unapologetically pulled me away from Finn whom I managed to get a wave to as I was pulled out the door.

'Who was that?' Tomás asked, as we walked into the quiet and the cool air of the night.

'A friend from college. He's the captain of the football team,' I said, sounding really proud as though that was a great thing because that was my college, forgetting I was talking to national sports star and super goalie Tomás Carrera. I'd had way too many margaritas, more than should be allowed for someone who had so little drinking experience.

Tomás made a sort of snorting sound as if Finn was playing the wrong code so was no threat. Or maybe it was a 'Finn's no competition for me' snort. He put his arm around my shoulder and pulled me into him again and then I didn't care who he snorted at. He looked at me and smiled, then kissed my forehead.

'Did I tell you that you were gorgeous, Cookie?' he said, with a grin.

'Uh-huh,' I said, somewhat pissy. 'You too, did I tell you that?'

'No you didn't,' he sighed. 'All you've told me is that I have to call you and be the hunter.'

'No I didn't,' I said, confused. 'Did I?'

Tomás laughed at me and squeezed me tighter. We stopped in front of a beautiful black Ducati motorbike.

'Is this your car?' I asked, yep, I said that.

Tomás smiled. 'This is my baby,' he said. He pulled a jacket from the under-seat storage and slid it on. He looked so good in leather and I was about to wrap my arms around him and that leather jacket. He grabbed a helmet; funny he had two on him; he came prepared to take someone home. Sigh, lucky me. He turned and put it on me, tightening the strap under my chin and then patted the top of the helmet.

'Okay?' he asked.

I nodded, my head feeling very heavy with the helmet on. I looked down at my dress.

'Yes, *Bella*.' Tomás looked as well. 'Might be tricky keeping that down on the bike. Good thing I won't be able to see you flashing while I'm driving,' he said, and I noticed before he zipped up his jacket that he had a sizeable protrusion already at the front of his pants – that thought must have been working for him. He noticed me noticing and gave me another of those sexy smiles. *Just kill me now, I'm a goner.*

I did my jacket up as well and watched as Tomás swung a sexy leg over the bike and straddled it. He looked so hot. He turned towards me and indicated I jump on. Hmm, I swung a leg over too, not that daintily given I had a dress on and the bike was big. Tomás started the bike and turned back to tuck my feet in and tell me where to keep them. Strappy sandals weren't great for the bike. I tucked my dress under my legs.

'All good?' Tomás asked.

'Sure,' I answered and he pulled the bike away from the curb. I clung to him for dear life; my life mainly. It was bloody cold on the back of the bike; luckily Tomás was warm and hard. I know, those two words together just take you places.

I'm such a bad drinker that I don't become fun or the life of the party after a few, I just get sleepy – I needed some serious drinking practice. Even with the cold air whipping against me, I was struggling to keep my eyes open. I clung on hoping the ride wasn't too long. My dad would kill me if he knew I was doing this – I would be the only twenty-one-year-old grounded for a year.

And then about ten minutes later, or when I was just frozen enough to not be able to stand, Tomás pulled into the driveway of a huge house, the gate opened and he drove in. The garage door opened, and he drove in there as well – it was as though it was all synced. I began to sober up and I started to get a bit nervous about what else was going to be synced.

Chapter 4

Tomás maneuvered the bike into the corner and turned the engine off. He pulled off his helmet and turned back to smile at me, still straddling the bike between his legs.

'Welcome to my home, Cookie,' Tomás said, as he swung his leg over the bike and unclipped my helmet too.

I pulled it off and handed it to him, then desperately tried to fix my flattened hair. Beside his bike in the large garage was a sporty little red Alfa. He put the helmets on a shelf in the garage and came back to lift me off the bike. It was as though the alcohol was a sedative. I was relaxed and willing; I didn't want to miss out on a moment with Tomás 'super goalkeeper' Carrera. It felt as though I was taking part in a love scene in slow motion; I was the one – the chosen one to be with him, he brought me home. He lowered me to the ground and I adjusted my red dress, pulling it down.

'Don't worry, *Bella*, I'll have that off in a minute.' He pulled me closer and gave me a breathtaking kiss, stopping only to whisper in my ear, 'I can't wait to have you, Al... iss, you are so gorgeous.' It was the first time he had used my name since the Cookie christening incident.

Tomás grabbed my hand and led me out of the garage, opening the door into his house and ushering me in. It was dark but I didn't have to worry about finding my way, Tomás steered me in and pressed me hard against a wall. The house was silent and all I could hear was Tomás's breathing and my heart pounding. The energy between us... the tension... he must have been feeling it too because his breathing was getting faster and my heartbeat was like a drum.

'I want you, Al...iss...' he moaned, his tongue slipping between my lips and his erection pressed hard against me. It felt enormous and I could barely breathe for the weight of him pressing me into the wall. I inhaled his scent, warm, spicy, so manly. His hands seemed to be everywhere – running across my back, in my hair, touching my face. My tongue touched his and he groaned.

Tomás grabbed my hand and pushed it down to his crotch to feel his erection through his jeans. He was pushing hard against the denim. I didn't know what to do with my hand there, whether to squeeze or rub. It felt like too much too soon, as if we had skipped five steps or something. I pressed on his hardness and his body twitched against my palm.

He roughly pushed against my lips and I jumped with surprise as he nipped my lip. The ladies at the *Shaken Not Stirred* bar were right – he could be rough. One of his hands pulled me tight against him. I could barely move now as his tongue pushed harder into my mouth. His other hand traveled down across my breast and I gasped as all my nerve endings were on full alert.

Suddenly, I felt an arm under my knees and my feet were swept off the ground as Tomás scooped me up. He hurried up the stairs with me in his arms without even getting just the tiniest bit breathless... that man was fit.

We entered a large room at the end of a corridor and Tomás took me straight to the bed – a king-size, black, four-poster wrought iron bed. I was dropped down into the middle and Tomás crawled straight onto me, kissing me and stroking my breasts again through the fabric of my dress. I couldn't get my breath; it was all happening fast, too fast for me to catch up. I wanted my first time ever – and my first time with Tomás – to be romantic. I had pictured a slow night, a subtle wine, maybe candlelight... I know, but they always have candlelight on *The Bold and the Beautiful*. Then plenty of long, slow kisses, slow undressing...

Tomás pulled his shirt off and began to unbuckle his jeans, all the time looking down at me. He slid his jeans off and I had my first sighting of an almost naked Tomás. I wasn't like a category one virgin... I had had boyfriends, kissed, sucked, done a few things, but I had never gone the whole way. Here was the most gorgeous body I've ever seen in a pair of fitted boxer-briefs and a huge bulge that was going to do some damage. I think I began to hyperventilate.

In a raging hurry, Tomás pulled me to a sitting position and began to zip my dress down. He took it off over my head. I had on a matching red bra and pants – nothing lacy because I wasn't expecting to go to bed with Tomás tonight... damn it, but they were satin. My dress was gone; it took all of a minute. He laid me back down.

'How do you like it, *Bella*?' he asked and tilted my face towards him. Tomás lowered himself on top of me again, holding his weight on his elbows. He pressed his erection between my legs, impatiently, expecting me to free him of his boxer-briefs I guess. When I hesitated he made a suggestion.

'Let's see your gorgeous behind and start there,' he teased and flipped me over. I felt his fingers hitch into my panties and I gasped. Tomás stopped. 'Unless you have something in mind?' He moved to see me side-on and raised his eyebrow at me suggestively.

'I've never had anything before,' I said, 'so...'

Tomás stopped. He turned me back over to look at him. 'What? Al...iss, what did you say?'

'I've never done it before, so you pick what you like,' I said.

Tomás's mouth fell open and he moved off me.

'No, no, not like this.' He shook his head. 'Why didn't you say you were a virgin? Fuck!' He took a deep breath. 'That is special Al...iss, it must be intimate... or at least a gift given to lovers.'

I pulled myself up on my elbows and Tomás, still in over-reaction mode, threw the quilt over my body. I was wearing my underwear; it was not as if I was naked.

'Why didn't you say?' he asked me again.

'Because...' I shrugged, '... I want you to be my first time.'

Tomás rolled his eyes. 'Saints in heaven, Al...iss, not like this. Your first time is not to be wasted when you are half-drunk with a guy who gives you a rough ride, shit.' He continued swearing under his breath for a few moments, and then pulled himself off the bed and went into the bathroom, closing the door.

I don't know what he was doing in there but I took a

guess he was relieving himself of the major erection that was just about to bore into me. I waited and listened but he was super quiet. I decided to just close my eyes for a few minutes; the bed was so comfortable and I was snuggled under the quilt. I could smell Tomás's manly, spicy scent on the pillow.

And that's how I ended up talking with Tomás's sister, Valentina, the next morning. I know hundreds, even thousands of girls would have been excited to have had Tomás's arm around them, leading them out of the club and being taken home to his place on the back of his bike. But in the cold, hard light of day, I felt a bit... slutty. How many people had seen me going home with Tomás and now, I was one of those girls. Maybe I just needed to get over myself.

Then, it got worse; no word from Tomás for days… even when I sent a message to say I was sorry that he had to abandon his bedroom for me, he shot back four words: 'It was no problem'. Kill me now.

Chapter 5

'I'm not here,' I called out as my bedroom door was banged on, again.

'Ali…' My annoying seventeen-year-old brother, Ryan, sighed. 'Dad said if you don't get up and show us you're still alive he's calling an intervention of all your friends or the police, depending on whether you're just faking it or really are dead.'

'Fine then.' I pushed the quilt off and realized I was a bit hard on the nose. I opened the door and my brother reeled back screening his eyes and yelling in terror.

'Very funny,' I told him. I went the two steps it took to reach our living room. Our whole house was the size of Tomás's garage... which reminded me of my new rule – everyone was now banned from saying the name Tomás to me.

'Dad, I'm alive.' I presented myself as evidence.

His hand went straight to his heart. 'Praise the Lord,' he said and Ryan laughed. Dad rose from his chair and walked towards me. He hugged me; a strong hug that said he knew all about the pain of relationships and he did. He had been through a few since he got back on the horse after Mom's death when I was fourteen. So in that respect, my dad was pretty in touch.

'Do you want Ryan and me to finish him off for you?' Dad teased.

I shook my head. 'No, I hope to do that myself, but thanks. I'm going to shower.'

'Good idea,' Ryan said.

I gave him a grim look.

'I bought ice-cream,' Ryan added, trying to cheer me up. I looked at my handsome brother, who I swear had shot up a foot in height in his last year of school and looked like a carbon copy of Dad – the strong, silent, bookish type.

I smiled at him. 'You're my favorite brother, Ryan.'

'I'm your only brother,' he reminded me, giving me a dark look.

'Then you've got less competition,' I said brightly and headed to the bathroom in our one-bathroom house. Twenty minutes later when I came out sparkling clean and with washed hair, Mia was sitting on the couch watching soccer with my dad. My brother, who has had a crush on Mia for most of his life, was hovering between the kitchen and lounge. He turned and went back into the kitchen and I nearly fell over when Ryan and Lucas came out of there together. The world's number one soccer star was carrying drinks for the family and Ryan was following behind with snacks. This was all too much; I wasn't up to it.

Lucas greeted me with a smile.

'Hey Alice, I've dropped in to watch the soccer with your old man, figured you girls had some talking to do.' He smiled that melting smile.

'Ease up on the 'old man' talk,' my father quipped from the couch.

Mia jumped up and took my hand. 'We'll leave you men to it,' she said.

I could tell Dad and Ryan were pretty pleased with the company. Dad was a soccer fanatic so could talk tactics. In between, he ordering pizzas taking topping suggestions from Lucas and Ryan as Mia led me back into my bedroom and closed the door.

'Right,' she said, taking charge. 'You've been locked in your room for two days, you haven't shown up at the cafe for your shifts, you haven't answered my messages and you skipped your lecture today. Alice, we need to talk.'

I sighed because she was right.

'I'm your best friend,' she reminded me.

'I know but you're busy with Lucas now...'

'Wash your mouth out!' she exclaimed. I don't know where Mia got these sayings from but she had a collection of good oldies in her vocabulary. She continued, 'I'm never too busy for us, never! Now sit.'

I sat on the edge of the bed and she sat next to me and took my hand. We both dropped back on the bed and looked at the ceiling. I had plastic stars stuck to the ceiling and if it was night, some of them still glowed.

'Tell me everything,' she said, drawing a deep breath in anticipation of the load I was going to put on her.

I ran through it all. She commented every now and then. 'Good... dangerous, you shouldn't have got on that bike... well that was gentlemanly... was Valentina nice? What's his house like?'

I filled her in. Then I told her the worse part. Since that night in Tomás's bed, I hadn't heard a word from him… three days and two nights now. Clearly, he didn't want to work that hard to woo a virgin.

We sat in silence for a short while as Mia processed it all. I had already regurgitated it in my mind five million times, now, make that five million and one.

'Maybe he just wants to play the field and respects you too much to take your virginity in his stride,' Mia suggested.

'Take it, take it, I'm begging for him to take it,' I whined pathetically. 'I don't care if he is rough; if the super gorgeous Tomás Carrera can take my virginity I'll live with rough, hell I'll live with not being able to sit for a week.'

'You don't mean that,' Mia said.

'Yeah, I do,' I said, turning side-on to face her. I didn't say it out loud but I wanted to see that huge mass in his boxer-briefs and feel what it would be like to have it inside me. I wanted to orgasm and open my eyes to see Tomás's dark chocolate eyes looking at me and if it was just the one night, then I'd live with that too.

But there was more, I was in denial pretending it never happened but it did, I had sent another message… I swallowed and looked at Mia. 'I told him that I wanted him to be the one to take it. Can you believe I did that the morning after I left his house? I am beyond mortified.'

'Oh no,' Mia whispered.

'I know.' I bit my bottom lip.

'Right, but you didn't say the virgin word in the text?' Mia asked.

I sat up, grabbed my phone, and thumbed to the text. I shook my head. 'I said that I wanted him to be the one to take me.'

Mia breathed a sigh of relief. 'Well that's okay,' she said and sat upright next to me.

'Is it?' I turned back around to look at her.

'Sure. If anyone sees that text or he tells, you can say you wanted him to be the one to take you to the college graduation ball or take you for your first spin on a motorbike or...'

'I guess so.' I felt a small wave of relief. 'I'm an idiot on so many levels.'

She rubbed my arm. 'You're not Ali. You've just fallen in... smitten.'

I looked at her. 'Do people fall in smitten? Who still says smitten?'

Mia started to laugh and I joined in and then I cried. 'How many days?' I sniffed, trying to remember the break-up or heartbreak pattern.

'Usually three,' Mia said. 'First day is shock and pain, day two is raw heartbreak, day three is when you start playing '*I will survive*' and can start rebuilding again. That's now.'

I nodded. 'I will survive,' I agreed. 'Finn Lalor called, but I haven't got back to him yet.'

'Really?' Mia brightened. 'We like Finn don't we?'

I smiled at her. 'Yeah, we do.'

There was a knock on the door and it opened a few inches. 'Is it safe to bring pizza in?' Lucas asked.

'Very safe,' Mia said.

I wiped my eyes and I tried not to look at Lucas as he handed Mia a box of pizza. Then he squatted in front of me, making looking at him unavoidable.

'Is there something I should know?' he asked looking from me to Mia.

I shook my head and Mia spoke up. 'It's all good, we've got it under control.'

Lucas's eyes narrowed. 'Alice? Did Tomás do something that I need to deal with?'

Mia smacked him on the arm.

'What?' he turned to her. 'I believe you, gorgeous, I just want to double-check with Alice,' he said, rubbing his arm dramatically.

'Tomás was a perfect gentleman, but thank you Lucas,' I said, sniffing again. I was pathetic.

Lucas looked confused. 'Well that's good then isn't it?' He studied my tear-stained face before turning to Mia.

'No,' I said. 'Yes, it's complicated.'

'Right,' he said, rising. He leaned down and planted a kiss on Mia's head before backing out of the bedroom slowly and closing the door behind him. I think he was scared to turn his back on me, sensing I was a lunatic.

Mia opened the pizza box.

'Come on.' She invited me to take a piece. 'Let's eat pizza, ice-cream and then I'll go for a jog to apologize for my carb sins and tomorrow, you can start the new day with a new view... a view of Finn maybe.'

I nodded and took a slice. I bumped it against hers. 'Cheers.'

I wondered what Tomás was doing right now.

'No checking for messages, no looking at his online stuff,' Mia ordered. 'You're now looking forward, not back. I think you should return Finn's text.'

I nodded again. The pizza tasted like cardboard. Did I mention that I was pathetic?

Chapter 6

The next morning I was back on top, so to speak. I fried some eggs, made a round of toast and a pot of tea for me, Dad and Ryan; even Dad said I was looking like my normal self again. I'm guessing that was a good thing.

I had one day of 'prac' a week in the final semester of my events management course – every Tuesday I worked with Josie from Planet Events. Trust me, Josie was a bit off the planet herself. She was a one-person, small business dynamo who supplemented her staff by using students like me. Josie was usually out of control – picture a thin, neurotic, hyped-up and highly-strung forty-something woman with bird's nest hair. Lord knows why she went into managing events, nuh, he's probably still wondering too.

That morning she lived up to her neuroticism and left me to meet with two brides while she went to woo a writers' group into giving her their three-day festival to manage. The first bride, Lucy, was a dream; everything was too easy, super relaxed and was going to be 'great fun'. I counted she said that eleven times, bless her. Bride two was bridezilla – okay her real name was Laura but I'm sure her surname was Bridezilla. It was pretty much downhill from her first question.

'So, Alice, how many weddings have you organized before?' she asked, folding her arms over her chest.

'Well,' I stalled, not wanting to lose business for Josie, 'while I have been doing my three-year degree in event management, I've worked on quite a few and I've seen some wonderful and successful weddings.'

She sniffed. It was one of those nose-up in the air sniffs. I think she was slightly curious about the wonderful weddings and how she could be sure hers qualified and that I'd be talking about it for years. Bridezilla took a deep breath, looked at her mother, then back at me and began.

'I hope you have a pen and paper because this is what I'm expecting. The table linen must be crisp white and I mean white... not washed, not tinged, not even the slightest mark of any former wedding. The bride and groom's seating should be slightly above everyone at the front of the room so we can be seen. I'll need my own large room to go to during the day to have some moments alone, not one of those small powder rooms, the bridesmaids can use that...'

She stopped to draw breath and her mother began to speak. Bridezilla held up her hand to silence her. 'In case you have forgotten, this day is all about *me*,' she told her mother. 'I have a vision for this day, *my* vision and I'll do the talking...' I tuned out and began to wonder if it was too late to change my degree to teaching instead.

*****

'Longest day in the history of the world and it is only lunchtime,' I told Mia over the phone as I stirred the froth on my cappuccino during my break. 'But on the bright side and there's always a bright side,' I cheered up, 'I don't have time to mope around thinking about certain sports stars and I have my health.'

'Well that's two bright sides,' Mia said. 'Hey, I called with some news.'

'You're engaged!' I said, holding my breath.

'What? No!' Mia exclaimed, 'we've only been going out a minute... but that would be cool wouldn't it? Mia Ainswright, yeah what a shame that Mia Carter sounds better. Mia Carter-Ainswright is too much, isn't it? Anyway, so not going there yet.'

'Sorry, I've been hanging around brides all morning, I've got weddings on the brain,' I explained. 'Promise me when you get married you won't turn into one of those brides-from-hell.'

'I promise,' Mia said. 'Actually we should have a word... you know so if either of us is getting insane-like during the wedding preparations we say the word and it reminds us to chill out.'

'Agreed,' I said, 'but not something obvious like Bridezilla.' I undid my jacket – I had to wear a suit to work on prac days – and slipped it off. 'News, what new?'

'Oh yeah, thanks,' Mia said. 'Saints' management is looking for an event coordinator.'

I sat up straight. 'Wow.' This was good, very good.

'Yeah,' Mia agreed. 'I'm reading it online now. They are looking for a junior or graduate to manage all the Club's events including the home game day entertainment, best and fairest night, annual gala ball, season launch, social media, and so on.'

'Wow,' I said again. Being an event coordinator for a national sporting team would be fantastic for the CV and since I would graduate in a few months, it would be good to beat the rush of jobless in the market.

'They'll get hundreds of applicants.' I pointed out the obvious. 'That's a dream job.'

'Yes,' Mia said, 'but not every applicant knows the game as you do and has been going to the game – that's impressive and they're bound to ask that at the interview. Plus, not every applicant can put Lucas Ainswright, captain of the Saints, as a personal referee.'

'I can't ask Lucas to do that, he doesn't even know if I'm good at what I do,' I said.

'It was his idea,' Mia said, 'and of course you're good at what you do.'

'OMG, Mia, he is the best, you have to keep him,' I gushed.

'I'm planning on it,' she said. 'You'll be working in the offices at the home ground so you'll be surrounded by all the atmosphere. You have to work game days of course, but...'

'But we both will be. You'll be in the PT rooms, and if I get the job, I'll be doing event coordination. This is so exciting, so exciting!' I said again, 'I want that job.'

'Okay, do the application tonight and call me after. Lucas said to let him know when you've applied and he'll put in a good word with the HR Manager.'

'Thank you, thank him,' I said, then stopped. 'Do you think it's wrong trying to get a job through the back door like this?'

'Are you crazy?' Mia said. 'That's how a lot of jobs are secured. It's not *what* you know it's *who* you know... my parents always say that. I got my part-time job because my boss knew my science teacher at school... I'm pretty sure they went out.'

'Must have ended well,' I mused. 'M, this is wonderful.' I used her nickname – there's not a lot to work with when it comes to shortening Mia. 'Can you tell Lucas I'm stoked and tonight, straight after I feed the men,' I said, referring to my father and brother, 'I'll do up my application. Thanks again for telling me.'

After I hung up, on a wave of highness if there's such a thing, I texted Finn back and said I'd love to catch up for a drink later in the week. The world was looking brighter.

And then my phone pinged with a message which was nothing unusual – except this was one from Tomás.

Chapter 7

Damn him and his sexy smile and hot body! It was day four... I was in recovery mode... I was like *'Tomás who?'*, okay that might be crap, but really, I had stopped thinking about him every minute and replaying the horror movie in my head. I had it down to about every couple of hours now. I was thinking survivor thoughts and feeling sorry that one day when he was an old, injured and retired soccer star, he'd figure out what he missed and it would be too late because I'd be swept up by some other fantastic guy.

I felt my stomach flip as I opened the message.

'Hi *Bella*, event job going at club. You should apply. Miss you. Tomás x'

What the hell? Miss me? Call me then! See me, take me out, do me, have me, unvirginize me or deactivate my virginity for crying in a bucket. I stopped now and took a deep breath. This required a serious girl discussion to decide on the return message – did I aim for warm and sweet, grateful, funny or a 'go screw yourself' text. I needed a straight shooter, not Mia this time because even though she promised not to share everything with Lucas, I didn't want Lucas having any quiet words with Tomás.

This was a job for Cassie. I hadn't seen her since we went to the *Shaken Not Stirred* bar last weekend and she witnessed me leaving the club with Tomás. But the best thing about Cassie was that she didn't pack any punches. She was a real redhead – fiery and a straight shooter. I texted her and met her for a coffee on the way home from my day with Planet Events.

'Reel him in like a fish,' she said, without hesitation.

'What, really?' I studied her trying to gauge if she was for real. Cassie looked gorgeous – she always looked gorgeous even as a poor student. She had on a green velvet dress and with her wild red hair, she looked like a beautiful witch.

'Are you going to eat your shortbread?' she asked, looking at the complimentary biscuit on the edge of my saucer.

'No, couldn't fit it in,' I teased her, and she smiled and grabbed it before I changed her mind.

'I'm serious,' she said with a mouthful of shortbread. 'You need to take charge with Tomás.'

'So you think I should be flirty?' I asked.

She nodded. 'Alice, get with the program. The hottest goalkeeper in the country sits with you and your friends at a club, is hot for you and he takes *you* home. He could have just done you there and then... but he didn't. How many guys would hesitate to take a girl's virginity? They all want to be the first and forever in your mind.'

'No?' I said, grimacing.

'It's true,' Cassie said. 'Instead, as soon as he finds out it's your first time, he doesn't take advantage of you. He steps away.'

'And then he goes completely off me. What's that about?'

Cassie leaned forward and lowered her voice. 'Maybe he doesn't want the commitment of a relationship and he knows that taking your virginity means you are going to be expecting that. Maybe he just wants to play the field while he can, while he's at the top of his game.'

I knew it, Mia knew it and Cassie knew it but Cassie was the only one who said it out loud.

'Thanks, Cassie.' I swallowed her words, trying to bury the hurt that cut me like ribbons.

'I'm sorry but...' she shrugged.

'No, I'm grateful, thank you for calling it like it is. No point kidding myself,' I said.

'So reel him in.' She leaned back.

'But if he doesn't want me, why would I do that?' I said. I know I'm not the most experienced relationship person in the world, but I was missing this one completely.

Cassie smiled. 'Alice, it's Relationships 101.'

'Damn, I missed that class,' I said.

Cassie laughed. 'We always want what we can't have. Look at you... last semester you would have wet yourself for a date with Finn Lalor. Now you've got one later this week and you haven't given it a second thought. In fact, Mia told me about the date, not you!'

'Right.' I tried to keep up. 'But Tomás could have me.'

'Tomás doesn't know he wants you,' Cassie said.

'Oh.' I nodded. 'Nuh, still not getting it.'

Cassie rolled her eyes. 'You're sweet and cute, and a virgin. He likes you, he's attracted to you, he's missing you – his words – and I bet you anything he doesn't want anyone else having you, but he doesn't want to go the commitment you require just yet.'

'Okay, I've got that loud and clear,' I said, with a smirk.

'So you need to show him that if he doesn't want your virginity, someone else does… and he can play around all he likes but look what he's missing out on.'

'I'm bribing him with my virginity?' I asked, just checking that I had the big picture here. It didn't seem like that big a prize.

Cassie nodded. 'Reel him in, Alice, starting right now. You're going to text him this back...'

I grabbed my phone, opened his text and looked up at Cassie, ready to type.

'Type this,' she said, 'Thanks T. Will apply tonight. Been so busy, hope all is well with you. Ax.'

I typed it, looked at Cassie, she nodded and I sent it.

'That just sounds boring to me,' I said.

'Ali, you've just said you're going for a job at a club full of fit, handsome soccer plays and you've been so busy you haven't had time to think about him. Hell, you're even looking more attractive to me.'

I laughed. 'Really? Thanks Cass, you're a lifesaver.'

'You'll see,' she said, 'nothing more desirable than an unobtainable woman. Wouldn't hurt to drop in the fact that you've got a date too, if you get the chance.'

I squeezed her hand and smiled with relief.

'He won't know other women exist by the time you're done,' she said, and sat back with a satisfied smile.

If only I was as confident in that thought.

Chapter 8

It was a buffet of good bodies... a smorgasbord of sexy shapes... a feast of flesh... okay, you get the picture – it was my first day on the job and who would have thought I'd be working in an office with so much eye candy. I was ruined for life.

Arriving at my first day in the office was a pretty easy process – the interview a few days earlier went well and I gave Deborah, the Human Resources lady, examples of my work experience and my results so far, including what subjects I had been studying. Deborah was also the accountant and managed the external technology contractor – such is the way with small companies. We pretended Lucas wasn't my referee but I got the job within a day; it helped I'm sure. So excited. I transferred my remaining subjects to night lectures and Deborah said I could have time off for study and exams. So excited, did I mention that? I gave Lucas a call to thank him and he brushed it off. Mia said he wasn't good at compliments that were personal, only professional. Fair enough. The best thing was that I hadn't time to think about Tomás or Finn while I sorted out my new job.

So, day one – I was now officially part of the Saints' marketing team and they were a great team. My boss was Jim Dixon and he was fun. He was mid-forties, short, wiry with a dry sense of humor… kind of like the Groucho Marx of sport admin. He looked after the advertising, branding, reporting and his team of three including me.

Also in our team was Kay who took care of the clubs' memberships from corporate sponsorships to the Saints' kids' club. She had the tough job of selling them, keeping databases and making sure all the benefits were delivered. Kay said it was an easy job when the team was winning; everyone loved winners. She was in her late thirties, a mom of two and a big lady who kept hugging me and telling me I would be just fine… I loved her already.

The other member of our marketing team besides me – Alice Peterson, events coordinator, the Saints… sorry I had to say it all the time until it sank in – was Sasha Saxon who looked after media and merchandise… you know, the hats, scarves, jerseys, headwear and so on. Plus Sasha also wrote the club publications like the fan magazine and annual report. I liked her too. She was about twenty-two-or-three and she had no airs and graces. Sasha had gorgeous messy blonde hair and was thin and fashionable; she designed and made her own clothes and loved hats. Everyone remembered Sasha… especially when she introduced herself as, 'Hi I'm Sasha Saxon from the Santa Ana Saints, try saying that five times fast after a night out!'

As well as events, I also scored the social media for the club – I was now looking after the Saints' website, Facebook page, Twitter account and more. Oh the damage I could do…

just kidding. God I loved my job and I'd been there only a day! And I scored – no pun intended, I was getting the hang of this, next I'd be talking about balls – I was also assigned player allocation for events and according to my new boss Jim, everyone out there wanted a Saint at their event.

Lucas was off-limits as nearly every single request asked for him and his contract stipulated he would appear at ten events only per season as determined by his management – these were mostly his sponsors' events. The rest of the team had to contractually give me five appearances a season and I was to work with the Football Manager, Shayne, to work these out. Give me five, oh yeah, I could just see me calling for that. I wonder if appearing at my place counted if I booked out Tomás for all five. I was so unprofessional.

As for the rest of the office... well it was very, very satisfying with a mix of current and former players holding office positions. The Saints had their own security staff who worked in a small office next to mine; the two men were both current Saints players – The Russian (I still didn't know his real name) who was a forward on the team and defender Eddie Mosley who I heard just got engaged. Both gorgeous, both just on the other side of the wall from me – a plaster sheet away. The Football Manager Shayne Williams was an ex-NY Red player who finished his contract and wanted to move back to California. He now worked in the Saints' admin and was eye candy if you liked your man a bit more mature. The coach, Johan, had his office in the same building and so did the assistant coach, the assistant football manager, the PT, the stats guy... too much to take in for one day. There were a few ladies as well, like Deborah in Human Resources, Brenda the Personal Assistant to the CEO and Suzie the receptionist. I'm sure they appreciated the scenery too.

Throughout the day players came and went as they dropped in to see whoever they had to see, but Sasha told me they didn't come to our side of the office much unless they needed additional tickets, merchandise or were visiting The Russian and Ed. Today though, just before training started onsite at four p.m., Lucas wandered in and dropped down in the chair in front of my desk. Kay and Sasha's mouth dropped open. Jim walked by and greeted him. Lucas knew Jim by name – I guess Jim was a bit of a fixture at the Saints.

'Hey Lucas.' I looked up at Mia's man and captain fantastic.

'How's your first day going?' he asked.

'Taxing,' I teased. 'Much harder than going to college for three hours a day. But I'm loving it. Hey thanks again.'

He held up his hand. 'They didn't even call me for a reference,' he said. 'I think Deborah knew your lecturer and that person you work with at... the lost planet or something.'

I nodded. 'Planet Events. Ah you're very modest, but I suspect you had some impact on me getting my dream job,' I said with a big grin.

Lucas smiled and shook his head.

'You've met Kay and Sasha haven't you?' I asked, introducing the two ladies in my shared workspace – technically it was their workspace, as I'd been there one day.

Lucas rose and shook their hands. 'Sure, Sasha's always trying to get me to talk with journos and Kay's scored me some merchandise for friends.' He smiled at them. My, he was charming.

'Anyway,' Lucas said, 'got to get to training. If she becomes too much trouble, ladies, just let me know,' he said with a grin towards Kay and Sasha. He turned back to me. 'I've got some tickets for Frank and Ryan for the next game if they want them,' he said referring to Dad and my brother.

'They'll love them, thanks.'

With a wave, he was gone. I saw Sasha Saxon of the Saints fanning herself.

'I am never washing my hand again,' she said.

'Eww,' I said and Kay grimaced.

'Isn't he a lovely boy?' Kay smiled. 'I would just love to hug him and feed him a roast.'

Sasha and I looked at her.

'My feelings are not at all maternal,' Sasha assured her.

And then The Russian went past – all six-foot-five of him – and we all stopped to watch. I caught Kay out.

'Was that maternal?' I asked, looking at her suspiciously.

She blushed and bit her lip before answering. 'I may be married with children but I'm not dead. Besides, I'm a big girl, I like them big,' she said.

Sasha and I giggled like naughty kids.

'No I didn't mean that, I meant tall, well-built... oh never mind.' She shook her head at both of us and looked away, still smiling but trying not to. 'You might be a bad influence, young lady,' she said with a look to me.

'I hope so,' I teased her.

Chapter 9

Finn Lalor looked very sexy in jeans and a black bomber jacket over a white T-shirt. Actually, he looked more like he was going to sign up for the Navy Seals. Finn had this new buzz cut which made his face look lean and angular and his eyes noticeably bluer. His fair hair was shaved to stubble length and it was the sexiest I'd ever seen him in our three years at college. He was so different to Tomás – fair to Tomás's dark hair, blue eyes to Tomás's chocolate eyes and broad while Tomás was trim, muscled and agile. I felt small beside him, which was kind of nice.

I was still in my work gear… a cream sleeveless dress with a full circle godet skirt and matching high heels. I got the dress on sale and just love it; there was a red version too but I've got so much red in my closet – where was I? I get a bit carried away when it comes to shopping, but I'm very, very good at it and I was dressing to impress in my first week given the office talent was so impressive.

'You didn't come to our game on the weekend,' Finn said, once we had settled into a booth at a bar near our college.

I'm sure that was the first time Finn noticed that I wasn't at a game. He didn't notice when I was present-and-accounted-for last season, and I bit my tongue from mentioning that. Saved by the waitress – I ordered a cola and Finn ordered a beer, producing his I.D. He placed a leg around each of mine – straight into the intimacy. How many times had Finn done this and how many girls had welcomed it? Might be best not to go there.

'So did you win?' I asked.

'Of course.' He grinned at me. Yep, he was the package.

I told him about my new job and he looked kind of impressed. He told me what he planned to do after college, how he was sweating on an NFL contract to play in the big league and how his parents wanted him to get his career started. I listened attentively like a good groupie.

The bar was getting noisier and when we finished our drinks, Finn glanced at his watch. 'Want to get out of here?' he asked.

'Sure,' I said, expecting him to say he had to be somewhere and ditch me. I reached for my purse.

'I've got this,' he said.

'Thanks, Finn.'

Nice, very nice. We rose, he took my hand and led the way out of the bar. My heartbeat was starting to pound again and just the feel of his skin on my skin had my girl parts very happy. Did I mention how good he smelled? An aqua scent; I could lick it right off him. And nice butt too... I was just far enough behind him to get a good glimpse of it and those broad shoulders.

We got to the parking lot and Finn moved towards his car. 'Let's go back to my room and hang for a while. I can drop you back later to get your car if you like?' he said.

I was so busy watching his arm flex as he reached into his back jeans' pocket for his keys that his words caused a delayed reaction – my alarm bells started ringing. God I hate being sensible but we weren't going back to his place to play Scrabble and if I said no...

'Um, that might be moving a bit fast for me.' There I said it. The night was still young enough for him to find a replacement.

'All good.' He shrugged. 'We'll just hang for a bit. We don't have to do anything you don't want to do.'

I nodded. 'Okay. Why don't I follow you there in my car and then you don't have to go out again later?' I suggested.

'Yeah, that would be good. Is that you?' He pointed to my small blue car.

'That's me.'

I looked at my Toyota Yaris – Dad had bought it for me when I started college. He was going to buy Ryan his first car too. Mom's life insurance was a bonus none of us wanted. When she died, it paid off the house, set up a college fund for Ryan and me, and gave Dad some money to help raise us. We would have given it back in a heartbeat to have one more day with her.

'Okay, don't lose me,' he said, with a grin. I kept his black car in sight and five minutes later we pulled up at his student apartment block near the college.

'I'll give you the tour,' he said, and again grabbed my hand and raced me through the building.

I hurried to keep up with him. Finn greeted other students as we passed through, some of which I recognized from classes or seeing them in the library or at games.

We got to Finn's floor and the door to the area was open. Two guys sat with consoles on their laps trying to beat each other at some war game and a girl sat on the arm of the couch drinking cola and watching them. She gave us a wave. It was like a large, open plan area with lockable bedrooms around the borders and a bathroom every few rooms or so. Finn unlocked a door and hustled me in. He relocked it.

'Welcome to my pad,' he said, taking off his jacket and throwing it over a chair.

It was a decent size room with a double bed, a desk near the window, a two-seater couch and a small table with a TV on it. I put my bag down on the edge of the couch.

'Kick your shoes off,' Finn invited.

I took them off and put them near my bag and suddenly he was right next to me. He cupped my face in his hands and I looked up at him. He was something, and so close I could see his body definition through his T-shirt.

'You're very pretty, Alice.' He smiled at me and then began kissing along the edge of my neck.

Oh God, this was good. Then his hand began to move down my body and up under my skirt.

'Finn,' I whispered. I had never had sex but I was pretty sure all my feelings were from pure sexual frustration. Virginity was such a curse sometimes. I wanted Finn, but this was just what I experienced with Tomás, this was just sex and if I was just into sex it would be great. But for the record, Tomás would have been my first choice in that category; Finn and I were still on our official first date if you could call it that and not quite at the jump-my-bones stage.

His fingers began to slip between my panties and my skin. Fuck, fuck, fuck.

'Finn,' I said, again trying to get his attention.

'Mm?' He moved to my lips and began to kiss me, wet kisses, his tongue touching my lips and pushing between them.

Just do it, my heart was saying. But then my brain joined in... '*Really, is this what you've been waiting for? This is what you call special?*' Shut up headspace, I argued with myself.

Finn steered me towards the bed and I felt myself falling back on it. He was on top of me, his hand making its way up my dress again which was an open invitation given it was a full-skirt and fairly short anyway. I was in serious trouble now, this was going places I wanted to go but didn't want to go, if that makes sense. I didn't mean to lead him on and I did follow him to his room to hang for a while... I think our definitions of hanging out were different.

'Finn.' I pushed his hand away and brought it up to my waist.

'Sorry,' he said. 'Too fast?' and without waiting for an answer he began to kiss me again – his hand running over my top, over the fabric of my dress and over my breast. I could barely think; the sensation was wonderful and I wanted that nipple to be free and sucked. Down below I was aching with a dull kind of vibration, a needy feeling. From the huge bulge pushing against my leg I was pretty sure Finn was thumping too. My brain was still issuing warnings that sounded like a car alarm.

There was a loud knock at the door and someone just barged in.

Finn looked up and frowned. 'Fuck, what?'

I quickly pulled my dress down.

'Sorry brother, but your car alarm is going off.' I recognized one of the team and he gave me a chin-up movement and a smile. He then ran his eyes down my legs. Finn jumped up and I followed.

'Fuck it,' Finn said. 'Sorry Alisha, won't be a minute.'

'Alice,' I said.

'Yeah, sorry, Alice.' He grabbed his keys and pushed past the guy at the door who continued to stand there. I straightened my dress and my hair.

'I'm Matt,' he said, still eyeing me up and down. I wondered if the team shared.

'Alice,' I said, and moving past him, I slipped my shoes on and grabbed my bag.

'You're leaving, so soon?' he said.

'Yeah, I've got to get home. Can you tell Finn I'll call him?'

'You could check out my room if you like,' Matt said. He gave a nod to the door across the room.

For fuck's sake, what am I? The college bike.

'Thanks, but I told my dad I'd be home by seven. I'd better shuffle.' I held my breath as I moved past him, hoping he didn't grab me or do anything stupid. I hurried down the stairs, expecting to see Finn but I didn't pass him on the way. As I drove out, I saw him at his car, leaning against it and talking to some girl.

Thanks Finn, you ass. I breathed a sigh of relief. Finn was never interested in me, just interested in a one-night stand and doing the girl he thinks one of the Saints is doing. It made me realize that Tomás had been a gentleman... he could have had me but he didn't. God, men! I wish I was a lesbian.

Chapter 10

The message ping woke me out of my complacency; I was in my bedroom doing my last college assignment – all four thousand words of it – and I had started to nod off. It was after ten and Dad and Ryan had already turned it and I should too with work tomorrow. I dreaded looking at my phone – I had spoken with Mia and Cassie earlier so I was expecting this to be a text from Finn asking if I want to hook up again. *No Finn, get fucked.* I wonder if that reply would be direct enough.

I picked up the phone and my heart stopped. The message was from Tomás. I took a deep breath before thumbing across the screen to open it... just in case I wouldn't be able to get my breath after reading it.

Tomás: 'Hey *Bella*, how is the new job?'

That was it. Wow, I could make a lot from this. Tomás is messaging me because he heard I got the job, and he knows I've started, and he's thinking of me, and he's not with another woman at the moment so he's got time to text me, and he thinks I'm beautiful. I wonder if he's lying on his bed with his phone. He could be lying there with no clothes on – no he'd be cold... don't want to think about shrinkage. He could be lying there with underwear on, and his muscles bulging. He could be...

I then remembered I had to answer the text. Cassie had said to play it cool, yeah, cool, that's me, super cool, I thought. Who am I kidding? I'm a twenty-one-year-old virgin who is surrounded by gorgeous guys and the inner voice keeps telling me to wait for a romantic, meaningful encounter to give it up. I suck big time.

I thought about the message and thought about it some more, and then I realized if I didn't send one back soon he'd be asleep. Here goes. *You go Alice*, I coached myself.

Me: I love it, thanks for remembering. All good with you?

Done. Right then, breathe again and wait. I wonder what Tomás's middle name is. Mm, maybe super-gorgeous. Well, Tomás 'super-gorgeous' Carrera was well-practiced at messaging as a response pinged back to my phone only moments later.

Tomás: Pleased for you. Been thinking of you.

Yes! He'd been thinking of me, this was so good. Hang on... you know I try really hard not to swear too much but sometimes you've just got to give in to it... for fuck's sake Tomás, I thought, stop thinking about me and do something about it. Saints preserve us, why was it so hard to find a romantic guy who would remove my virginity?

Right, a response, let me think here. I looked to the clock; a bit late to text Cassie, I was on my own. *I can do this*, I continued to coach myself. I could tell him I miss him too but I bet every girl on the planet would miss Tomás Carrera, I took a different tack – I'd follow on from his comment.

Me: What have you been thinking about me?

Yeah, that was good. Good job me. He shot back a text.

Tomás: When I can see you again?

You're killing me Tomás Carrera. KILLING ME. No, I didn't text that, but I wanted to. Okay, think, Alice, think.

Me: You can walk past my office every day and spot me hard at it. Working gal.

I put in a few emoticons, God that was a good response, I surprised myself and hit the send button. Tomás volleyed a text back to me seconds later.

Tomás: Love that cream dress today

He had seen me! But he didn't come in and say hello. Where was he? Did he see me leaving in the parking lot maybe? Never mind, keep it light and fun. I can do light and fun.

Me: Were you hiding behind the photocopier?

Tomás: Sprung me Cookie. I'd like to hide under your desk

Okay, I was going to have to take matters into my own hands shortly. Why couldn't I be a slutty girl or a promiscuous girl, or hell, any girl that wasn't a virgin? I shot back a reply about work.

Me: As Mae said, come up and see me sometime, top of desk.

Tomás: Who is Mae? I'm up already.

Ah there it was. I stopped to think about this one. Kind of figured we'd get there, God knows I want to get there in the flesh.

Tomás: *Bella?*

And then my phone battery died.

No! Seriously. I plugged it in, trying to get it to turn on again but there wasn't enough charge to even open the screen yet. My life was hell. Tomás was going to think I was offended – crap, shit. It hadn't been a good day with the guys; I was truly screwed but not, if you know what I mean?

Whatever, just give it up and become a nun. Are there any nuns left in the world? On the bright side, at least I was following Cassie's advice and playing hard to get… accidentally.

Chapter 11

'Looking good,' Sasha Saxon of the Santa Ana Saints said, as I walked into the office in a red tartan skirt, black boots and a black knit top.

'This old thing.' I grinned at her. 'You're looking pretty hot there yourself.' I took in her full-skirt, ankle-length, navy velvet dress set off by the bleached blonde hair. On her desk was a velvet fedora in the same color – very bohemian.

'I made this; I make a lot of my own stuff.' She stood and did a twirl before plonking herself back on her chair behind the desk. 'I sell my fashions online and at the markets. I'll send you the link.'

'Please,' I said. 'I love shopping, did I mention that?'

Kay entered in a hurry, flustered from the school run, and Jim walked in from his office.

'Alice!' he exclaimed. 'You've come back for day two; well this is a good sign.'

I laughed but no-one else did. I noted Jim's pin-striped suit should have been retired last century.

'Umm, don't they usually come back?' I asked Jim. The three exchanged looks. 'No, really?' I asked again.

'Jim's scared a few away,' Kay said with a grin in his direction.

He put his hands up in surrender.

'I did no such thing, but there is a bit of a mice and rat problem in the office, and sometimes the reality sinks in that they are not going to meet the players, and they are pretty much working seven days a week on home game days.'

'How exciting though – not meeting the players – the being involved on game days,' I said, 'but not so excited about the mice and rats.' I lifted my feet a little higher off the ground onto the chair frame and thanked the Lord I had boots on.

Kay addressed me. 'Don't you worry Alice, I've put bait around... although it is a terrible way to die,' she said and sighed.

That killed the mood until we turned at the sound of someone walking towards our department. My eyes grew huge as Tomás Carrera, my Tomás, walked into our area.

'Ah the most beautiful women in the most important department, and Jim,' Tomás said, entering our area.

Jim laughed. 'Yes, thank you Tomás. Are you well?'

'Very well,' he said, hitting Jim on the shoulder and towering over him. Jim seemed to know everyone; he definitely was a fixture.

Tomás looked so edible in jeans which hung perfectly on his slim, muscular hips, a light black pullover and a white T-shirt underneath. His hair was a bit of a spiky mess as if he had just got up and forgot about it but it looked so cute. I wanted to run my hands through it.

He looked at me. 'I came to see how Al...iss was settling in.'

.I felt them all looking at me. If according to Jim, players rarely came into our part of the office, I was going to have absolutely no credibility left after this. First of all the Santa Ana Saints Captain visits me on day one; now the best boot in the country drops in on day two. It looks like I've slept my way to the job.

'Settling in just fine thanks, Tomás.' I smiled, awkwardly.

'You know each other?' Sasha said, her eyes huge.

'Ah, would you believe we're cousins?' I asked.

'No,' Kay said, smiling sweetly at Tomás.

'Kissing cousins,' Tomás said and leaned over to kiss me on the cheek.

'So...' I tried to restore some sanity to the situation even though I was sure my cheeks were burning red. 'Tomás you've obviously met Jim, and you know Sasha and Kay?'

'I have not had the pleasure of meeting Kaa...hh, but Sass...sha and I have done a few media interviews together,' he said in his smooth Spanish tongue, accentuating the 'a's and softening the rest. He turned his gaze to them and gave a smile that pretty much melted them to their seats. They both returned a smile, looking much sweeter than I knew they were... ah the effect a gorgeous man can have on a woman, shameful really.

'Ah, a short but sweet visit,' he looked to his watch. 'I have a meeting with Shayne.' He turned to me. 'I'll see you before I leave.'

'I'm really busy today,' I said, shaking my head and trying to tell him not to get me fired on day two.

'Nonsense.' Jim stepped in. 'Player management is important and I'm sure there are a few player appearance requests in that folder for Tomás.'

Tomás grimaced. 'Ah, I might be busy after all.'

Everyone laughed and he departed, not before stopping and whispering in my ear.

'Are you mad at me, Cookie?'

I shook my head. 'Definitely not.' Then I remembered that I hadn't returned his message.

'Good,' he said, and with that he was gone. There was never going to be a dull moment in this office.

*****

Jim answered a few of my questions and disappeared back into his office. As soon as he was gone, Sasha began on me.

'Okay, Alice, spill it, how do you know the Latin lover?' She crossed her arms in front of her and gave me a look that said an interrogation was coming.

'I don't know him that well.' I tried to play it down. 'I met him a few times and we've hung out in the same circles, that's all.' Meanwhile, I could feel his kiss on my cheek still and blushed every time I thought about it.

'It seems to me he likes you a little more than friends,' Kay said and gave me a knowing look.

'Right then.' I looked at my computer. 'I've got heaps to do.'

'Mm, we'll continue this later,' Sasha said and waggled a finger at me. 'You know I'm a qualified journalist, Alice. I don't give up on my interview subjects that easily.'

I grimaced at her. Lunchtime with Sasha was going to be hell but for now, I was saved by The Russian walking past to his desk.

'Morning ladies,' he said, and we answered in unison, all three of us silently watching like clown heads in a sideshow carnival – our mouths opened, our heads turned – as the six-foot-five vision passed us.

Then the messages started on my phone. I was lucky it was on silent and Kay and Sasha were hidden behind their computer screens.

Tomás: You look gorgeous, *Bella*.

Me: Aren't you in a meeting?

Tomás: Yes, but Shayne is on the phone. Were you mad at me last night?

Me: No my battery went dead.

Tomás: On your vibrator?

Me: Eww. On my phone.

Then there was blessed silence for a short while and I got to work. Ten minutes later, the messages started up again. I took a deep breath to calm myself because all I could think about was Tomás, and I didn't want to think about Tomás at work.

Tomás: Did you think of me all night?

Me: Bighead, I'm not telling you

Tomás: Cookie, that's not nice

Me: Okay, maybe I thought of you a few times

Tomás: More than 10, less than 50

Me: Are you still in that meeting?

Tomás: Yes but Russian interrupted and is talking to Shayne. So?

Me: Sigh. 10+. Did you think of me?

Tomás: No

Me: Thanks

Tomás: Kidding. Of course, I told you I was up. Aren't you flattered?

Me: I have to work, you'll get me fired

Tomás: I want to take you out

Me: Good

Tomás: I will call

Me: Great

Tomás: Bye for now, Cookie

Me: Bye Tomás

Tomás: Did I tell you that you are cute?

Me: Bye Tomás

Chapter 12

Cassie was on my case to move out with her now that I had a job – a job I had for three days mind you. Dad knew I was going to do my own thing as soon as I finished college and got a job; I had done one of the two at least. He joked it would be a bachelor pad now with him and Ryan, and he'd be able to bring a few ladies home at last. I knew Dad had had dates since Mom died but no one serious. My aunt said it was too easy for him just to come home to Ryan and me every night and not get on with meeting someone, but eventually, he had to. It helped to make the move out a little less painful knowing he might date – I worried about him. Ryan on the other hand pretty much lived in his room.

Cassie and I had always talked about flatting together. Actually, we talked about the three of us flatting together – Mia, Cassie, and me – but Mia had gone straight to first-class, moving in with Lucas in his posh beach mansion as she called it. Cassie had a great apartment; it belonged to her family, which meant her rent was way less than the industry standard. Up to a few weeks ago, she had shared it with another student until they graduated and she hadn't found another housemate yet. It had three good size rooms and two bathrooms – luxury, I would have my own bathroom. Only one car park but Cassie didn't have a car so that worked out just fine and I could afford half the rent now with my new job.

We'd put it off until Monday week because I had to work for my first weekend at the Saints and anyway, I could move in one carload – I only had clothes. Cassie's place was fully furnished and Dad wanted to keep my room the same in case I ever needed to come back. So, as well as the new job and moving out on the cards, I was saving the best until last… I had an official date with Tomás on Wednesday night. Big news!

*****

Wednesday at last… I never thought it would arrive. It was the night of the great date. Seriously, that's what Tomás called it when he messaged me on Monday night to say he wanted to take me on a date and I should dress for all things. What does that mean? Am I wearing heels or running up a mountain? Sipping champagne or playing soccer? Men, they just don't get it.

I was going on a date with Tomás Carrera, pause, I was just letting that sink in – okay, now I was too nervous to form a sentence and he'd be here in fifteen minutes.

I re-read his message again; thank God text messages don't fade from wear and tear or this one would have disappeared two nights ago. I kept studying it, looking for meaning between the lines, words within the words,

65

picturing Tomás composing it and looking at the screen with his gorgeous eyes and kissable mouth, turning up in a smile as he fired off the words to me. Sigh.

Tomás: Bella, pls allow me to take you on a date.

Me: Tomás, that would be great

Tomás: Yes, it will be a great date

Me: When, where, what shall I wear?

Tomás: Wednesday, I'll pick you up at 7

Me: It's in my diary

Tomás: Are you that popular that you might forget?

Me: I'm very busy and important Tomás

Tomás: Ha. Then I'd better make it a great date

Me: A hint? Do I wear heels or sneakers?

Tomás: Dress for all things

Me: Want me to meet you?

Tomás: No I'm picking you up. I won't bring the bike

Me: I look forward to it

Tomás: Me too. See you then, Cookie

I hardly slept since getting that message on Monday night and when I did my sleep was full of lustful dreams of Tomás and his hands, body, lips, tongue and other parts. Let's face it; I was exhausted; I was running on pure adrenalin here. With the pressure of starting a new job and now my first date with Tomás, who only a few weeks ago left me hanging after an uneventful night in his bed... I was so wired I was bound to orgasm if he held my hand. I wondered if his sister Valentina told him to pull his head in. I wondered if he was sick of beautiful women... ah yeah, that must be it.

'Ten minutes love, are you ready in there?' my dad asked from the other side of the door. I couldn't look at myself any longer or I would change clothes again, so I took a deep breath and opened the door to Dad.

'You look lovely, absolutely lovely,' he said.

'Thanks Dad, but you're only a little biased,' I teased him.

My brother Ryan walked past. 'You scrub up all right.'

Yep, that's more like it.

'Now do I need to have a word to this boy?' I knew Dad was teasing but really! I was wound tight enough. I rolled my eyes at him.

'No Dad, and he's not a boy, he's twenty-three and – '

'And he has the best foot in the country,' Ryan finished.

'I don't think your sister is too enamored by his foot,' Dad said.

So wrong – I was enamored with every appendage belonging to Tomás. I heard a knock at the door and my heart stopped.

'I'll get it,' Ryan said, keen to meet another soccer legend.

Dad squeezed my arm. 'Be careful and most importantly, have fun.'

I nodded. 'Thanks Dad.' We both were thinking of Mom. How she would have loved to be here to fuss over my hair or offer some jewelry and to meet my date. It was not as though I hadn't dated guys before but I hadn't had many come to the house before to pick me up and none that were Tomás Carrera.

I heard Ryan and Tomás talking as Dad and I came around the corner of the hallway to the front door and living room. Oh my God, there was a Latin model in the lounge room carrying a dozen long-stemmed red roses. Red means passion, I think. At this stage, it could mean smelly socks and I wouldn't care. They were beautiful and would impress Dad too with the touch of old-fashioned charm. Tomás looked amazing in a dark suit with a white T-shirt underneath – the perfect mix of dressy and casual. I could have eaten him then and there and licked his bones clean... wow that was a weird thought... hmm I'd been watching way too many zombie programs.

I couldn't form words quickly enough to introduce Dad but he took care of it himself, extending his hand, and the men shook.

Tomás gave me a breathtaking smile. '*Bella*, you look, well *bella*.' He grinned and handed me the flowers.

'Thank you, Tomás, they are gorgeous.'

'I'll put them in water for you so you two young people can get away,' Dad said, taking them from me.

'You had a great game last weekend,' Ryan said.

'Ah thanks, sometimes it just comes together,' Tomás said with a hint of modesty. 'Are you coming to the home game this weekend, Ryan?'

'Yeah, Lucas got Dad and me tickets.'

I saw Tomás's eyes narrow slightly. He couldn't possibly be worried about Lucas in my life – Lucas was living with my best friend.

'Ah, good,' he said and turned to me. 'Shall we?'

'We shall,' I agreed. I smirked at my brother because even though we're close, that's what we do, and I kissed Dad on the cheek goodnight. As we walked out, Ryan nearly bowled me over at the door.

'Wow, a Mercedes AMG GT S!' He came out to circle Tomás's car. 'I didn't know they were released yet!'

'Yeah, it drives very nicely,' Tomás said, as though the six-figure car in our middle-class driveway was no big deal. It was sleek; two doors, smooth lines and being red, no doubt very fast.

'I've never seen you on anything but your bike,' I said.

'Mercedes are one of my sponsors so I just borrow a car when I need one,' he said, with a shrug.

'Of course, silly me. Yeah, Toyota is my sponsor,' I teased, and the men laughed, as I glanced towards my little Yaris in the garage.

Tomás turned to my brother. 'Another time, I'll take you for a spin if you like?'

'Hell yeah, that would be great, thanks,' Ryan said.

Tomás was doing all the right things to make a good impression – flowers, calling my dad Mr. Peterson, winning my brother over for life with a promised ride. And he had me at first sight.

'Well, have a good night,' Dad said and hustled Ryan inside with him.

Tomás gave them a wave and turned to open the car door for me, I slipped in. This was so good – the new car smell and new guy smell and trust me, he smelt gorgeous.

Tomás slid into the driver's seat and put on his seatbelt. He stopped to look at me. 'Hello Cookie,' he teased. He leaned over and kissed me full on the lips, hovering there for just a moment.

'Hello Tomás,' I said, barely getting the words out. I was gone, maybe never coming back to reality. 'Thank you for picking me up.'

'The pleasure is all mine, *Bella*.' He eyed my outfit. 'You look very adorable.'

'Thank you,' I smiled wishing everything would go as slowly as possible now.

I spent a lot of time picking my outfit for tonight... more time than I probably spent studying in the last few weeks. It was a big dilemma – a dress or skirt? You don't want to look too dressy but I didn't want access to be too easy either if you know what I mean? Sandals or boots? Seriously; were we climbing sand dunes or not? Jewelry or was that too dressy? I wish we had all been born with fur coats like dogs and cats and all we had to do was pick a collar for the night. Wow, another weird thought... where did that come from? Mm. Meow.

Anyway, I decided on a hot pink fitted wraparound dress that fell just above my knees with three-quarter length sleeves which felt very girly. I figured Tomás might like a feminine type and I selected strappy sandals – I could always take them off to run across dunes. As for the underwear, well I spent a whole day on that not knowing if I'd be leaving it on or taking it off but I went for white, seamless, fitted, and satin fabric. Didn't want lace marks ruining my dress line. It was so complex. I wondered if Tomás spent any time thinking about his underwear; Lord knows I spent plenty of time thinking about what was next to his skin.

Tomás started the car and pulled out. It glided along the road and he looked like the master behind the wheel. I think we might have been the first to sit in these leather seats and the silver and black interior was so beautiful. I looked at him, so in control, so stunning, and I wondered what it must feel like to be in his body, to be Tomás Carrera. I admired his beautiful arms, his hands on the steering wheel, the way he wore his watch – this guy was going to kill me.

'Now, the great date,' Tomás said, getting my attention and musing over his words. 'Well, I plan for it to be great. We have a lot of things to do.'

'Do we?' I asked, surprised.

'Yes. We are starting with drinks at one of my favorite bars... you'll like it I'm sure.'

As he drove, he reached over and took my hand. I am going to remember this moment forever. And the next moment and the moment after that. Tomás drove along the harbor and took his hand back to do a reverse park opposite a bar with water views.

'A friend of mine just opened this little bar a few months ago.' He ducked his head a little in the car to look out the window and up at the sky. 'We have probably twenty minutes.' Tomás opened the door, jumped out and raced around to my side to open the door. He extended his hand and helped me out.

'Why? What's happening in twenty minutes?' I asked.

'You'll see.' Tomás smiled at me. He locked the car, took my hand and we crossed the street. It was such a buzz walking beside him – tall and handsome, my hand in his. People called out greetings to him as they passed and he returned them. Some snapped photos with their phones. Wow, these guys never got an off day.

We entered the trendy little bar and I saw the reserved sign along the bench table at the front.

'Ah, here's Rocco.' Tomás shook hands with a small, nuggety man all dressed in black.

'Rocco, this is Al... iss.'

'Pleasure,' Rocco said, and shook my hand. 'The seats you requested are waiting,' he said, indicating them. He looked pretty pleased to have Tomás in the front bench seat of his bar.

Tomás led me to the timber bench and stool.

'Now Al... iss, you must sit this way,' he said, facing me to see the water and the sunset but also very close to him. He put his legs on either side of mine and sat facing me. I was overwhelmed by the view – the ocean, the sunset, and Tomás with his legs pressed against me. I felt like a bundle of nerves. Everything was heightened; I was not sure I would be able to swallow, let alone form a sentence.

Moments later two tall glasses appeared, with the most delicious mix of champagne in red and gold colors and trimmed with mint. Tomás thanked Rocco and now, it made sense.

'Wow,' I said.

Tomás nodded. 'I know. Beautiful, and you dressed to match the pink in the sunset,' he teased. The cocktail was the same red as the sunset and we had a front-row seat to it.

'It's called Beach Sunset, a Rocco creation with orange juice, grenadine, champagne and a few other things. You don't have to drink it if you don't like it, but it's not too lethal,' he teased, remembering my last encounter with alcohol and my night in his bed where nothing, and I mean nothing at all, zilch, zero, happened. I think I went as red as the cocktail and Tomás laughed.

He raised his glass. 'To beauty,' he said.

I clinked glasses with him and had a sip – divine. Behind us the sun was a huge ball of red, pink, orange and gold hues sinking into the ocean and if we did nothing else tonight, this would have been enough – so perfect.

Chapter 13

'Next, I'm going to dine you, Al... iss,' Tomás said, in his sexy Spanish accent, 'but I will make you work it off later,' he teased. He left some dollars on the table and I noticed a very generous tip, waved goodbye to Rocco and we went back to his car. From there we spun into town to a tiny tapas bar called *Granada*.

We left the car, he took my hand in his, and we entered a small but crowded restaurant. Again Tomás knew all the staff and there were kisses and handshakes as we were led to a private little room and seated in our own booth. That didn't stop the flow of interruptions, but in a way I welcomed them. I could watch Tomás without blatantly staring; watch the way he smiled, laughed, related to people. The way he dipped his head just a bit shyly sometimes, the way his eyes lit up and became guarded when he wasn't sure.

And I was introduced as the woman with him; everyone was checking me out. I wonder how many of Tomás's women they had met in the year that he had been with the Saints. Most of all Tomás was a good guy, a really good guy. To me, he was sweet and generous with his affections. The only bad things I had discovered so far about Tomás were that he liked to play the scene and was, according to the ladies at the *Shaken Not Stirred* bar, a bit rough. I guess if he was not in a relationship and was hot, single and in demand, there was nothing wrong with that. Except, I hoped to change his relationship status. I wondered if playing the field had a use-by date. Was a couple of years enough or did some people want to do it for life? I wondered what Tomás wanted.

'*Bella*,' Tomás said, getting my attention, 'this restaurant has a tapas-only menu, an excellent one. Do you trust me to order for us?'

'Please,' I said, and within minutes a very attractive Latin American waitress joined us and greeted Tomás as if she knew him, carnally. I watched and internally panted as he ordered in Spanish without opening the menu. We both ordered colas – Tomás was driving and training early in the morning and I wasn't going for a repeat performance of last time, even though I'd be happy to revisit Tomás's bed.

Tomás sighed and took my hands across the table. 'This place, the food is very authentic,' he said, with what I thought was a hint of melancholy.

'Where is home?' I asked, studying his beautiful features.

'Buenos Aires.' The words rolled off his tongue. 'Beautiful city, very European, it is often called the 'Paris of South America' – think the tango, artists, writers, theatre, historic architecture, wild nightlife and of course, beautiful people.' His eyes looked soulful as he spoke of home.

I was still working on the image of Tomás dancing the tango in my head, with its dominant, long sensual moves. I cleared my throat. 'When did you last go home?' I asked.

Before he could answer, another attractive female walked in with our colas and slid into the booth next to Tomás, nudging him with affection.

'He doesn't go home enough, or so Valentina tells me,' she teased him. 'How is Tina? Are you keeping an eye on her?'

'She is well. And you look well, Lucia,' Tomás said and they kissed each other on each cheek. 'This is Al... iss.'

The beautiful Lucia gave me a warm smile. 'Welcome to our restaurant, Al...iss.'

'It's wonderful,' I said, trying not to stare at the way she snuggled into Tomás. She had straight dark hair, large lips and large brown eyes.

'Thank you. My business partner and I like it, but it takes over our lives. So, Al...iss, is he behaving?' She winked at me.

Tomás rolled his eyes.

'Unfortunately yes,' I said, and Lucia laughed out loud.

'Ah but the night is young,' she said and wrinkled her nose at me in a teasing fashion. 'I could tell you some tales.'

'But you won't of course,' Tomás said, ushering her out.

Lucia laughed again and shuffled off the bench. Before leaving she turned back to Tomás. 'When does Julieta arrive?' she asked.

I noticed Tomás stiffen and his eyes flicked quickly to me and then back to Lucia.

'Sunday,' he said.

'Good, I look forward to it. Make sure you bring her in.' With a wave, Lucia disappeared.

I reached for my cola and had a sip, a thousand questions buzzing in my mind that couldn't be asked because it was our first official date and I had no right to be territorial. But who was Julieta? His sister, cousin, friend, or more? Well that sucked and threw a bucket of water on my dream date. I had to pull myself up and out of that thought.

'I am sorry for the interruptions,' Tomás said, 'but it is the best tapas restaurant I know.'

'It's all good,' I assured him. 'I love being here with you and meeting the people you know.' His fingers interlaced with mine. 'You're quite distracting Al... iss,' he said, with a shy smile.

I cocked my head on the side and studied him. 'What does that mean exactly?' I asked.

He drew a breath and I waited for his response.

'I confess I didn't want to think of you,' he said and cleared his throat. 'But you kept invading my headspace. I tried for a week not to think about you.'

I frowned. 'But, why didn't you want to think...'

We were interrupted by the arrival of several small tapas dishes, this time delivered by a waiter that Tomás greeted as Felipe, who named each dish for my sake and left us to it.

Tomás moved on as though he hadn't just dropped a huge, intriguing bombshell on me.

'You must try this one first,' he said and, taking my fork, put a little of the spicy dish on it and brought it to my lips. He watched my mouth as I took the offered bite. His eyes met mine.

'Mm, so good,' I said.

He smiled, took his fork and helped himself to a serve.

Tomás made me taste each dish and waited for my reaction before having a bite himself: bacalao, slow-roast pork shoulder in chipotle, shredded duck tortillas and chargrilled chorizo.

'Rich, but delicious,' I said.

'You wait until you try my mother's cooking... I almost didn't accept the contract here because I'd have to go without,' he joked.

I waved off another bite; it was hard to eat when Tomás was sitting opposite me looking so divine and his legs were pressed against mine under the table. Plus he was talking about me meeting his mother... I could be reading a bit into that but I was running with it.

He leaned forward. 'Maybe coming here was a mistake,' he said.

'Why?' My eyes widened. 'It's wonderful.'

He shook his head and I bit my lip with concern.

He moved several of the plates out of the way and reached for my hands again. 'I'm going to scrap the next part of the great date,' he said, look intently into my eyes. His brown eyes were so compelling.

My mind was going through a thousand scenarios in milliseconds, thinking of what I might have done wrong or didn't do at all.

Tomás ran a finger around my palm and up my arm, giving me tingles. He lowered his voice.

'Sitting here and not being able to have you to myself is...' His breathing increased and as if on cue, Felipe arrived again to clear the plates and Tomás sat back, thanking him.

I cleared my throat and found my voice. I made some conversation so it wasn't awkward in the silence.

'So,' I asked again, 'when did you last go home?'

Tomás drank some more cola before answering. 'At the end of last season, about four months ago.'

'Do you miss it?' I asked.

Tomás exhaled and leaned forward, looking me in the eyes.

'No.' He shrugged.

'No, not a bit? No, not this week? Or no, not ever?' I asked, studying him.

'Don't get me wrong, I love my family, but there's a lot of them.' He smiled. 'When my family visited last year, someone at the club said it was like seeing a Pez dispenser of Carreras.' He smiled and shook his head. He was so adorable. 'But I am free here. My only responsibility is to play well for the team and to keep my contract. At home, it is always duty.' He finished his cola and chased it down with a half glass of water.

I did the same because the meal had been spicy.

I started to put two and two together about us – Tomás and me – but before I could explore it further, Tomás pulled out his wallet and put more cash on the table.

'Come Cookie, let's get out of here.' He rose and hurried me along. 'I'm scrapping the next part of the great date... no more people around us. I want to show you something.'

'Thank you, Tomás for tapas,' I said, accepting his hand as he helped me out of the booth. He pulled me into him, kissed me, and grinned.

'The pleasure is mine,' he said, stopping to look at me for just a moment. 'Let's go.'

He kept my hand in his and I hurried to keep up with him. We left with the same raucous round of greetings – farewells this time – and Tomás stopped to sign an autograph and appear in a selfie with a young fan at the entrance. We returned to Tomás's car and he saw me in again before coming around to the driver's side. This time, he took off fast and we headed towards the beach. He parked away from the madding crowd.

'You might want to leave your shoes,' Tomás suggested. He pulled his black leather dress shoes and socks off and rolled up his suit pants a few inches. I left my bag and shoes in the car and exited. He met me at the front of the car, and taking my hand, walked me towards the beach. He leaped the two steps down to the dune, turned around, and lifted me down. When my feet touched the sand, he didn't let me go but pulled me closer.

'There's nothing here but the waves, moonlight and solitude,' he said and sighed.

'Perfect,' I whispered.

Tomás put his hand in my hair, and leaned into me, kissing me softly then deeply. I slid my hands into his open coat and onto his white T-shirt. I lightly ran my nails down his back and he stiffened... everywhere.

I could hear the waves crashing and Tomás's controlled breathing. My heartbeat sounded as though it could lead the school band. He slowly pulled away, wrapping an arm around my shoulder and we walked down the beach. I left my arm around his waist, inside his jacket.

'I couldn't concentrate before with all those people around and your legs inside mine,' he said.

Thousands of pins and needles tingled me everywhere. He was so smooth, very dangerous for a young blood like me. But I soaked it all in, trying to capture every minute in my mind's camera. I shivered, not from the cool air, but as tingles from being near him rushed my skin. Before I had time to explain I wasn't cold, he slipped his jacket off and held it out for me to put on. I slipped my arms in and he took my hand, smiling at how his jacket drowned me.

'Isn't this magic?' I said, feeling the cold sand between my toes and the light spray of the ocean on my face.

'I come here often at night,' he said. 'Everyone is down the other end with the bars and lights, but here is so quiet.'

'By yourself?' I asked. I wasn't sure if that was good or a sad thing.

He nodded. 'I like the time out.'

'Tell me, Tomás,' I started.

'Yes, Al... iss,' he looked at me with a hint of a smile.

'Why can't you be free at home?'

'Ah.' He pulled me in closer again. 'I can now I guess. But that's a fairly new thing.' He hesitated, putting his words together. 'You see, my father cleared out one day... when I was twelve, just left.' He did a vanish-into-thin-air motion with his hands. 'My mother, God bless her, was left with five of us under twelve. I was the eldest, then I had twin sisters a year younger, a brother who was nine then, and Valentina – Tina – is the baby, you met her... she was eight when my father left. So I guess we all stepped up and grew up a bit, but I feel like I've helped raise a family,' he shrugged. 'Now, everyone has finished school, my contract has bought my mother a good house and she won't have to work again and I am free.'

I nodded and looked at him with new admiration.

'If I go home, I am pulled into all the family stuff and while that is great, I just want to be me for a while.'

'I get it,' I said. 'You've had so much responsibility from such a young age.'

'They are my family, it's what you do,' he said, and shrugged; Tomás wasn't good at taking compliments.

'But you were a boy,' I said.

'I was the man of the house when my father left.'

'You are such a good person, Tomás. Your father was irresponsible, but clearly, you didn't get that trait,' I teased him. 'You deserve some time off for good behavior.'

He grinned. 'That's one way of looking at it. Let's sit,' he suggested and dropped to the sand, suit and all. He raised his arms for me and lowered me between his legs, wrapping his arms around me. Nothing else existed in the universe at that moment; it was perfect. We sat that way in silence for a little while until Tomás broke it.

'I have something for you,' he said and reached into the outside pocket of his jacket that I was wearing. He pulled out a little black velvet pouch and gave it to me.

'What's this?' I asked looking from the pouch to him. The words of the models at the bar came back to me... *he gives good gifts*. Was this going to be my first and only date with Tomás and this was a payoff?

'Open it,' he insisted.

I pulled open the black cord on the small pouch and

pulled out a beautiful Pandora bracelet in silver with half a dozen mosaic blue and green ball charms. I knew it would have been expensive – far too expensive to give a girl on a first date.

'Wow, it's beautiful,' I sighed, admiring it. 'I love it, but I can't accept it,' I slipped it back into the black velvet pouch. 'It was good of you to think of me.'

Tomás frowned, a look of confusion on his face.

'Why can't you accept it, Al...iss? It's for you.'

'I know, but why?' I slipped it back into his jacket pocket.

He shrugged. 'I thought you would like it. Don't girls always like jewelry?'

I turned so I could see his face. 'I like you, Tomás. I don't want anything from you,' I said, and studied him.

He looked bewildered. His eyes narrowed. 'Oh, I understand, you think it means something? It doesn't have to mean anything, it's just a gift.' He shrugged.

I realized where he was going now; he assumed I was scared that I would have to 'put out' in return. Wow, this guy really traded in favors.

I shook my head. 'No. What I think is that you don't realize that not everyone wants something from you.'

He laughed. 'Yes, they do. Everyone.' He had the good grace to look a little sheepish then and pulled me against him so I wasn't studying his face anymore. He looked back out to sea, his cheek pressed against mine.

'No, Tomás,' I said, softly. 'I'm just happy to be in your company. I don't want or need a single thing from you.'

I felt him swallow and he didn't say anything, processing it all. I imagined he would run that through his mind a few times in the future. I suspected he was so used to family and lovers all needing him or expecting something from him that he didn't know how to just give himself. Maybe he thought that wasn't good enough? I wonder if he knew how to ask for what he wanted in a relationship or how to receive. We sat in silence listening to the waves crashing. A breeze picked up across the ocean and I realized he might be cold while I sat wrapped in his jacket.

'Are you cold? Do you want your jacket back?' I asked.

'I'm not cold,' he said. He continued to press his cheek against mine. 'Tell me, Al... iss, where is your mother? She was not there tonight to meet me.'

'No.' I swallowed and was pleased I didn't have to look at Tomás. 'Cancer took her when I was fourteen – seven years and two months ago.'

'It is still very raw?' he asked.

'No, not raw anymore, but I miss her every day. They say it gets easier, but it doesn't, it just gets different. Does that make sense?'

'Yes. I understand,' he said, tightening his hold on me.

I told him about how Dad, Ryan and I all had a role to play but I was never burdened by it the way he was; we just all did our bit to contribute. Financially Mom's insurance meant we never struggled.

'Can I ask you another question?' I said.

'I thought you were doing events, not journalism,' he said, with a smile.

'Yeah, I might have missed my calling,' I said.

'Ask away,' he invited me.

I took a deep breath.

He prodded me. 'Hurry up and ask because I have to kiss you and once I start, I can't stop for question time.'

I laughed. My heart was telling me to forget the question and go straight to the kissing, but I asked anyway.

'You know when I slept in your bed and you didn't go all the way with me...' I began.

'Oh, I know it well,' he said. Like a trigger reaction, I felt his erection pressing into the back of me. My own breathing increased... I kept going. 'Did you not do it with me because you thought I would be...' I tried to find the right words, '... not good because I'm inexperienced or... you thought if we did it, you'd have some sort of responsibility to me after?' There, I had put it out there. I felt my stomach drop as he hesitated to answer.

I guess I was hoping he would say that wasn't the case and he would say it really quickly to assure me, but he didn't.

'I'll tell you when I take you home,' he said. 'And I am going to take you home tonight Al...iss, but I am not going to take your virginity.'

'Okay,' I said, slowly. 'Why?'

'Because the first time I did it, it was awful, she was such a bitch. I don't want that for you and that's partly the reason why I pulled away,' he confessed.

I didn't say anything, I wanted him to keep talking, keep sharing what 'partly' meant and his reasons for not contacting me for over a week since that night I slept in his bed.

Tomás continued. 'I wasn't sure if I wanted something regular. Okay, that's not quite right. I was sure I didn't want a regular girlfriend.'

I felt my heart drop; I think it fell into my stomach. I didn't speak as I tried to work out what to do with this information.

'But I couldn't shake you.' His voice cut through my overactive mind. 'You kept coming into my head. So, here we are. Are you prepared to continue the great date knowing what you know?'

I breathed out. 'I'm prepared to take that ride,' I said, leaning my head back further onto his shoulder, cheek to cheek. I heard him laugh a little and my heart felt lighter again.

Chapter 14

I can't remember the trip to Tomás's house; he drove and my stomach fluttered the whole way. I was running through scenes in my head – so, we're going to his place but he's not taking my virginity... hmm? What will we be doing? Maybe it will be like a Finn ambush and he won't be able to hold back when we get there. When exactly is he planning on taking it? I was thinking way too much. He spun the car into the driveway and I noticed Valentina's level of the house was in darkness.

'We have the house to ourselves. Tina is away for a few nights,' Tomás said, and turned off the car engine. 'Are you sure you want to be here, Al...iss?'

I turned to face him. 'Tomás, there is nowhere else on the entire planet that I want to be right at this moment,' I said, looking into his eyes and holding his gaze.

A slow smile spread across his face. 'Ah Bella, you are something.' He leaned in and kissed me. 'Let's go inside.'

I opened my car door and before I was out of the car, Tomás had come around to close it and had taken my hand. He opened the house door at entrance level, flicked on a few lights and led me the way we came last time, although my memory was a bit blurry.

'I would offer you a coffee, but that would waste time and I want to explore you,' he said, and continued to lead me past the kitchen and living area to his bedroom.

'No coffee,' I agreed. I started feeling terrified and excited and, aagghh, well lubricated. Did I just go there? But it was so true, I was overheating for Tomás. I wanted him but I didn't want to be one of his wham-bam girls.

Why now? Why not the other night?

Maybe because I was sober now he felt better about it. Stop thinking, I ordered myself.

We entered his room and he slipped his jacket off and placed it over the back of a chair – so sexy in a white T-shirt and suit pants. I stood, feeling like a spare lamp.

'Can I use the bathroom?' I asked.

'Of course, Cookie. Next door to your right,' Tomás said turning on a small lamp which gave the room a soft glow.

I nodded and retreated to the bathroom. Thanks to Mia, I had a handy pack of supplies in my purse, all miniatures. I dabbed just a little perfume on and did a quick brush of my teeth. Nose powdered, dress straightened, underwear on correctly – all systems go.

I returned to the room but now Tomás was missing. I put my bag down and wandered around taking in his room – again. For a man who can dress himself so well, his taste in bedroom furnishings was surprisingly ordinary. The stripes and patterns, miss-matching sheets and quilt covers – it surprised me that Valentina hadn't offered to decorate his abode for him. On the bright side, the bed was huge, king-size with a big four-poster bed frame around it. I wasn't going to go there but you know where I'm going.

I turned on hearing a noise and found Tomás watching me. He was leaning up against the door like a model in a fashion magazine.

'Okay?' he asked, with a mixture of smile and frown.

'Very okay,' I assured him.

He looked relieved and moved towards me. Tomás lowered his head and kissed me, placing his other hand on my throat. I had a rush of passion and fear; how easy it would be for a man of his size and strength to take my life, but he moved his hand down my neck onto my chest and to the line of my bra. I stopped breathing.

Tomás stepped me back onto the bed and laid me across it. I watched as he slipped my shoes off and just as quickly removed his belt, lowering himself onto me. I ran my hands along his arms, feeling my insides flutter with the feel of him, the definition of his muscles and how his body reacted to my touch. I felt his erection swell and harden against me as he pressed it into the fabric of my dress. He was so relaxed; he knew all the moves while I was extremely unchoreographed in the bedroom – I'd get better with practice.

Tomás knelt up, pulled his T-shirt over his head and lowered himself on to his side, returning his arm to around my waist. His chest was beautiful; so well defined, and with golden skin. I ran my nails lightly down his back and he moaned, leaning into my mouth to kiss me. His tongue flicked between my lips. God, I wanted him to touch me so badly that my body ached for him. I was so wired that I was sure that I was going to lose it completely the moment he touched my naked skin. If he wasn't planning on taking my virginity, he was definitely going to take me to orgasm in a heartbeat.

'Al...iss,' he said.

'Yes,' I answered in a lusty haze.

'I promised I would answer your question and I've only answered it partly,' Tomás said, continuing to kiss me as he spoke.

Seriously, how does he expect me to concentrate on the words coming out of his mouth when he's kissing me and lying next to me? He was the only man I'd ever been with so far that I wanted to be with in every sense. Still he was talking...

'I could have easily have taken you last time you came here,' he said, and then his hand started up my dress. I think I stopped breathing.

'And, I would very much like to take you now,' he said. His thumb traced the inside of my thigh. I gasped and he stole the only air I had left to breathe, covering my mouth with his lips. He pulled away only slightly.

'I don't feel responsible to you if you came here of your own desire and you did, but...'

I waited patiently, barely able to hear his words as his thumb moved away from my thigh and his fingers touched the fabric of my panties.

I moaned softly, and he stopped.

'Tomás... please, touch me,' I begged him.

He gave me the hint of a smile and moved his hand out from under my dress.

'No, where are you going?' I wailed and he chuckled.

'You are so cute, Al... iss.' He reached to the tie at the front of my wrap-around dress and released it.

'Ah, that's what you were going,' I said, and smiled at him. He didn't open my dress, just left the tie undone and looked at me.

'Please, just listen to me for one moment,' he said. He ran his tongue over his lower lip.

'What?' I asked, leaning up on both elbows.

'You girls always want to talk and now I'm talking you don't want me to,' he said.

I smiled. 'I got distracted by that other stuff you're doing.'

'Making love to you stuff?' he teased, his brown eyes laughing at me.

'Yes, that stuff. Please, finish.'

'Which one?'

'Both. The words and the actions,' I said, a little more insistently while placing my hands on his bare chest. 'I heard what you said and I'm pleased you don't feel responsible for me.'

'Well when you say it like that it doesn't sound right,' he frowned. 'I feel responsible for getting you home safely but I'm saying you are a grown-up, as am I, and you choose who you want to lose your virginity to without that guy having to marry you or commit to you.' He shrugged. 'But that is not quite how I wanted to say it.'

I touched his face with my hand, keeping my other free to roam his arms. I agreed with the marry sentiment, but I wasn't sure I liked the idea of no commitment. Regardless, I wasn't going to ask for the definition right here and now for fuck's sake, I thought, let's move on.

'I get it,' I assured him. 'I've had to grow up a bit fast too and I'm not looking for a guy to step in and save me. I just want...' I stopped – I really didn't want to get into relationship talk on the first official date. 'I just want you to touch me.'

'I can do that,' he agreed. 'What I want to say, Bella, is that you are very different from the girls I have been seeing. They are like me, just in it for some fun. I do want to take your virginity, but I want it to be special for you. I want you to be romanced and no matter what happens for the rest of your days, you will look back on that experience and feel it was special, as you are. Yes?' he said.

Tears welled in my eyes and I didn't risk speaking. I nodded. He leaned in and kissed me again. I quickly blinked away the tears. When he stopped kissing me, I opened my eyes and he was looking at me again. He brushed under my eye and removed a tear, putting the wet finger on his lip. That act of kissing my tears was so sensual.

'So I will seduce you and then take your virginity when we are ready. Tonight, only my hands will have the pleasure,' he said.

Thank God I was lying down because I'm sure I would have melted to the floor and needed mouth-to-mouth resuscitation. Now, he undid the flaps of my dress and, pulling me up off my elbows, he slipped it off me. He rose, placed it on a chair and took off his suit pants at the same time. I fell back in shock.

'What?' his eyes widened.

'It's enormous; it's never going to fit!' I exclaimed, teasing him. What a body, OMG. Slender hips, defined six-pack, strong arms, tall and lean and... hard.

Tomás laughed. 'It will fit; didn't you get that birds and bee talk? You expand and your lips below swallow it whole inside you,' he said and grinned. He lay back down beside me and admired my underwear.

'No,' I looked at his enormous erection pressing against the white fitted boxer-briefs he wore. 'I'm sure that won't fit inside me. I'm very tight, you know?' I continued to tempt him. 'No one else has been in there before.'

Tomás dropped his head to my chest and groaned.

'Al... iss, if you keep talking like that one of two things is going to happen.'

'What?' I teased, keen to make him say it.

He looked up at me and said quickly, 'I'm going to blow my load or I won't be able to let you leave here tonight as a virgin.' He covered my mouth with his hand before I could respond and then his lips began to trace my body, leaving a trail of goosebumps.

Surfacing for air, he smiled, removed his hand and shook his head at me. 'Beautiful, Cookie,' he said, and ran his hand down over my bra and satin pants, taking my breath away.

He moved his thumb under my bra and electricity ran from my breast to everywhere in between. Tomás slowly pulled the straps down off my shoulders, and then reaching behind, unclasped my bra and removed it. I tried not to gasp, but this was it, I was half-naked in front of him and so self-conscious.

He made a satisfied sound like a low growl and began to suck on my nipple. My back arched and I exhaled sharply.

Holy fuck that was good. Why hadn't I been getting nipple sucks before? I'd wasted so much time. I thought that was the ultimate until his teeth grazed me and sent a new wave of glorious shock waves through my body. With a free hand, he began to trace the fabric of my panties. I could feel him urgent and pressing into me. I grazed my fingers up the fabric of his briefs along the length of him and Tomás breathed in sharply, as his body shuddered.

He put a finger into my panties and began to slide them down over my hips. My breath was catching; the world didn't exist at this moment, just Tomás and me alone on his bed. He moved his lips to my mouth and his finger slowly teased me.

'Tomás,' I moaned.

'Al…iss, it's okay,' he assured me. He must have thought my reaction was nerves but it was just the opposite. I wanted him to continue, to take me now. I wanted all of him, inside me, over me, under, around, just bring it home.

His repositioned, all the time, his tongue explored me. I froze.

'Al…iss, relax your body a little, you can trust me,' he said.

Electricity and emotions coursed through me while Tomás played my body.

I suppressed a cry, gasping, as my back arched and still Tomás wouldn't release me. He kept up the motion, slowing it down, and his touch becoming gentler. I begged him to stop and he edged off, holding me and gently kissing me.

'It's okay, just let yourself go,' he said.

I tried. I was frightened to be uninhibited, to release my feelings and cry out in orgasm. Was it normal?

He began to increase the pace and I groaned with pleasure and embarrassment. I had never lost control like this, ever.

'Good, relax my Al…iss, it's okay, trust your reactions,' he whispered and then I relaxed and trusted him. It seemed to go on for ages – a heated ride of extreme pleasure like nothing I had ever experienced or could describe and all by his hand. He worked me until I pushed his hand away as it became agony. Tomás moved up to press me against him. I couldn't even see him for the lust haze in my eyes.

'That was… orgasmic,' I whispered.

'It was,' Tomás agreed.

'Tomás…'

'Yes Al…iss?'

'You're so good,' I said, still feeling dreamy.

He laughed. 'Cookie, that is only our first play with hands. Next time my tongue wants to take you, then after that, I want to enter you and then we will try all different positions and places and we will try some very bad stuff.'

'You are the master,' I said. 'I am a very willing student.' My heart rejoiced at the future dates lined up in the 'classroom' with Tomás.

'I'll have fun teaching you,' he teased, flashing me a sexy smile.

I moved my hand down to his boxer-briefs; I couldn't believe he hadn't burst out of the fabric it was so hard and tight in there.

'Your turn to be released,' I said, my voice husky with satisfaction. I saw his surprised expression. 'I have a few skills,' I assured him, rolling him onto his back, 'and I'm a quick study. You can tell me what you like and want too.'

'I think you'll do fine,' he said, smiling and dropping his head back on the pillow with his hands behind his head. As I ran my fingers along his body he omitted a low growl which seemed to come from deep inside his chest.

I straddled him, and began to do my part, what a tough job.

'Oh Tomás, you are a work of art,' I said.

'Hands only!' Tomás warned me.

'But...' I pouted.

'No, Al...iss, the teacher has spoken. Everything in good time.'

'Okay,' I sighed and then began.

He inhaled sharply and muttered my name. 'Don't get ahead of the teacher, Al...iss.' He leaned up, grabbed the back of my head and pulled me towards him. I fell onto his chest, not doing any damage – he was so hard I think I bounced. He stuck his tongue in my mouth, hard and fast and needy. It was a powerful kiss; I thought about the ladies at the bar saying he was rough. I looked forward to a bit of rough.

He pulled away. 'That's the only place your tongue is allowed tonight,' he growled and gave me a warning look. I swallowed and nodded. He pushed me back. I resettled and licked my lips; it was subconscious, honest.

'Behave,' he said.

'Shh, Tomás, I have work to do here,' I said, trying to focus.

He chuckled and stopped abruptly when I touched him

lightly everywhere, and I mean everywhere. I looked at Tomás lying on his back looking so beautiful. His eyes were closed and I felt I had all his power in my hand.

'Saints be praised,' I heard him whisper or something in Spanish that sounded like that.

'Al...iss,' he cried out as he came. He pulled me over to lie beside him and I traced my hand gently over his chest as we lay quietly.

Eventually, Tomás spoke. 'I think you are head of the class, Al...iss,' he said.

I smiled. 'I have a very good teacher. He makes me want to learn, such a rare gift.'

We lay in blessed silence again for a while longer, just enjoying the post glow.

'So,' Tomás eventually said, 'how was that date?'

'Just great,' I assured him. 'So great.'

'Our lesson continues on Friday night, does that work for you, Cookie?' he asked.

'Yes, sir,' I snapped with glee. 'Any homework before then?'

'Oh yes,' he said, with spice in his voice. 'I'll be messaging you your homework instructions.'

I think I giggled like a twelve-year-old. Study had never been this much fun.

'But there is one more thing you must do tomorrow.'

'Mm?' I asked suspiciously.

'We have the press conference in the morning. What will you be wearing?' he asked.

'Our office team has to wear the uniform... navy skirt, white shirt, blue and gold Saints silk scarf. It's nice actually.

They make us wear that so you can tell us from the players.'
I poked him in fun.

He laughed. 'Yes, it would be hard to tell you and The Russian apart. Then your homework starts tomorrow. No panties.'

'What?' I turned to look at him.

His eyes laughed as his smile began to widen.

'You heard your teacher, no panties under the skirt.' He ran his hand down and I stopped it midway. He pushed on and started circling around my butt, making his way to the front. I couldn't speak while I followed the pattern of his hand. 'When I look at you tomorrow at the press conference, I will know that under that skirt you are naked.'

I felt the rush of desire and fear. 'Have mercy,' I told him.

Tomás laughed.

'What if I have to go up a staircase or I collapse from excitement and my skirt rides up?'

'That would be unfortunate,' he said. His fingers made their way back up to my face and he stroked my cheek. 'No panties, Alice, or you'll make your teacher very cross.'

Chapter 15

Sasha Saxon from the Saints was in the office before me when I rocked into work Thursday morning; Jim was in too but he was always in early and Kay arrived ten minutes or so after me, harried as she always was after the school run. Could they tell I wasn't wearing panties? Good grief, the things I do for a guy, well this guy. I should have just worn them and slipped them off before the press conference but there was something so sexy about knowing I kept his secret. I did bring them in my handbag; I wasn't planning on going commando all day!

It was Jim and Sasha's job to pull together the media conference at ten; Kay and I were on hand to help. The club didn't do the full-on media event very often but there was this weekend's game to talk about, a new substantial sponsor to announce and a few other bits of club news including all the recent media hype about the drain the club would face as players were tempted by European clubs. No wonder they had signed Lucas up as tightly as they could and wanted to keep him happy – it helped that he wanted to stay near his friends, and now Mia too.

I should have been exhausted but I was on a natural high. I got home late from my date with Tomás, or early depending on how you look at it. I fell straight into a deep and satisfying sleep only because my body couldn't take any more lying awake thinking of Tomás, and I woke up at seven a.m. I allowed Dad and Ryan two questions only answered those and was at the office at eight-thirty, ready for a day of Saints and scenery. God, my life was great.

Except for one small thing, I didn't ask Tomás the question I wanted to ask – *who was Julieta?* The Julieta that was arriving on Sunday. My mind went to the date last night, again – who was I kidding, I'd thought of nothing else since I opened my eyes. What a wonderful night, what a kind, sexy and wonderful man. I was so happy I was scared... I know that might not make sense but anyone who has ever fallen in love will totally get it.

Sasha's eyes narrowed as she looked at me. 'You look particularly happy this morning.' She studied me.

'I am particularly happy,' I agreed.

I'd be happier if I had my panties on, but seeing Tomás would make up for that.

I continued, 'I'm in a job I love, I get to work with you, Sash, every day, the scenery is great and...' I heard the coffee van pull up outside, '... the coffee van is here! Kay, can I get you one?'

'May God bless you, Alice,' she said, fishing some coins out of her top desk drawer. 'A double shot latte made on soy please.'

'Like I could forget that order,' I teased her, rising and taking the coins. 'Sash?'

'I'll come with you,' she said, still eyeing me off.

I stuck my head into Jim's office. 'Coffee, boss? The van is here,' I said.

'Why not? Thanks,' he said and pulled his wallet out and offered me a few dollars.

'Cappuccino with one sugar,' I said.

'You'll go a long way, Alice,' he teased me.

Sasha and I walked out of the admin offices and joined the staff already in the queue at the coffee van.

'Nice uniform,' I said, admiring her outfit.

'Right back at you,' she said, 'you wear it well.'

I sighed. 'Bit sad when we have to deliver our own compliments.'

'Undo a few buttons and lose the bra and I'm sure we'll get plenty,' she said.

My heart rate went into overdrive. I hoped she didn't have an inkling that I was going commando from the skirt down. Thank God it was knee length. Mm, Tomás Carrera would pay for this one. I bet he was secretly laughing right now – I bet he didn't believe I would do it. It did feel pretty sexy though, in the right company.

Sasha sighed and looked to the top of the queue. 'C'mon Russian, how many coffees are you ordering there?'

The enormous Saints player cum security officer turned and looked at us.

'Sasha, I'm not built for speed, but if I can get before you in the queue, then you deserve to wait,' he said. The queue waiters laughed along. It was hard to tell most times what The Russian was thinking or if he was joking; he was so dry and nothing really changed in his expression, his tone or his speed. He was a walking wall; a muscle-built, huge wall.

Sasha gave him her best 'you'll pay for that' look.

'I have one word for you, Russian,' she called to him. 'Merchandise.'

'Oh yeah, about that,' he said and turned to her, 'have you got a kid's jersey I could send my cousin?'

'Ah, have you got a cappuccino with my name on it?' she asked.

He picked up the two he had ordered; one for himself and his fellow Saints' player and security officer, Eddie Mosley who shared the office with him. 'If you had just got here a few minutes earlier I would have ordered you one,' he said, with a shrug.

'Hmm.' She smirked at him, as the line moved along.

'Morning Alice,' he said as he passed me.

'Morning Russian,' I said, with a smile. I'm sure I was radiating a post-orgasm glow.

'Good to see you girls in uniform,' he said, 'love a woman in uniform.' He continued to the office.

I looked at Sasha and lowered my voice. 'You get on well with him. Shame he's taken. Leesa, his girlfriend, is gorgeous though.'

'I heard they split. Anyway, uggh, I'm not going out with a player,' she said, quietly. 'How incestuous... working here, hanging out with one after hours. I'd have Saints on the brain. Besides, I've got my eye on someone.'

'Really? That's good,' I said, pleased for her. 'So I wouldn't know him then?'

'Yes, your brother,' she said, then laughed.

'Oh, ha, you're very funny, he's not even legal age yet.' I

rolled my eyes at her and she broke up laughing at her own joke. She was a bit 'out-there'.

When I got back to the office and finished delivering Jim and Kay their coffees, I threw myself into the game entertainment that was required for the weekend – luckily my predecessor had set that up for the next few months and I was just required to follow up and tick all the boxes, an easy learning curve. I checked the rundown of events was still correct and posted a round of updates on the Saints' social media sites. Next, I had some player appearance requests to wade through and approve or deny – they seemed to be never-ending, and then we had the media event at ten and our own weekly marketing team meeting at three p.m. I went to the ladies' and forgot there were no panties to pull down – super weird.

Back at my desk, my phone vibrated with a message and I reached for it. There was only one person I wanted to hear from this morning and I wasn't disappointed... make my day!

Tomás: Hi Cookie, my very promising student, thinking of U

I grinned and then tried to hide it. My stomach flipped with excitement and I messaged back quickly.

Me: Morning 'T' for Tomás & teacher. Thank you for a wonderful night. Truly was a great date

Tomás: For me too. Are you panty-less?

Me: Yes sir, as instructed

Tomás: You're going to be begging me to take your V

Me: I'm begging you already

Tomás: It must be memorable, a V-trip, I insist

Me: I don't think I'll ever forget

Tomás: See you at the press conf. Then, I will send you homework for tonight.

Me. Don't make it too hard.

Tomás: Trust me, it's hard right now.

Ah Tomás, Tomás, Tomás. Thank God I don't have male parts. It would be hard all day thinking of Tomás, so uncomfortable sitting down and I'd get absolutely no work done. Another weird thought... wow, I'd never need drugs for tripping.

Chapter 16

The press conference was in the Saints' club room and there was a good turnout. A small group of the key players was in attendance – they got rostered to attend a few during the season and it was compulsory – along with several television camera crew, and staff from the two newspapers and radio stations with their microphones set up at the front of the room. The players were in their uniform too – a navy suit, white shirt and club tie. Men usually always looked good in a suit especially when they were fit and gorgeous to begin with and the Saints' boys didn't disappoint. It was an effort to not drool. Where was I? Oh yeah, Sasha and I manned the door; then I took a pile of press kits from Jim and circulated, handing them out. Winning brownie points basically – it was my first week, and I wanted to be a hit.

I saw Lucas arrive and begin to circle the room and as he passed me, he squeezed my shoulder and I gave him one of those smiles that said 'you're adorable – but don't hurt my best friend because I am now in charge of the Saints' Facebook page'. Amazing how much one expression can hold.

Kay had taken over at the welcome desk and Sasha swanned past and nudged me. 'Show off,' she said.

'What?'

'Friends with the legend, hey?' she said, with a glance to Captain Lucas.

'You mean... the legend dress designer?' I asked wide-eyed looking directly at her.

She laughed. 'Yeah right, that you are. One day you may just be saying that.'

A female journalist about my age wearing a beige suit and dangerously high heels walked up to Sasha and me.

'Can I have one of those?' she asked, looking at the press kits in my hand.

'Of course,' I said, and gave her one. She looked at my name tag and job title and it wasn't a friendly look – it was like the look a carnivore gives a bunny in those National Geographic TV documentaries.

'Oh, you got the event coordinator job; I went for that,' she said. Her lips thinned as she appraised me as though it was my fault I applied.

'I was really lucky,' I said.

'What do you know about soccer?' she asked.

I bristled at her rudeness and I felt Sasha arc up next to me.

I took a deep breath. 'I'm a bit of a regular at the games.'

She smirked and raised her chin defiantly.

I continued. 'But since there's an entire management team and several dozen contracted soccer players that know a lot about soccer, they don't really look to me for advice on the game, they just needed someone who can do events.'

Her smirk soured and she turned and walked away. I exhaled.

'Good for you! That was great. What a cow,' Sasha said. 'Lucky she moved on, I was just about to see what soccer skills she had and it wouldn't have been pretty.'

Sasha's loyalty was comforting especially given it was only my first week. We went our own ways and I grabbed my camera to take some photos for the social media pages.

And then I saw him arrive; Tomás Carrera was in the building – oh be still my beating heart. His eyes searched me out and widened on finding me. The look he gave me undressed me there and then; I'm sure I went three shades of red.

I cleared my throat and returned the greeting to the journalist in front of me, offering him the last press kit I was holding. I returned to the welcome desk to help Kay. Tomás moved in front of me.

'Hello Al...iss.' He smiled. 'You look lovely today.' His gaze ran down my body.

'Tomás, it's good to see you again,' I said as if we were strangers passing in a room full of strangers.

He moved closer to my ear. 'Are you panty-free because I will be checking up later?'

I swallowed and nodded at him, and he grinned.

'Well done. I want to touch you,' he said into my ear which sounded even hotter with a Spanish accent.

I saw The Russian walking towards us. He was doing both of his roles – club security and appearing as a Saints' player – worth every cent that man. He eyed up his teammate Tomás.

'Is this guy hassling you, Alice? Do you want me to move him along?' The Russian said, his smile twitching slightly. He crossed his enormous arms over his bountiful chest.

'Um, yes, he is distracting me, Russian. If you could move him along that would be much appreciated,' I said, deliberately fluttering my eyelashes at him.

'Oh please,' Tomás said, 'you and whose army, Russian?'

The other half of the security team, Ed, wandered over. 'The Russian army?' he suggested.

'I wasn't going to get my hands dirty, as I'm the manager. Ed, throw this gate-crasher out,' The Russian said to Ed.

Ed rolled his eyes. 'You see what I put up with every day and that office is so small.' He hit Tomás on the back in a casual greeting.

'How's the ankle, Ed?' Tomás asked the wiry defender, and I took the opportunity to sneak away and get back to work so I didn't get the evil eye from the boss.

I went back to help Kay who was opening a box of Saints' scarves to offer as a takeaway gift for the media.

'Sasha is very protective of her merchandise; she won't let us put them out in advance because she thinks all the journos will take several and clear out,' Kay said. 'So it is just one each.'

'Got it. Don't want to mess with Sasha,' I said, with a half-smile.

Kay shuddered. 'Strange one that, but we love her.'

I looked over at Sasha and began to wonder just how strange we were talking about here. Kay brought me back to earth by stacking half a dozen scarves in my hand. She took the rest herself. We stood near the door and over the next thirty minutes, as people left, we offered them a scarf.

'You can only take it if you wear it in your office when you get back,' I told one of the older journos who laughed and put it on straight away.

'That do?' he asked.

Jim passed by and heard my comment. He turned to the journo.

'Alice is tough, but she gets results.'

Out of nowhere Tomás appeared at my side. 'Yes, she does.' He smiled at me, shook hands with the journo and I looked away quickly to hand out another scarf.

'I need to speak with you,' Tomás said in my ear. 'It's work-related.'

I narrowed my eyes at him. 'Really?'

'Really. I'm a player and you work for the club. I need assistance.' He looked around. 'It's over now anyway, and Jim can spare you for ten minutes.'

Kay was smiling and trying not to listen in.

'Hey Jim,' Tomás called, 'can you spare Alice for ten minutes?'

I gave Tomás a dark look that Darth Vader would have been proud of if I had been his daughter.

'Sure,' he called back, 'have her for fifteen if you like.'

Kay reached for my few remaining scarves as Tomás hurried me off. He led me by the elbow down the hall whispering, 'Oh I will have you all right, *Bella*.'

He knew his way around the club because in a matter of moments we found ourselves in a large room. At the far end were a sink and mirror, paper towels, and a shower you wouldn't enter without brandishing a bottle of bleach. At the end closest to us were tables, bike and storage racks.

He shrugged. 'We lock our bikes up in here some days if we ride to training.' He locked the door.

'So I'm your bike now?' I teased. 'Tomás, you're going to get me in trouble at work.'

'It's an office, you're not in the army. Now take your skirt off,' he said, and leaned back against the wall, folding his arms.

'What? Never! We're in... public.'

Tomás looked around. 'It's just you and me, Cookie.' He moved over to me and pressed me against the wall. He leaned down, not taking his eyes off my face and ran a hand up under my skirt. I gasped. Tomás pulled his hand back out from under my skirt and rose to full height; a very satisfied smile on his face. He took my hand and guided it to the front of his suit pants where he sported a very hard package.

'I have had that all morning thinking of you naked under that skirt. Even worse once I got here. Don't make me suffer anymore Al...iss, I want you.'

'I can feel that,' I said, my breath catching. 'Is that why you kept your jacket done up?'

'Yes and I tried to think unsexy thoughts. Seeing The Russian helped,' he joked.

'Poor you,' I said, pouting.

'Come on, it's part of your education on the virgin trip,' Tomás said. He pushed my hair back behind my ear and ran his thumb along my lower lip. I almost melted to the ground. 'It's important, this road to losing your virginity.'

He leaned down and kissed me, depriving me of the

small oxygen supply I was getting between my heightened breaths. He pulled away and I leaned into him, barely able to keep standing. Was it like this when everyone fell in love... the feelings and the passion? The sexual tension and attraction? No wonder everyone wanted to be in love.

'It is so good of you to dedicate yourself to my journey,' I said, holding his gaze.

'If I have the honor and pleasure of educating you and taking your... gift, then I take the responsibility very seriously. But you have to have the whole package,' he said.

'I love the package.' I rubbed my hand down over the front of his suit pants again and worked him just a little; he straightened, his breath hissing through clenched teeth.

'For the love of God, Alice, you're either a natural or a very naughty girl.' He kissed my neck. 'Or both,' he moaned.

'Teacher, I have this ache,' I tried to explain and Tomás smiled.

'Good, excellent,' he said. 'But hands, we're on hands until the next class which is tongue. You must get it right before we move on. Lucky that you are a very good student and we can move on so quickly,' he said, his voice breathless as I continued to stroke him.

'Hands, got it,' I whispered and then I began to undo his pants, pulling his shirt up and I put my hands to good use.

'I think you've forgotten I'm the teacher,' he said, panting slightly.

'Shall I stop?' I asked and kept up the good work. He didn't answer that question and I tried something new.

'Fuck, Al...iss,' he panted, 'where did you learn that trick?'

I didn't tell him that I had read it in a health magazine

and didn't realize it would come in so handy. Tomás didn't stop me, so I kept going gently, using my hands, getting a rhythm going until I felt him buck. God, I loved controlling him.

He pulled away momentarily and I gave him a confused look.

'No tongue, no mouth,' he said, trying to focus as I kept him right on the edge of coming.

We were both still half-dressed but it didn't deter my efforts… I know, I am such a hard worker. I kept going.

He was so close; he grabbed the shelving above me, put his head back and his jaw locked as he tried to control his loud groaning. I kept up the momentum until he couldn't hold it in any longer and then I watched the beautiful Tomás reach the heights. Eventually, he dropped his head to look at me.

'Fuck me that was good, Al…iss,' he said, sounding surprised.

I smiled. I loved good reviews. We stayed like that for a minute while he caught his breath and then I was no longer was in charge.

He began with his hands, and lips, his eyes all glazed and relaxed. What a hard day at the office, and to think I got paid for this, even the breaks.

'You have graduated in hand technique with honors, *Bella*,' he said. Then he gave me a deadly smile. 'I'm going to enjoy this.' He removed his coat and laid it flat on a table in the corner. I was guessing I would be lying on that coat in a matter of minutes.

I bit my lip, worried about the fact we were on office

property and I had no panties on. I didn't mind Tomás being revealed, but I wasn't so keen on being exposed myself.

He grabbed my hips and in a few quick moves, spun me around, pushed me over to the table in the corner and bent me over it. My chest was pressed onto his jacket on the table and my face turned to the wall, away from the door. I gasped with the quickness of it all. I felt Tomás behind me, leaning against me and restricting my movements. He pulled the zip down on my skirt.

'Don't move, *Bella*,' he said, and I felt him peel my skirt off me. It pooled at my feet and I could only imagine the view he had of my naked white butt looking up at him. I felt completely exposed. I couldn't see his face, but I felt his hand as it began to circle gently over my butt cheeks. My breathing was fast and I'm sure my face was red with embarrassment.

I braced as I felt his hands move over me. Oh my God I wanted this – the exposure, the pleasure, the embarrassment, and the thrill, all fighting each other while Tomás breathed near my ear and stroked me below. Then I felt his hardness again.

I arched up.

'Shh, it's okay, I promise,' he said, and placed his hand on the center of my back, gently pushing me down again on the table. 'Trust me, I'm not going to enter you today… it's our hands lesson.'

His pace increased finding his mark again, I was only seconds away from coming as he moved his hand off my back and slid it around past my throat, down the front of my work shirt and straight into my bra.

I was gone, exploding in a full-throbbing orgasm, pleasure overwhelming me. I rode it forever and when I pulled his hand away from me, unable to take any more, Tomás held me from behind in an embrace. I moaned and managed to mumble a few grateful words.

When I was back on earth, Tomás lifted my skirt off the floor, pulled it back up over my hips and zipped me up. I tucked in my shirt, straightened my scarf and patted down my hair. Unfortunately the flushed, happy look on my face gave it away.

'I am speechless,' I said, still slightly breathless and he grinned.

'Best press conference ever,' he agreed and pulled me closer for a kiss.

'They'll all know,' I bemoaned. 'Look at me. I look like the most satisfied woman on the planet.'

'My beautiful Cookie, let them be jealous,' he said.

I took a deep breath and nodded as Tomás checked us both.

'Ready?' he asked.

I nodded and he unlocked the door, looked out and gave the all-clear. Sometimes, I wish I smoked.

Chapter 17

Luckily when I returned to my desk, Sasha had gone out for lunch and Kay was in the lunchroom talking with Ed. I snuck in, grabbed my can of diet cola from the staff fridge and returning to my desk, touched up my make-up before they both arrived back. Wow, what a day at the office – they never taught this at college. Sasha and Kay returned not long after and we did what Sasha called a 'post-mortem' on the morning's events. Sasha was satisfied it went well. I thought it had gone particularly well, especially the part with Tomás.

Interrupting my thoughts, Kay, Sasha and I jumped as a huge bellow came through the wall from the security office on the other side to us.

'What the hell?' Sasha said and ran towards the office door. Kay and I followed.

Sasha pushed opened the door to the security office and we found The Russian standing on his chair. His head was bowed so it didn't go through the ceiling given he was six-foot-five and add another couple of feet for the chair. Ed was under the desk and we had a good view of his very fine, firm butt.

'Got it cornered,' he yelled. 'Someone pass me the biscuit tin.'

'Mouse!' Russian told us.

'What the fuck?' Sasha looked at him. She grabbed the tin, took the plastic bag of biscuits out, and passed it under the desk to Ed.

'I hate rodents,' Russian explained.

'What are you; an elephant?' I asked, and Kay broke up laughing. 'It's probably terrified of you.'

'Yeah, well I don't like it either,' he said. '*Mythbusters* proved that's not a myth you know... elephants really are scared of mice.'

'Good to know,' Sasha said.

I raced out, grabbed my phone and came back to snap a pic of Russian on the chair and Ed under the desk. Moments later, Ed crawled back out from under the desk with a closed tin in his hand.

'Got it, buddy, you can get down now,' he assured Russian. 'I'll let it go outside.'

'Way outside,' Russian said and Ed nodded.

'You poor darling,' Kay said, watching Russian get off the chair. 'Want a cup of tea, love?'

Sasha and I shook our heads and Russian grinned. 'Thank you Kay, that would help a lot.'

She took his mug and patted his shoulder.

'I could use a massage on my shoulders too, Alice, to release some of the stress,' he said, looking at me.

'Gee, sorry Russian. I'm an events girl, not a masseuse. Sash?'

She rolled her eyes. 'As if.' She turned and walked out.

I shrugged and followed her out.

'Yeah thanks for nothing you two,' he called after us.

Never a dull moment in the office. Well, tick that box – Jim wanted good 'behind the scenes' Saints' pics for the fans on Facebook and Twitter and now I had another good one. Always on the job even when I'm having to look for photos of good looking men.

*****

That night, I was in my room working on my final assignment when my 'homework' assignment from Tomás came through in a sort of text 'shorthand'.

Tomás: Hello Cookie, home from training, showered, & lying in bed thinking of you. Confirming you want to hang out Fri night?

Ah, this man made my heart race. I think I hugged my phone to my chest. Just one small problem, being the new girl I found out today that Jim had signed me up for two half-day marketing workshops on Friday and Saturday which included two night functions and lots of good networking opportunities. It was good of him, but I really wanted the Friday night tongue class with my favorite teacher. My heart raced just thinking about it and I was thinking about it a lot.

Me: Would love to hang with you, but found out this pm, I've got conference Fri & Sat nights. Won't finish until after 10pm

Tomás: All good. Got Sunday game so will be training both days & having quiet nights in. Come around after

Me: Might be late

Tomás: I'll be up, really up and waiting

Me: Cute. Will do

Tomás: Ready for your homework?

Me: Ready, teacher

Tomás: Answer following... honestly

Me: Okay, shoot

Tomás: Would you rather I made love to you in a crowded restaurant or in a cinema?

My breath caught and I almost fanned myself for the heat level that had just risen in my room. I had to think about these answers carefully in case he really made them happen; this could be a research mission after all.

Tomás: You can only pick one

Me: Cinema

Tomás: Would you rather I made love to you in nature or in a scented bath?

The way this was going, I was going to need relief sooner rather than later.

Me: Nature. Can I ask research questions?

Tomás: No, student. Would you rather sleep your first night next to me naked or in lingerie?

Naked, I think. But then again, maybe I really would prefer lingerie so I wasn't totally exposed, but somehow I suspect Tomás would prefer naked especially as that implies we've already done it. And if I was naked, it would be skin on skin. Tough one. I decided to go for the naked option and hope he was still awake.

Me: Naked

Tomás: Would you rather be tied up or spanked?

Ooh tough one, I hadn't ever considered this proposal.

Tomás: Clock is on. Don't make me delay tongue class because you haven't done your homework

I quickly messaged back.

Me: Umm, I haven't done either... I don't know. Need experimenting

Would he now do both? Damn, I should have chosen.

Tomás: Very good answer, Cookie. Flowers or chocolates?

Me: Flowers

That's an easy one.

Tomás: Class over. See you tomorrow night late, for tongue class. sleep well, Cookie. xx

Me: How can I sleep after that?

Chapter 18

I was so lucky to be in a new job otherwise the time I spent waiting to see Tomás would have seemed like a hundred years. But with so much new stuff on the agenda, it was a great distraction. The Friday conference was fun; people shared their event experience, clever themes and results. I didn't have anything to share except a few bridezilla tales which I kept to myself; most event people had had those experiences.

On the first afternoon of the conference, I wandered in to find about fifty other people like myself, all looking lost. I picked up my nametag and got adopted by a similarly lost person.

'So, here to present or here to learn?' a male voice asked.

I turned to find a guy about a head taller than me and a few years older holding the events welcome kit and offering me a smile that would have had any normal girl thinking, 'hello this conference is looking up'.

'Um, to learn. I've got nothing,' I said. 'And you?' I looked to his name tag, '...Dane Frazier.'

'Well, Alice Peterson,' he said reading my name tag. 'I'm

here to do both, but thank God I'm presenting on the first day so I can have a drink tonight and stop freaking out about it.' He frowned. 'Well that was uncool; I wish I hadn't said that out loud.'

I laughed. 'I love your honesty, Dane Frazier.'

I checked him out; no one could compare to Tomás, but I was always looking for potential match-ups for Cassie, Melissa and now Sasha. Still, a guy who looked as hot as Dane Frazier probably had a girl. Dane had prominent blue eyes and dark hair that looked as though it hadn't seen a comb but which suited him. He was slim and tall. He might have had some muscles but I couldn't tell with the black jacket he was wearing over a white button-down shirt with jeans and boots. He had a good head – OMG, I had been at the club a week and I was talking like some of the players.

'What do you do?' I asked. 'Or have I got to wait for the presentation?'

'No, I'll treat you to a preview,' he teased. 'I work for the major film companies. I do events for major sponsors and benefactors before the film launch.' He shrugged. 'Sometimes they are fundraisers, sometimes just publicity events or to thank sponsors.'

'Wow, that sounds fantastic,' I said. 'I've just started work for the Saints, but when I grow up, I want to create great events for movie companies too!'

Dane laughed. 'I wouldn't mind a gig with the Saints. They're having a good season.'

'Three wins out of four,' I agreed.

'Got to be happy with that,' he said.

'Are you into soccer?' I asked.

'I'm more of a football guy, but I'll pretty much watch any sport.'

The room was filling up around us and two women joined us and introduced themselves as conference organizers. I kept the cards they offered; who knew when I might be looking for my next job. A voice over the speaker invited all of us to enter the main room for the conference to begin.

'After you,' Dane said, and we headed into the huge room which had been set up for the delegates. There were probably three hundred or so people in attendance. Tonight was a get-to-know-you dinner and tomorrow night was an event ball. I'd hate the pressure of preparing an event ball for event people! It really was good of my boss Jim to send me to a conference that must have cost him at least a thousand dollars or so from his budget, especially when I had been there for only a week. It was a show of faith that made me determined to give him good value for money... in the work sense of course. I shuddered at the thought of anything else with Jim. Thank God he was happily married, or so Kay told me.

Dane sat next to me and we planted ourselves about halfway up the room and at the end of the aisle so that he could get out of the row quickly to give his presentation. It was nice to be sitting next to someone I knew sort of, even if we met only a minute ago.

'When are you on?' I asked.

'Third speaker, so in about an hour,' he said with a glance to his watch. I couldn't blame him for being nervous presenting in front of a huge group like this. Every now and then his leg kept its own beat until he realized, straightened up and harnessed his nerves.

The first speaker finished, the second speaker followed and was much quicker. While Dane waited to be introduced a gorgeous blonde seated in front of us, and I mean gorgeous, turned around and had a quick chat with Dane. She didn't notice me, which is fair enough and I had a quick chat with the super fit looking woman in her late thirties sitting on the other side of me. She explained that she ran her business from home and specialized in events for the health industry.

'You know, fun runs, open days, trade shows, major boot camps, that sort of thing,' she explained. 'I like to get to a couple of conferences a year just to see if there's anything new happening.'

'It's my first,' I explained and I complimented her, telling her that she looked super fit, which she did – I had won a friend. Then I heard Dane's name being called and I turned and wished him luck. He got a warm round of applause and he glanced towards me, giving me a look that said 'notice me'. He began and I realized he needn't have worried; he turned on the charm and was a bit of a ham. It definitely wasn't the first presentation Dane had ever done. At the end, a few people raised their hands with questions

The gorgeous blonde in front raised her hand and asked, 'What has been your favorite event, Dane?'

I had the feeling she wanted to organize her own event with Dane after hours.

'Well, Kelly, the *Titanic* might have sunk, but there was no iceberg in sight for the event our agency did; it was a huge hit.'

The audience laughed and a few people called for more details. Dane obliged.

'Our film publicity agency wanted to celebrate ten years in business so we picked one of the biggest films in history as the theme. Two hundred guests – all VIPS – were invited and had to come in costume representing the era of the *Titanic*. We gathered everyone for drinks in the foyer of the five-star Grand Hotel and then moved them in for dinner by opening the grand ballroom doors. We hired actors in costume to stand on the level above them and throw streamers as they moved through the doors, as though the ship was departing.' Dane stopped for effect as we all oohed-and-aahed at the fun of it.

He continued. 'We had a small orchestra playing and the staff was all in costume. At the back of the room was a huge Styrofoam iceberg with dry ice so it gave the appearance of being very cold and very threatening. We did lots of things, as Kelly will remember.'

Kelly stood up. 'One of the waiters came to my table and told me it was time for my swimming lessons.' The audience laughed again.

Dane wrapped up and came back to sit beside me. Kelly turned and gave him a winning smile.

'Bravo,' I said to him, 'that was great. Your job sounds amazing.'

'Thanks.' He shrugged modestly. 'Now I can chill for the rest of the conference.' He exhaled.

The convener called for a break.

'Let's get a coffee.' Dane nudged me.

Kelly turned and gave me a territorial look.

'Coming for a coffee?' I invited her and she cheered up no end. Hey, I was happy to share; I had my hands full right now with a certain soccer superstar. A week earlier, Dane might have been on my shopping list.

*****

There were a few hours break after the conference and before the getting-to-know-you dinner so, I raced home, had a shower and packed an overnight bag for staying at Tomás's place, in Tomás's bed, with Tomás's tongue working wonders. Right, I was back now but that was a great trip... I sent him a message.

Me: Can't wait to see you tonight. Don't reply I know you are at training

My phone beeped moments later.

Tomás: Just heading there now. See you tonight. Bring your tongue

Well that was tonight's event shot – I'd have Tomás and his tongue on my mind for the rest of the night. I changed into underwear to impress Tomás – how lucky that Mia and I had gone lingerie shopping just before I met Tomás – it was fate! Sure, anyway, I was wearing a flesh-colored lace bra and panties set in floral semi-sheer mesh, with scalloped edging. I was hoping not to have them on for long tonight. Over the top of my new lingerie, I slipped on a black silk flowing dress that was not too dressy but which would get me through cocktail hour at the event and into bed with Tomás. That was the main event after all.

Drinks and the dinner were scheduled to kick off at seven p.m., so I rocked in around quarter past the hour to minimize the amount of small talk I'd have to do. I'm a people person, but I'd been 'peopling' all day and small talk wasn't my thing. I entered the room and heard my name called. I turned to find a fellow student from my events classes at college. We all juggled part-time jobs and now I was juggling a full-time job for the last few months of the semester.

'Katie, hey, I didn't know you were working this gig!' I said.

'I do Friday and Saturday nights here every week. Drink?' she asked.

'Yeah, thanks.' I grabbed a glass of champagne off her tray. 'Wish you could have one with me. I'd love the company.'

'Me too,' she sighed, 'but have tray, must roll.'

I grinned, gave her a wave as she headed off and turned to find Dane waving to me from across the room. He looked hot, very hot, and luckily I only had eyes for Tomás and I didn't notice. There were quite a few hotties at the conference but more women than men, so Dane wouldn't go home empty-handed if he was on the market. I waved back and was about to head over when Josie from Planet Events arrived. Her eyes lit up on seeing me which was kind, but she was always a bit neurotic.

'Daarrrlliing, how I miss you,' she said, rolling her eyes and reaching for a glass of champagne as it went past. 'The student who has replaced you is vacant.'

There's the pot calling the kettle black but it's always nice to be missed.

'I had hoped you would come and work with me after you graduated,' she said.

'That's so good of you Josie,' I said. Praise the god of small mercies for sparing me that. I tapped my glass against hers in a cheers salute. 'I didn't see you today,' I said.

'No, I only bought the function pack which includes the two functions so I can mingle and network but not attend the presentations or workshops. I don't have time for those. You know what it's like,' she said, rolling her eyes.

Dane interrupted us. I appraised him in his dark suit and red patterned tie – he looked very suave. I introduced him and Josie, and I saw her eyes examine him with interest – she was old enough to be his big sister with five siblings in between. Which reminded me of Tomás, ah, Tomás. I glanced at my watch; when would this be over?

'You look a bit like that guy from the all-boy band, but an older version,' Josie said, clicking her fingers and trying to recall his name. 'The *One Direction* guy.'

'Yeah, I get that a bit,' Dane said and turned to face me. 'You look great.' His blue eyes appraised me.

'Ah, thanks,' I said, surprised. I'd forgotten Dane was a guy; I only had a heartbeat for Tomás at the moment. Seriously, I'd fallen into Tomás way too fast... danger, danger Will Robinson or Alice Peterson.

'Harry!' Josie said, looking pleased with herself. 'That's it, you look like an older version of Harry.' She continued to appraise Dane.

'Ah thanks, I think.' Dane smiled at her.

'Oh yes, definitely a compliment,' she said.

Dane turned to me. 'So, sit next to me tonight?' he asked without it being a question.

'Sure, that would be nice,' I said, pleased I wouldn't have

to work too hard, especially if Kelly worked her way on to the other side of Dane.

Just before eight p.m., a little bell rang and we were seated. Dane led me to a table and Kelly did a record dive across the room to sit next to him – it was a fine effort on her behalf, I took my hat off to her. On my other side, a very large and homely lady took the seat. She told me she organized children's events and then proceeded to tell me in great detail about it. Luckily, Dane saved me a couple of times.

I wanted to leave a few times during the night but I couldn't duck out when the speeches were on or when I was required to play networking team games. Sigh. I sneaked to the ladies' just after ten-thirty and thought I would keep going but Dane was onto me as I rose from the table.

'You're escaping aren't you?' he asked. He looked even better after a few champagnes and with his tie off, his tan showing through the open V of his shirt.

I grinned and nodded. 'See you tomorrow.'

'Alice, come on!' He gave me a pleading look.

'I think you'll be just fine.' I raised my eyebrows to the interest he was attracting.

He shook his head. 'Fine then, abandon me in my hour of need.' He grinned at me.

I patted his arm with a mock show of sympathy and got out of there. By the time I cleared the parking lot and arrived in Tomás's street it was nearing eleven-fifteen. I knew his training schedule and he had a seven o'clock session in the morning, which would mean he had to be up after six or so to get there. I didn't want to rush tongue class but I'd happily cancel that and just curl up with him for the night. The guys couldn't afford to party or have too many late nights in-season; a lot was riding on it – million dollar contracts.

As I drove down the street, I saw his entire house was in darkness. Damn, did I go in or not? I pulled over and reached for my phone. There were no messages from him. I debated what to do... even if he had one light on I would have felt better. Was he cheesed off because I was super late? My finger hovered over the send button but seriously, the whole house was in complete darkness. If he wanted to see me he would have left a light on somewhere, or messaged me to check up on my arrival time.

I turned and headed home. I know it was only one day since I saw him at the press conference but it was a lifetime to my heart. I felt an overwhelming wave of disappointment bringing me down. I had thought of nothing else all day but seeing him but I couldn't bring myself to be a selfish bitch and wake him, or risk his wrath since he'd packed it in without waiting for me. He might have been exhausted and crashed early. I hoped he was home and not... no, that was just silly. I buried that doubt.

I headed to my lonely bed where I would take off my lingerie and go to sleep.

Chapter 19

My phone rang at just after six o'clock in the morning, startling me into the wake zone. I grabbed it quickly so I didn't wake Dad and Ryan.

'Hello?' I mumbled, not even looking at the caller I.D.

'Cookie,' the voice said. It was low and threatening.

'Tomás.' I sat up. 'I missed you last night.'

'Why didn't you come? Did you get a better offer? Meet someone at the conference?' He was pissed off.

'What? Don't be stupid. You are all I thought about all day and night. But it was so late when I got to your place – ' I tried to explain.

'I don't care how late it was, what happened?'

I took a deep breath. 'I came to your house after eleven last night and it was in complete darkness. Complete darkness, Tomás. You'd gone to bed, not even left one light on to tell me you were waiting for me and not even a message to say for me to wake you when I arrived. I didn't know what to do so I went home... I thought it would be selfish to wake you, sorry...' My voice trailed off.

He thought about it for a moment.

'I see,' he said. 'I'm sorry *Bella*, I thought you would just knock when you arrived and I would let you in. I just lay down on the bed to rest while I waited for you.'

'I desperately wanted to come in,' I assured him. 'I waited in the car out the front for a few minutes looking for signs of life.'

He chuckled. 'I wanted to wrap my arms around you and wake up with you this morning.'

'Tomás, shhh, I can't hear that, it just makes me depressed that I've missed out.'

'What time does your conference start this morning?'

'Ten,' I told him.

'Hmm, I finish training about then. I'll have to wait until tonight to see you. Probably a good thing. Got to do a clean-up for a guest coming and Valentina is being bossy about it.' He sighed as though there was no escaping his family responsibilities.

I hated to sound needy but I wanted to know who this Julieta was and what she was to him.

'Ah, that's Julieta?' I asked. 'That lady at the restaurant mentioned her,' I reminded him.

'You have a good memory, Cookie.' He cleared his throat. 'Yeah, a friend of my family coming to stay for a while.'

'Right,' I said, but he didn't elaborate and I didn't want to appear clingy or possessive even if I was feeling that way.

'Did you want to come to the game with me on Sunday morning? I'll leave after nine.'

How good did that sound coming off his lips and how I would love to go with him and arrive on the back of his bike – I didn't know how the office skirt would cope with that.

But I didn't need to go that early and I imagined it made for a really long day just waiting around.

'No, I don't start until ten-thirty,' I said, 'but thanks.'

'Tonight then, Cookie,' he threatened, 'knock, text, drive-in, just come to me.'

'I will and I am getting away earlier tonight. Expect me sooner.'

'I'll be waiting.'

He signed off and I lay back on the bed, relieved. I didn't get to sleep until the early hours of the morning for stressing I had cheesed him off, but now all was well again. I hope I could stay awake at the conference today.

*****

After talking with Tomás I fell straight back to sleep and didn't wake until after nine. Then it was a race to the bathroom, to dress and to get to the venue for the events workshop. I arrived ten minutes late... maybe it was a good thing; it gave Kelly more time to hit on Dane. I sneaked into the back of the seminar where a session was already underway on social media to promote conferences.

I planned out the rest of the day: after the workshop which was scheduled to finish at three o'clock, I would head home, shower and dress for the conference dinner tonight which was an event-themed ball starting with drinks at six o'clock. I would also have to iron and hang my work uniform in the car to go straight to the game the next morning – my first game in the event role! I wasn't going to need any special underwear for Tomás as the dinner theme was superhero.

I might have forgotten to mention that to him that I would be arriving in costume – I wanted to see that reaction for myself.

So, the plan – I would leave the ball around nine-thirty p.m. – that would allow me to be seen, eat the main course, skip dessert, and be in Tomás's arms by ten. God I'm good, the master of planning, no wonder I went into events. It would be my first night sleeping over at Tomás's house with him in the bed with me, with luck. Everything was happening at once.

I made sure my phone was on silent and sent Mia a quick hello message while I tuned into the conference; it was about social media after all. She messaged back that she was doing 'prac' for her physical therapy qualification today and wanted to catch up tomorrow night after the Saints' game. I replied saying affirmative to that. I sent Cassie and Melissa a greetings message too and checked out their Facebook posts – it was social media practice, honest.

I didn't see Dane until the conference broke for lunch. He was more casual today – in Saturday attire of jeans and a button-down navy shirt. He still looked hot in that dark, smoldering, boy-band way but hey, I didn't notice much.

'Alice,' he greeted me, strolling towards me with a coffee and a finger sandwich in hand. He munched away, sizing me up. 'If I was the suspicious type, I'd think you came in late to avoid me,' he said with a smile.

'Damn, you've exposed my plan,' I said. 'Finish up late last night?'

'As a matter of fact, yes. I got hijacked... there are too many women at this conference. The dancing started and it appears that every female needed a dance partner. I got home after two.'

'Ooh, nasty,' I said. 'I was in bed by midnight.'

'And you can tell,' he flattered me.

'So how does your girlfriend feel about you being swamped by event beauties or is she confident enough in herself not to care?' I asked.

He smiled and took another bite of his sandwich, considering my question.

'Mm, yes, I'd be attracted to a woman who was confident enough in herself not to care, but sadly I am single at this moment in time.'

He said everything with a hint of humor, playing me.

'Not for long if you were inclined,' I said, looking around. 'I'm surprised I got to sit anywhere near you yesterday especially after that masterful presentation.'

'I could do it again for you, as a private presentation.' He raised an eyebrow.

The bell rang for the conference to continue.

'Damn, another time,' I played him. I suspect my lack of interest in Dane was an aphrodisiac for him. Men! 'Um, it looks like Kelly is trying to get your attention.' When the gorgeous Dane turned to look at her, I sneaked away before he turned back.

Lucky I had Tomás on my radar because I suspect Dane would be a hard act to resist... there's something about those blue eyes that draws a girl in. But tonight, I'd be looking into the deep, dark, chocolate eyes of my Latin lover and experiencing my second sex class – the many wonders of the tongue.

Chapter 20

I easily escaped from the ball at nine-thirty. I wanted to say goodbye to Dane but he was preoccupied on the dance floor, so I just took the opportunity between mains and dessert to flee. He had made the conference fun and with his handsome good looks, just a little bit exciting.

It was nearing ten o'clock as I approached Tomás's house – much better on the timing, and neither of us would be as exhausted. I turned into his street. His house was way down the end – private and on a large, secluded block of land. Then I saw it; his house looked like a Christmas tree – every single light that could be put on in the house was on. I started laughing because it was so adorable. It looked all the odder as the street was so dark but yet down the end was this huge lit-up building that looked as if it was draining the power from the neighborhood.

This man was gorgeous. I couldn't wipe the smile from my face. I parked my car against the curb out the front of his house and grabbed my overnight bag, before alighting and locking the car. I walked up the path to the front door.

Tomás answered before I raised my hand to knock and I dropped my bag and threw my arms around his neck.

'You are so gorgeous,' I told him. 'I love that you did that, thank you.'

'What is this?' He pulled me away, his eyes lit up, taking in my costume. I had forgotten in the excitement of the Christmas tree lit house

'It was a superhero-themed ball,' I explained. 'I love Catwoman, she's so... capable.'

'Al...iss, you're a danger to yourself and you don't even know it. Have you any idea how sexy that looks? Turn around,' he ordered. I did a full rotation in my Catwoman costume – it was a sleek and fitted black jumpsuit with a cool utility belt, long black gloves to the elbow, high black leather boots to the knees and a little cat's ears headpiece.

I turned to face him again after pirouetting and gave him a soft meow.

'I think I've just lost control.' He grinned, and then pulled me closer and kissed me. His hands ran over my fitted suit, across my back, butt and hips.

He kept kissing me as he picked me up with one arm under my butt, grabbed my bag with his free hand and closed the door with his foot.

When he stopped kissing me and let me breathe I had tears in my eyes. 'Thank you for the Christmas treehouse,' I said.

He grinned. 'I didn't want you to drive by and go home again,' he said, still holding me against him. He kissed me again. 'Did I mention you are cute?'

'Never,' I told him and his eyes narrowed. He began to carry me upstairs.

'Um, lights?' I said. 'You might be draining the power from the neighborhood.'

'Ah, right,' he said and lowered me to the ground. He did a quick run around on the lower level turning off the lights, inside and out. He returned, took my bag and my hand, and led me upstairs to his room, turning off more lights along the way. Eventually, there was only one light left on – a soft lamp in his room.

He put my bag down on a chair and pulled me closer. 'You look super sexy in this outfit, pussy, too good to take off, but I will anyway,' he said.

I laughed and snuggled into his embrace. I inhaled him and felt my body begin to relax. I sighed. 'I've needed this. I've missed you. You've dominated my every thought,' I said, then wondered if I had put too much out there.

'I haven't had a sensible thought in days, you're a very bad influence on me and very distracting,' he said matter-of-factly. Ah, the beauty of direct translation. 'Leave those kitty ears on but the rest is coming off.'

I purred as I pulled off the long gloves one a time as though I was in a strip show, and threw them over the chair. I worked through the outfit until I stood in a black lace bra, matching boy-cut panties and my cat ears. Tomás had been lying back, enjoying the show.

He moved to sit on the edge of the bed and he pulled me between his legs. 'Magnificent. Can you wear that every time?' he teased.

'I was thinking of being a private investigator next time and just coming naked under a trench coat,' I said.

'Stop talking now or the consequences will be very bad,'

Tomás said in a low growl. He pulled me onto the bed and positioned himself on top of me.

'Tonight's lesson, Cookie, is the power of the tongue.' With that he leaned forward and slipped his tongue between my lips, kissing me passionately. He moved away from my mouth and I wanted him back immediately.

I shuddered. 'Wow, powerful tongue,' I murmured feeling a bit giddy.

Then, encouraged, he began to work his magic… he wasn't only good on the sports ground, I promise. It was so achingly good that I realized how important these lessons were… the wait to get to tongue class was paying off.

Tomás lowered me back onto the sheets and moved closer. He worked his way around my body, I could not only feel his magic tongue but his warm breath on my skin as he took his tongue odyssey all over my skin. I was so close that I almost went to the edge and over several times. I was also crazily self-conscious; it was such a vulnerable position to allow someone to discover you, especially when you had never before exposed such much of yourself!

'How do you know to do that? That thing with your tongue and thumb... it's so good.' I was ranting like a virgin high on sex. Different parts of me were sending sensation signals to my brain and body simultaneously. It was unbearably good and I tried not to writhe too much.

'It's okay, my Al...iss,' he said once or twice when I tensed, before returning to his tongue work. And that work started getting faster and more heated; I was panting now with pleasure.

'Oh God,' I moaned. 'I'm going to...' and I dug my fingers into his shoulders and reached that place, most spectacularly. Heat rushed everywhere, like nothing I'd ever felt before. Like nothing I could compare or explain – chocolate, ice-cream, hot baths, my own handiwork, nothing. He held me while the shudders rose and faded and I got my focus back. It took a while. I was weak.

'Oh, it's you,' I teased him when the haze was lifted from my eyes and I could see him clearly again; my heart was still pounding.

He shook his head and stroked my face, watching my reactions with a smile on his lips. 'Al...iss, are you a happy kitty?' he asked.

'Oh yes, thank you, I'm a very, very happy cat,' I told him and then I looked at him from head to toe.

'Tomás, you still have clothes on.'

'It appears so,' he nodded. 'But lucky for me, you don't.'

'Well, get your clothes off,' I insisted. While he pulled his T-shirt over his head, I leaned over and pulled down his black track pants. He laughed in surprise.

'Oh my, it's my turn,' I said.

Tomás smiled and stepped away from his clothes pool. He grabbed me and we fell back on the bed, with me on top of him where I could see first-hand those tight muscles. He used his muscled arms to pull me up to his chest for a kiss.

'I'm going to start my tongue class,' I told him when he released me and to make sure I had his attention.

He nodded in agreement. 'Right, well good luck Al... iss,' he said, encouragingly. 'Don't hesitate to ask if you need guidance.'

I grinned and worked my way down his body just a little to get into a good straddle position; his body reacted with a quick shudder.

'Hurt?' I frowned, concerned.

'No... an electric charge,' he explained.

I smiled like a student encouraged and kept going. I felt the tremor in his muscles as my tongue traveled along them; I loved it when I got a reaction. I glanced at his beautiful face – his eyes were closed and he looked so edible. He was hard and perfect and breathtaking.

I'm new at this but my tongue seemed to know what to do, what it wanted to do more to the point. Warm skin, beautiful scent. He coached me a little – softer, harder, faster, careful – I felt his whole body stiffen and he held his breath – I'm not sure if he was worried that his student would bite him or he was totally pleasured.

I increased my tempo, time to bring it home, so to speak.

'For the love of all that is holy,' he muttered.

'Are you religious?' I asked between licks.

'I am now,' he said, breathlessly, his hands gripping my legs or the sheets alternatively.

Tomás's whole body looked so taut; it was magic to see; I could look at it all day. He began to moan as the urgency increased and moments later I knew he was close; his hand worked a handful of my hair, gripping and releasing.

I wasn't sure how to bring it across the line but then Tomás must have sensed that.

'Keep the tempo up now, Al...iss,' he coached in a husky voice.

I went a little faster and a little more intensely.

He groaned and when he couldn't take any more, his body released its energy. My work was done!

That was the most amazing experience ever and pleasuring someone you are crazy about is as satisfying as being pleasured. Sex school was the best.

'Come up here to me,' he moaned.

I moved up the bed and wrapped myself around him. He looked at me with a mixed look of astonishment and satisfaction, a growl rumbling in his chest like a satisfied lion. I couldn't help but grin.

'Was that okay?' I asked.

'Fuck, Al...iss, you are a very gifted student.'

'Maybe you should move me to the scholarship program,' I teased, trailing my fingers along his chest.

'Oh *Bella*, you are there, my number one girl,' he said.

The rush of excitement filled me and I wondered if he meant I'm his girl, his only girl or just his top student. I didn't want to think about it now, I just wanted to enjoy this, because it was fun and delicious and I was in love – the truth hit me – and Tomás was right... it was memorable. I would never, ever forget this experience and the journey to losing my virginity.

But tomorrow, Julieta – whoever she might be – was arriving.

Chapter 21

Game day and my first working game day for the Saints – I was a little nervous even though I was mainly in gatekeeper mode looking after what had already been set up. There was no post-morning glow and snuggling up to Tomás – he had a game to play and he was up super early. I felt his hand on my back, he nuzzled into my neck and told me not to get up, and after touching his lips on my neck, he rose and got to it. I wished him good luck and watched his superb body as he strode out of the room. I heard him down in the kitchen for a while and then in the shower but I kept out of his way to let him do his pre-game routines. I was happy to enjoy his scent in the bed just that little bit longer. I heard his motorbike start and he was gone.

I stretched out in his huge bed for another fifteen minutes or so before getting up. No hot yoga for me today, I had already enjoyed a good workout. Mm, I felt weak just thinking about it. Our next sex class was going to be penetration – Tomás's words, not mine – the official deflowering. I couldn't wait, just take it Tomás, the sooner the better.

I forced myself out of his bed and away from the scene of the sex crime and into the shower. I put on my work outfit, this time with panties, and headed out. As I locked the front door, Valentina drove up in a sporty little red convertible and gave me a wave. She jumped out of the car, locking it.

'Alice,' she said. Bless her for remembering my name. That was hopeful.

'Hi Valentina,' I said, 'I'm just heading off to work. Tomás has already gone.'

'Call me Tina, everyone does. I'm sorry we didn't get a chance to catch up.'

'Thanks, me too.' I smiled. 'Are you coming to the game?'

'Not today,' she said. 'I often do but I've got a rehearsal. I sing at a jazz club on a Saturday and Sunday night,' she explained.

'Oh wow, that's fantastic.'

'Come if you can; it would be great to see you there.' She sat back, leaning on the bonnet of her car. 'Tomás is picking up a family friend from the airport this evening so he won't be able to come with you, but bring a friend if you like.'

'I'd love to,' I said. 'I used to love Sunday jazz afternoons at Clifton Street; I'd go with some of my college friends.'

'I've sung there,' she said. 'It's a good little venue. I'll leave two tickets at the door under your name at the *Buzz Club*. I'm on early from six to seven, then a jazz swing band comes on from eight. Don't sweat it if you can't make it, there's no set seating, they're just entry tickets.'

'Thanks Tina, sounds great. I'd best get to work then,' I said and gave her a wave, departing. I still felt like a kid beside her, she was so voluptuous.

*****

I had gone to the first few Saints' games with Mia on Lucas's tickets but now that I was working with the Saints, I had my own two tickets allocated to me. I gave those to my brother Ryan and one of his friends. The staff seats weren't as good as the WAG seats but they were still damn good.

I parked in the staff area and being nice and early, it was still easy to get around the grounds. The crowds wouldn't start to arrive in earnest for about another thirty minutes or so. I took a few moments to get my mind on the job and check I had everything I needed – I wanted to make sure my boss Jim was happy with my performance today.

My predecessor had done a good job; today for my first day I just had to follow through... check that the Saints' mascot showed up – another college student doing a part-time job in a large Saint Bernard dog suit – check the kids' entertainers arrived and the post-game band was sorted, check the catering had arrived for the trainers and PTs, and a few other bits and pieces were in place. It was all going like clockwork.

In no time the crowds were pouring in and thirty minutes before game time, I finished the event work I had to do on my checklist. I checked in at the VIP membership marquee to see if Jim and Kay needed a hand, then checked with Sasha in the media box to see if she was okay. Everyone was good, so, I was free to head up to the grandstand and sit next to Mia as her plus one.

Earlier, Mia was doing work experience in the PT rooms but Lucas wanted her seated before he ran onto the ground so he could look for her, like a lucky charm. Tomás and I were new at this and we weren't official, so while he offered me his complimentary seats in the WAG section, he didn't mention anything about needing to spot me in the crowd. Damn shame.

Spotting Mia in place, I dropped into the seat next to her. She gave me a quick hug. She was always nervous before a game, and now we both were. And then the boys took to the grounds. The crowd was full on and the rival team – the Columbus Cats from Ohio – brought their own fans with them. They must have flown in by the thousands. The atmosphere was electric and only added to the tension. We gave the Cats a round of applause as they ran past our stand, but not everyone was as generous.

Then our Saints appeared, coming out of the run with Lucas in the lead. We saved our cheers for them and now my vested interest was even bigger. Behind Lucas, I could see The Russian. Ed was in the pack, and I recognized German Nik from meeting him fleetingly at Lucas's pre-season party and then my man Tomás appeared. Lucas looked our way and Mia smiled at him. He didn't return it, just took it in and kept moving. Tomás didn't look my way, but he was the picture of concentration; I guess there was a lot of pressure being a goalkeeper – if you let an opponent's ball into the net and they score, it could be all over for your team unless the boot of Lucas and other players put more through the net at the other end. The game was much more exciting to me now that I knew some of the players personally and one in particular intimately.

Our team looked so good; so fit and ready as they did their warm-up around the grounds. The crowd was enormous, and the stadium was bursting; it must have been both exciting and daunting to play in front of them. It was the first time we had played the Cats this season, but we had won against them twice last year and lost one, so they weren't going to be a walkover. The players got into position and the siren blasted. The game was on.

I didn't breathe for the first quarter, so it's a wonder I'm still alive. Twice the ball went towards Tomás and he was totally on guard, not making any mistakes. The Cats were doing all they could to get the ball past him, and Tomás had the area well and truly covered. The Saints were having a good game but there was nothing in it yet. Neither team had scored until Harry in the striker position slipped one past the Cats' goalkeeper and scored. It was his first ever goal for the Saints as a new kid on the block and the team and crowd loved it.

By halftime, Lucas had put a goal in and it was a big score by soccer standards. Tomás had been under enormous pressure and the guys seated in front – I was eavesdropping for their commentary – said he had done a brilliant job. I smiled a satisfied smile – great on the ground and in bed... what more would you want?

I held my breath as the Cats worked the ball back down their end of the ground again and Tomás came alive, moving in for the attack before they came too close to the goal.

Backing him up, Jackson in defense was holding his own but the Cats still had a shot at goal and I inhaled sharply, watching the ball travel through the air as if it was in slow motion to the goal.

Tomás intervened, stopping the goal, and you could hear a collective sigh of relief followed by the roar from the Saints' fans. He held the ball as if he was born with it in his hands, looked around for an unmarked Saints player, and kicked it well over forty yards down the field, landing it in the secure orbit of Nik or the Kaiser as the boys called him. I breathed again. I didn't know how I was going to get through the season. The Russian was having a solid game too, he was solid in every respect – that man was a wall.

When the full-time siren went – thank the Lord because I was exhausted from watching – the Saints had won the game two goals to nil. The players were pumped, celebrating in a huddle, and the fans streamed onto the ground. Security tried to keep them back and get the players off the field but they had their work cut out for them. Mia and I hugged each other with relief. Praise the Saints for our Saints winning! I squirmed with pleasure, thinking where one Saints' player had been last night.

Chapter 22

I didn't see Tomás after the game; he had to go to the clubrooms for the usual post-game discussions, PT and media interviews. Then he was going straight to the airport. I sent him a message to congratulate him on a brilliant game. I wasn't expecting a message back until he had access to his phone later and got sorted.

The usual post-game drinks were on at the *Shaken Not Stirred* bar, but I decided not to go this time; now that I worked in the office I didn't want to O.D. on Saints – I saw plenty of some of the guys and didn't want to look like a major groupie. Besides, my college friends weren't going either because exam week was upon us. I was lucky that my final assessments were assignments and I didn't have to cram for an exam.

Mind you, if I was with Tomás tonight, I would have gone to the post-game party, but he had to pick up *that* friend from the airport. Julieta – I wondered how friendly she really was. Luckily, I didn't have to worry about going alone though to hear Valentina. Mia wanted to come with me at six and then she organized to meet Lucas at the *Shaken*

Not Stirred bar at seven-thirty. Valentina was performing for only an hour and I could drop Mia off to the bar on my way home and have a much-needed early night. It had been a huge week with work, Tomás's sex classes, and the conference – I was seriously wiped out. It didn't help that I hadn't been sleeping because Tomás dominated my every thought... so worth the sleep deprivation.

Mia looked up the address of the *Buzz Club* on her phone, while I drove in what I thought was the general direction.

'I love that you are coming with me, but you don't have to,' I reminded her.

'I want to,' she said, with a quick glance in my direction. 'We haven't been to a jazz club for ages and with work and study we don't see much of each other now, and I see plenty of Lucas. He won't even notice I'm not there for the first hour while he dissects the game with the boys,' she said, pointing to the right hand turn up ahead.

'Oh he'll notice, he likes to keep you in sight,' I teased. 'It's cute.'

'It is kind-of in a non-stalker way.' She grinned. 'Do you see him in the office much?'

I shook my head. 'Only once in my first week. My department, marketing, is on the other side of the building from football management, so unless they're coming to see us about appearances or wanting merchandise, or to visit Ed and The Russian, we don't see the players much.'

'What's it like working next door to Ed and The Russian?' Mia asked. 'They're both hot.'

'I'm sorry, but aren't you with the hottest guy in the team, except maybe for my Tomás?' I nudged her.

She laughed. 'Yeah but I'm not dead, I can appreciate good art when I see it. The Russian is so big and Ed... mm, that velvety skin and those big soulful eyes.' She sighed.

I shook my head.

'What? You haven't noticed?' She narrowed her eyes at me.

I bit my lip while I thought about it. 'I might have.'

She laughed. 'Yeah, right. I heard The Russian has broken up with Leesa. She hasn't been at the last few games.'

'I noticed. I only met her once though, and she was nice,' I agreed.

'Turn next left and we should be there,' Mia said. 'He hasn't said anything? The Russian?'

I shook my head. 'No, he probably wouldn't mention it around me or the girls anyway. You know what guys are like, they hardly wear their hearts on their sleeves.'

I pulled my car into the parking lot of the jazz bar, which was already packed and found a spot. We exited the car, I locked it and we made our way in. The doorman marked my name off and welcomed us. Inside the *Buzz Club* was great; moody and atmospheric. We grabbed a wine from the bar and found a few seats along the bench rows that faced the small, elevated stage. Tables were dotted around the room and a large oval dance space had attracted one slow dancing couple in front of the stage. Valentina was already on stage and her voice was perfectly soulful; she was all woman as she swayed and played up to her three-piece band – one on the keyboard, another on the sax and one on the horn. Her sound was rich and throaty and she wore a fitted black dress, low cut to show her full figure. I bet she was one of those girls at school who had curves years before the rest of us.

'Is that her?' Mia asked, whispering in my ear.

I nodded and touched her glass with mine in a toast.

'Wow,' Mia said. 'I can see a bit of resemblance with Tomás, but she's something.'

'I know.' We tapped along as Valentina started a new song: 'Someone to Watch over Me' attracting whistles and applause – it must have been a favorite of her regulars.

More couples moved onto the dance floor, swaying in rhythm. She was mesmerizing and the song was so beautiful it made me a bit teary. Next, she was joined on stage by an older man in a three-piece suit wearing a hat that suited him no end and they did a wonderful duet of When I Fall in Love.

'I'm so glad we came,' Mia said, her eyes wide.

'I know; how good is the mood in here?' I agreed. 'I just wish Lucas and Tomás were with us and we could slow dance.'

Mia scoffed. 'Yeah, not sure I could get Lucas on the dance floor unless he had a guitar in his hands.'

I imagined Tomás in a dark suit slow dancing with me to this song – I was in heaven just thinking about it. His sister was so talented. I wondered if she moved here to try and get more work or to launch her career.

Valentina had just started her third number when Mia nudged me. 'We better get going then,' she said, finishing off her wine with one large gulp.

I looked at my watch. It was nearing quarter to seven and Valentina was only on until seven; still, plenty of time to get Mia to the Shaken Not Stirred bar by seven-thirty.

'Oh, okay. Aren't you enjoying this?' I asked, wondering

why she wanted to cut early when she had been happy to stay for the one hour set beforehand.

'It's great, but I've got to go to the ladies and it's getting packed in here,' she said, looking over at the ladies' toilet. 'Perhaps we should start exiting.'

'Sure.' I shrugged. I finished my few sips of wine and grabbed my bag to follow her. She grabbed my arm with some urgency and then I saw why. I heard why first – someone yelled out the name 'Tomás' and I looked to Valentina whose face had lit up as she looked to the door. Tomás was standing there and under his arm and wrapped around him was a beautiful woman – slim, with dark long-flowing hair, big breasts and a tiny waist, she just came up to his shoulders. I turned to Mia and she was biting her lip, looking at me.

I looked back. I couldn't take my eyes off the scene at the door. Tomás grinned at Valentina as if he was delighted to get there in time while she was still performing. A waiter showed them to a small reserved table at the front right of the stage. Tomás and Julieta – assuming that was her – were more than friends by the look of it, much, much more and Valentina was delighted to see them. Then, to put an end to any of my doubts, Valentina said, 'ah ladies and gentlemen, my brother Tomás who you may know and his girlfriend, Julieta. Did you win?' she asked him.

I couldn't see Tomás for a moment but everyone cheered acknowledging he did. Mia said my name and I nodded.

'Let's go,' I agreed. We forgot about the trip to the ladies' toilet and made our way towards the door. I wasn't sure I was going to make it. Tides of nausea and grief were riding up from my stomach. I had fallen in love with this man; my lips were on him late last night and early this morning. Was he seeing other people all that time and just making sure I had a memorable loss of virginity experience? Had I read it so completely wrong? Was it completely my fault and was I a total idiot?

Mia's hand looped through my arm and she took over, leading the way to the door – I walked there in a daze. There were lots of people moving around and I tried to blend in behind them and not make eye contact but I couldn't help but look at them. They were this beautiful, sexy couple, the royalty of the room – it was a horror movie. I expected everyone to turn and look at me in unison and laugh.

As we got near the door Tomás looked away from her and towards the waiter who passed me. His eyes flicked from the waiter to me and realization dawned. I saw his eyes widen and his lips said my name and then I was gone, through the door with Mia and racing towards my car. I unlocked it and we fell into it. I just wanted to get away as fast as I could. I started the car, drove forward and turned right up the street. Mia said nothing; she reached over and put her hand on my leg which was shaking.

'I'll come home with you,' she said.

I shook my head. 'Thanks, M, but there's nothing you can do. I have to process this.'

'We can talk, have a wine or a coffee, work through it,' she insisted.

I touched her hand on top of my leg and squeezed it. I

knew I was white. I could feel the color draining from me and that awful clammy feeling of vacillating between hot and cold.

'I appreciate it, really, but I need to be alone. I'm okay.' I glanced at her and back at the road. 'I just need to process it all and I've got work tomorrow. I'll be busy. I'll keep busy.' I felt like I was having an out of body experience – it was so surreal.

Why did he go there with her? Because he knew I would probably be at *Shaken Not Stirred* with Mia or at home? Why didn't he tell me? If I hadn't seen them, when would he have told me? After we'd done the final 'class'?

I heard my phone ringing in my bag.

'Do you want that?' Mia asked and I shook my head in the negative.

She knew how badly I'd fallen for him. She'd had daily reports except for the sex classes and she had promised it would all stay in the vault. Thank God no one else in the club knew we were an item other than a bit of flirting. How humiliating that would have been.

'Do you think Valentina knew when she gave you the tickets? Do you think she knew they would be there?' Mia asked. 'Maybe she really likes that other woman and wanted you to back off Tomás.'

I shook my head. 'I don't know, but I don't think so. Tina seems so lovely and she told me Tomás wouldn't be there because he had an airport run. I doubt she even remembered to tell Tomás she gave me the tickets. He was gone when she got home this morning,' I said.

I could be wrong, but I didn't believe that of her, she

seemed so genuine and I wanted to give her the benefit of the doubt. She hadn't been judgmental of me the first time she found me in Tomás's bed; she had been really accepting.

I pulled up outside the *Shaken Not Stirred* bar and left the car running as I turned to Mia. 'Thanks for coming with me, thank God you were there,' I said.

'Why don't you come in for a while? Just have a drink and dance, distract yourself,' she suggested.

I thought about it for a second but I knew I would be terrible company; totally in my head analyzing it all and morose.

'No,' I whispered, 'I'll just go home and...' I let the sentence trail off.

'I'll leave my phone on and I'll be up, so no matter what time you need to talk, you call me, okay? No matter what time,' she said, with emphasis.

I smiled and nodded. 'Thanks. Please don't tell Lucas or anyone.'

'Never,' she said, and leaning over Mia kissed me on the cheek and got out of the car. I saw her watching me drive away.

I wanted to do something but I didn't know what – I felt like crying but the tears wouldn't come. I wanted to scream but nothing would come out. I think I might have been in some sort of shock if it applied to love. I didn't know what to do and so I drove home on automatic pilot. I now knew why people avoided being in love too; so painful, so excruciatingly painful... why would anyone put themselves through this? The highs were great but the lows were just so very low.

I pulled into the garage at home and I heard my phone ringing again. I turned off the car ignition, grabbed the phone from my bag, and put it on silent. It was Tomás calling and there was another missed call and a message. I didn't want to hear from him that it was over before it started with us and I didn't want to hear his excuses. He knew she was coming and yet he didn't tell me, he still dated me and slept with me. What could he say now?

If he had been honest with me, I could have chosen to keep it casual or not progress with him but he didn't give me that option. He held all the cards. I couldn't get the picture out of my head of her snuggling into Tomás's body as if she was designed to fit against him. Then again, maybe it was my fault… maybe I read way too much into what we had going on.

I took a deep breath, exited the car and went into the house. Ryan was in his room on his computer and probably would be for the rest of the night. Dad was having a coffee in front of the golf on the television.

'Hello love, great game today, your boy did well,' Dad said.

'He did. It was a great win. I'm so exhausted…'

'Of course, it's been a big week for you,' Dad agreed.

'I'm going to shower and turn in now.'

'All right love. I've got a seven o'clock meeting onsite in the morning so if I don't see you, I'll see you tomorrow night? I'll be home at six to help you with the move to Cassie's place.'

I couldn't think about that right now.

'Thanks Dad. Night,' I said, and kissed him on the cheek as I passed.

Dad was an engineer who had to do onsite reports throughout construction processes. I guessed the first few weeks without me around were going to be hard for him because I'm adorable, okay, I cooked dinner, so it was good if he was busy. I'm not sure if Ryan would notice I was gone. At least the move was another thing to look forward to and focus on – so much was happening so quickly.

I went into my room, closed my bedroom door and fell onto the bed. I curled into a fetal position which was surprisingly comfortable and wished Mom was here. Still no tears. I'm sure I was in shock... I could barely hear my heart beating. Twenty minutes later, I forced myself up and to the bathroom for a shower. I came back, turned down my bed and got in. With the lights off, then I cried a river. It poured out of me. Grief, pain, embarrassment, hurt, loss, all the emotions. My face was swollen and my eyes stung.

My phone vibrated again and I looked at it. Still, Tomás trying to reach me. I listened to his phone messages.

'*Bella*, it's Tomás. Answer for me.'

'Al...iss, please return my call. I want to tell you what is happening.'

'Al...iss please don't do this, take my call. Call me anytime tonight, anytime.'

I think you have enough on your hands Tomás without worrying about calling or messaging me, I thought.

There were also several messages from him and one from Mia checking up on me. She must have sent that when I was in the shower. I shot her back a quick text telling her

I was okay and not to worry and that I was turning in. I mentioned I was going to ignore my phone for a while so as not to panic if she couldn't reach me.

Thank God I had my work to go to tomorrow – a blessing to be busy in my new job and to have the company of Kay, Sasha and Jim. Otherwise, I would have had to be in my own space all day, in pain and alone, or at college lost in a lecture, trying to focus and trying not to think of him.

I took a deep breath and opened Tomás's messages. I didn't want to read them but I wanted them to have some explanation in there that would make everything okay again and ease the ache in my chest.

TOMÁS: Alice I need to explain. It's a history thing. please

TOMÁS: *Bella*, don't do this I am sick about it. Call. Need to talk to you

Wow, you feel sick Tomás, imagine how I feel and I don't even have a back-up guy.

I sat upright in the dark of my room and made a plan. I would message him back, then I would move on. Tomorrow I would throw myself into my job with gusto and into my studies to get the semester finished. I was busy, too busy to think about Tomás or Finn or any of these guys who wanted something that was more than me, clearly more than I could give them.

I wrote a reply in my head and then tapped it into the phone. I knew he wouldn't come around – it was late now and he knew I lived at home. I read it again and then, signing off, I sent it to Tomás.

ME: Hi T, it's ok. I understand, no explanation needed. It

was fun and thanks for the great dates. See you around the club maybe.

Tomás rang me within a minute of me sending that message. I don't know how he was explaining to Julieta about the texts and phone calls and I didn't care. I didn't want to answer, I didn't want to hear his voice again especially when I was weak and pathetic and likely to believe anything fed to me. The phone beeped to tell me there was a phone message and I listened to it.

'Al...iss, I need to explain. Please take my call, *Bella*.'

A few minutes later, a message arrived.

TOMÁS: A, please, I know you are awake reading this, call me. Tx

I put my phone on the charger and decided to turn it off altogether. I had never done that before, but disconnecting from the world was just what I needed. And then I slept fitfully, seeing in the morning light.

Chapter 23

Thank God for hot showers and makeup. The water took some of the swelling out of my face and I practiced smiling to try and get my eyes more open and less swollen. I don't know if that is scientifically proved to work but I was kind of desperate.

It sounds weird but I felt as if I grew up overnight, as if I had been let into a new club and had a bucket load of life experience poured on my head. Dad had left for work by the time I got up and Ryan and I moved around each other with our usual morning grunts.

I arrived early and found Jim in; he seemed oblivious to my slightly swollen face but I wouldn't get it past Sasha Saxon of the Saints. Jim and I talked about the game for a few minutes and I thanked him for the conference opportunity on Friday and Saturday. Within fifteen minutes Sasha and Kay swanned in. It was going to be a great week for the team – Jim said the office morale was always up after a win and it made our job with the media and marketing so much easier. Kay gushed about the game and we all joined in again.

'Do your boys play soccer?' I asked after her two young sons.

'They do.' She lowered her voice. 'But Spencer prefers track and field and Cooper likes swimming... don't tell anyone,' she joked with a wink.

'My lips are sealed,' I assured her. We sat and logged in, getting Monday underway. I hadn't turned on my phone, as I didn't want to know if he had called or not called. Later, when I was feeling stronger, I'd clear my phone of all that. Sasha studied me but didn't say anything initially until Kay went to photocopy a document.

'Are you okay?' she asked. 'You look sort of... drained.'

Yep, she nailed it – that's just how I felt.

'I am thanks, Sash, big weekend,' I said by way of explanation. 'I had the conference too,' I reminded her.

'Oh yeah, any talent?' she asked.

'Yeah, there were some great presentations,' I teased.

She gave me a wry look; that wasn't quite the talent she was talking about. We heard the coffee van arrive outside and Jim shouted from his office.

'I can't do Monday without a coffee,' he said, appearing and waving a twenty dollar note at us. 'My shout for Monday if you girls order and collect?'

'Done!' Sasha jumped up and took it from him. 'C'mon Alice, help me carry. The usual?'

'Please, but make it a large,' Jim said, returning to his office.

Kay came around the corner and nodded. 'Oh yes, yes,' she said as if the coffee was an orgasm. She reached for her purse and we told her it was Jim's shout. A coffee orgasm might be the closest I came to one for a while... already with the pathetic jokes and it was only nine a.m.

We exited the building and joined the coffee queue at the van again. It was a smaller queue this morning. Most of the football staff wasn't in yet, but the security team was – somehow The Russian had beaten us to the front again. I was beginning to think he had some sort of spy network of alerts going with the coffee van crew.

Sasha appraised me while we waited. 'Mm, cute .. schoolish. I like that pinafore.'

I had on a grey pinafore, white dress shirt, black tights, and black shoes and it was one of my favorite outfits, even if it did look a bit like a school uniform.

'I like that too,' I said, admiring her outfit. She wore a houndstooth short skirt, black tights, and a black zip-up jacket.

'I have a matching houndstooth hat too, but it's a bit much for the office.'

'Did you make it?' I asked.

She nodded. 'I sold two of my designs last week.'

'Good on you,' I said, impressed.

The Russian – all glorious six-foot-five of him, ambled past with a coffee for him and Ed. He checked me out.

'I like the schoolgirl look, Alice,' he teased. 'Most becoming. An all-girls' school?'

'Of course, The-Bless-Me-Now-College-for-Wayward-Girls,' I said, looking down at my pinafore.

The Russian burst out laughing, a huge, booming laugh that matched his size. He shook his head at me – no comeback for that one – and continued.

Eventually, back at my desk and with my skinny cappuccino in hand, my priority was to select some of the great shots from the weekend's game as they came in from our official photographer and drip feed them on our website and Facebook page over the week. I wanted to start the morning with a brilliant shot and of course, amongst the photos was the beautiful Tomás Carrera in action. I tried not to look at them but I was drawn to them like a magnet. It would get easier, I knew that. I picked a Lucas shot – the fans wanted to see their captain in a hero pose.

Shayne, our football manager, appeared in our area. He said a few words to Jim and then came out to see me, greeting us all.

'Got a gig for you this morning Alice; could be good for some social media exposure,' he said.

'Sure, great.' I looked up at him. Shayne, as a former player, had kept up his fitness and still looked damn good.

He continued, 'Ed's got a junior clinic from ten o'clock at the school down the road. It's only an hour and Ed could use a bit of profile-raising. It would be good to get some shots of the young kids in action having fun too – we need to keep the youth recruitment and clinics in the spotlight.'

'Sounds good,' I said. 'I'll go catch Ed and attach myself to him.'

Shayne laughed. 'Yeah, that's a plan, thanks.' He turned to Sasha. 'Maybe, Sasha Saxon from the Saints, you could use the shots for a small story in the next newsletter?'

'Super, for sure, Shayne,' she said, with a grin.

He moved over to have a chat with Kay about getting

some extra tickets in the VIP area and I stuck my head into Jim's office.

'All good with you if I go with Ed?' I asked and he gave the thumbs up and also handed over the camera from the bottom drawer of his filing cabinet.

'Might be better than your phone,' he said.

I took the camera and went to the office next door to mine to catch Ed. I rapped on the door and opened it when Russian's voice boomed out a request for me to enter.

'Alice, twice in ten minutes! What a pleasure.' He grinned.

'Yeah, thanks, Russian. I'm just here to see Ed,' I said and laughed as The Russian's face fell.

'First visitor ever for Ed.' Russian smirked.

Ed gave him a rude hand sign and a grin and turned to me. He was shy and quiet spoken.

'Shayne suggests it might be good if I tag along with you to the clinic this morning and get some pics of you and the kids in action for the clinic promotions. That okay?' I asked.

'Sure,' he said, 'leave here in thirty minutes? I'll pick you up at your desk.'

'Perfect,' I said. 'Well thanks guys, sorry to interrupt the engine room.'

The Russian grinned and Ed laughed.

'The place would shut down without us,' The Russian agreed.

I walked back to my office to find a huge delivery of flowers had arrived and was sitting on my desk. I inwardly groaned. Don't do this Tomás, I don't want everyone to know that we've started and you've got two on the go.

Sasha grinned at me. 'Well, who did you impress on the weekend?'

I cringed. 'I did wash the car, maybe Dad sent them,' I joked. They were beautiful, a huge bunch of mixed flowers of all colors and scents – I had Tomás's roses at home and now flowers at work; it was either a feast or a famine.

'So come on, tell us,' Kay said.

I moved them to the spare table against the wall where we could all enjoy them and opened the envelope with dread.

What the...? The card read: *Didn't get to say goodbye but would love to say hello again, Dane.*

I breathed a sigh of equal relief and disappointment. I didn't want them to be from Tomás but I kind of did too. I was pathetically torn. There should be a manual for this stuff. I looked up to see Kay and Sasha looking at me expectantly.

'They're from a guy who was at the conference. A nice guy, he's a film event promoter,' I said.

'What's his name?' Sasha asked.

'Dane...' I had to think about his surname for a moment. 'Dane Frazier. I'll have to call and thank him. They're divine,' I said and buried my face into them.

'He's hot,' Sasha said and I looked up and over at her.

'How do you know?' I asked.

'I found his Facebook page,' she said.

Kay and I both moved behind her.

'Very nice looking young man, Alice,' Kay approved. I swear sometimes she forgot she was only a decade older and instead, had taken the office mother role. 'And not cheap... I like a man who sends flowers.'

'He's lovely, but I'm not the only one who noticed at the

conference,' I assured them. And he had made my morning a bit brighter, thanks Dane.

'I think you might be the only one he noticed though,' Kay said, with a glance to the flowers.

*****

Before I knew it, Ed appeared beside my desk carrying a bag full of soccer balls for the clinic. Sasha looked up at him.

'Got the address and the first aid kit?' she asked him. I looked at her, surprised, and she explained. 'I always do a checklist before I leave home and the office.'

'Got them,' Ed confirmed.

'Got your phone?' she asked me.

I nodded. It wasn't on, but I guess I had to bite the bullet and put it on since I was leaving the office and should be contactable.

'Camera? Clean hanky?' Kay asked with a wink.

'Yes thanks, Mom.' I smiled, waving the camera at her.

'Got Ed?' Sasha asked, and Ed smirked at her.

'I've got Alice, come on,' he said, nudging me out.

I grabbed my bag and followed Ed to his car – a sedate sedan but fairly new. 'A work vehicle,' he explained. 'Tax deduction for the business.'

'Ah-ha,' I nodded, not that his driving preference required any explanation but the guys seemed hung up on car appearances and their contracts allowed them to spend big on a car if they wanted to do so. He stuck the bag of balls on the back seat and we got in the front and belted up.

The god of broken hearts must have been protecting me; I

saw a black Ducati motorbike turning into the club grounds and coming towards us. It was Tomás – I don't know if he was coming to see me, the football manager, or get PT, but thank goodness I wasn't in the office. That's all I needed. I ducked a little, pulling down the sun visor, and watched in the side mirror as he turned past us, not seeing me in the car.

Ed started the car and checked the address on the sheet supplied by Shayne. I sat dying, willing him to drive – move it, let's go, put the foot to the floor for pity's sake.

I watched in the mirror as Tomás parked and pulled off his helmet. He ran his hand through his hair. Oh my, he was gorgeous sitting straddling that big black bike with his jeans on and a leather jacket. Ed saw him – *damn, can we just get going here? Please don't come over to the car, please, pretty please.*

Ed put down the window and called out a greeting and Tomás replied. I sat far back in the seat, staying out of sight. I breathed a sigh of relief as Ed put the window up, and turned the car towards the road.

I put the sun visor back up and turned my attention back to the lovely Ed. I hadn't spoken more than twenty words to Ed since I started at the club – he was sweet and shy and I was the new girl, so it would be good to get to know each other. It would help with my job too. We started talking about the game and I congratulated him on a good performance, not that I'd have a clue, but that's what you usually said.

'Thanks.' He smiled. 'This is my second year with the club and it's coming together now; it takes a while to learn to play as a team, but they're a good lot.'

'Are you a career player?' I asked. I was pretty sure Tomás was a professional player, you know full-time and no college qualification.

'Actually, I'm an accountant,' Ed said, surprising me. 'So is Kaiser... uh Nik. Have you met him?'

'German Nik?'

'Yeah, that's him. I look after our business books and some of the players' finances as well.'

'So how did you get into security?' I asked.

'Well The Russian was working part-time just doing some security work when we first met and he'd roped some of us guys in if they were short-staffed.' Ed shrugged. 'Easy work, just hustle a few people along and look as though you don't want to be messed with. He had the idea to take over the Saints' security and it just built from there. We have about eight clients now including the Saints and we rent that space from them. I do the accounts and a bit of security work when needed.'

'Really? I didn't realize the business expanded out of the Saints' office. Most impressive. So what are The Russian's qualifications?' I asked.

'He's tall,' Ed said, delivering the line without a smile.

He glanced at me and we both laughed.

'He's got a management degree,' Ed said. 'He's handy with the contracts and a few other things.'

'Yeah, I wouldn't want to run into him in a dark alley,' I said.

'His size is handy for a security company,' Ed agreed. 'Jackson is a carpenter, Josh is a full-time player...' he rattled off names and I waited, dreading the name he would get to eventually. '...Tomás, he's a whiz at I.T. can fix anything, but I don't think he's qualified, Lucas has a history degree...'

I tuned out. A whiz at I.T., so he could fix my laptop, phone, or anything else that needed tweaking. What I needed him to do was fix my broken heart, but he wouldn't be getting a chance to do that any time soon unless he had a good story to spin.

I guess if we had gone the whole way, it would be memorable for the pleasure and the pain. I wished we had. As some poet said, maybe Tennyson or was it Shakespeare, no Tennyson I think, whatever... '*Tis better to have loved and lost, than never to have loved at all*'. At the moment I didn't feel that way because the pain was too much, but in a week, or two, or a month, maybe I'd agree with him.

Chapter 24

I had all the photos I needed and there were some super cute shots of Ed instructing some of the kids in technique and a great shot of them all chasing Ed, and then sitting on Ed as he lay flat on the ground underneath them. While Ed wrapped it up and spoke with the sports teacher, I braved a glance at my phone. I had turned it on earlier but avoided looking at it until the job at hand was done. I guess I would have been disappointed if Tomás hadn't tried to call again – which was pathetic I know because I told him not to – but he had. I thought it would be easier if we didn't talk and just moved on, instead of dragging it out and prolonging the agony for me.

I thought a lot about it overnight, about whether I could just have sex with him, keep it casual, no commitment, and enjoy having him take my virginity. I know guys can do this – separate sex and emotion – but I wasn't sure I could. As much as I wanted him, I didn't think I could be his casual fling. I hadn't the heart for it; I was either all in, or all out, so to speak. Maybe if I didn't care for him so much I could just have had a fling and walk away.

I saw two missed calls and two messages from him this morning and another call and text from last night. There was a call and message from Mia and I texted her back to say I was at work and all was well. I replied to Cassie's message confirming I would be moving in tonight and I'd arrive with my car packed full of gear just after six or so. At least Tomás wouldn't know my new address and wouldn't surprise me with a visit.

I took a deep breath and opened Tomás's first message. His call and the text came in last night just after I sent him the text saying: *It was fun and thanks for the great date. See you around the club maybe.*

TOMÁS: Don't do this Cookie. I beg you to let me explain

I sighed. I couldn't think of any explanation that would satisfy in my head what I had seen. I opened his second text message.

TOMÁS: I am falling in love with you

Holy crap. I promised myself no tears especially since I was at work. Ed appeared and I jumped up, grabbed my bag and camera and followed him to the car, blinking furiously to clear my eyes.

What did I say to that? Why was he with her, why were they all over each other if he was falling in love with me?

*****

We got back to the office and I was looking out for Tomás's bike as we drove in. It was gone and I breathed a sigh of relief – I didn't want the drama at work. I thanked Ed. It had been fun spending time with him and I parted ways with him at the door while I lingered outside the office to call Dane and thank him for the flowers. I dug his card out of my bag and called. It went to message bank and I breathed my second sigh of relief in minutes; I was too drained to turn on the charm this afternoon and I didn't want him asking me out just yet. If I could just have one drama at a time thanks Universe, that'd be appreciated. Being heartbroken took so much energy.

Not saying being asked out by a gorgeous guy is a drama – I don't want to piss off the universe and the love karma vibes – I just wanted to be in a good headspace if it went that way with Dane. Phew, glad we got that sorted. I left a message: 'Dane, hi, it's Alice here. Wow, well thank you. What a gorgeous surprise… I didn't even present and I get flowers! Um, I'll try and catch you later and hey, thank you again, you've made my day.' That should do it for now.

I walked back into the building and turned left down the hallway to our marketing area. I was accosted by the scent of the flowers as I entered our partitioned area. They made the office look quite lovely.

'You two look beautiful with those flowers beside you,' I said, teasing Sasha and Kay and appreciating the scene.

Kay chuckled.

'It helps that we were beautiful to start with,' Sasha piped up.

'Ain't that the truth?' I agreed. 'I got some great pics that I'll stick up online now. Want me to send you some words and a few shots for the newsletter too?' I asked Sasha.

'Please.' She nodded, enthusiastically. 'By the way, you had a visitor.'

Here it comes.

'Oh?' It's hard to make that sound nonchalant when your heart is beating like a drum and the pain in your chest is so overwhelming that it clouds all rational thoughts.

'Tomás the Latin lover was looking for you.' She smiled. 'He didn't look happy even after the great game on Sunday.'

'He was very polite and charming though,' Kay said, with a dreamy look.

That was my Tomás, charming.

'What did he want?' I asked. I tried to keep it cool. 'I've only got three players at events this week and he's not one of them... yet.'

'He didn't say,' Sasha said. 'He just strolled in with that leather jacket on and those well-fitting jeans and looked at your desk expectantly. Then he said our names...'

'Rolled off his tongue like honey,' Kay said and fanned herself.

Good grief.

Sasha continued, 'He asked where you were and admired the flowers.'

I cringed. I didn't want to ask questions but I desperately wanted to know what Sasha and Kay told him. Sasha filled in the blanks without me having to stage an inquisition.

'I told him they arrived for you this morning,' Sasha said, 'and he seemed pissed by that, didn't he Kay? I think his jaw sort of locked.' She tried to impersonate him and I couldn't help but smile and shake my head at her.

'What?' she said. 'It doesn't hurt a guy to know he has competition.'

This wasn't going to be good, but then again, maybe that would help him move on.

'I don't think I'm in Tomás's league,' I said.

'Not slutty enough?' Sasha said, and we both grinned.

'Yeah that's it,' I agreed. 'Nice girls come last or something like that.'

'I wouldn't know.' She shrugged and gave me a wicked smile.

Yeah, I believe Sasha wouldn't know; she was a strange one and I suspect she was into some strange stuff too.

'His girlfriend has just arrived from Buenos Aires hasn't she?' Kay piped up.

Sasha and I both turned to look at her.

How the hell did she know that?

She continued like the proud source of all good gossip. 'Yesterday at the game, I heard some of the WAGS mention it when I was working in the VIP marquee. They said that the two of them had been going out since school but one of the wives said he wanted to come here by himself first before bringing her to live here.'

'Looks like she's checking up on him,' Sasha said.

And he didn't think to mention that to me when he was kissing me, teaching me! Men. My phone rang again and I looked at the screen and it was Tomás. I turned it on silent and let it ring out.

Get screwed Tomás, preferably by your girlfriend.

Chapter 25

'You're here!' Cassie screamed as she opened the door and I stood there with an armful of clothes and a suitcase.

'Here and deaf now,' I said and grinned.

'Hi, Mr. Peterson.' She opened the door wider to let me and my dad in. 'Isn't this exciting? Our first flat together! But we'll be sensible about it, Mr. Peterson.' She caught my eye and reeled her enthusiasm in.

'I'm sure you will be Cassie, clever young women like you two,' Dad said. 'I've just come to help with the move in and check your security.'

'Sure,' Cassie said. 'My folks got someone in to put better security on the windows. I think we'll have more trouble getting out than someone will have getting in.'

Dad chuckled and did a quick look around. He looked for smoke alarms too; an occupational hazard.

We took my first lot of stuff through to my new room. It was a bit bigger than my current room and bare except for a double bed. A large built-in closet featured mirror doors and there was a three-drawer chest next to the bed.

'Perfect!' I exclaimed and dumped everything on the bed.

We went back for a few more loads out of my car and Dad's, and then he said goodnight with a reminder that I was coming for dinner Thursday night. We agreed we would do that every week, it made the parting easier. I watched him drive away and for a moment wanted to run behind him; I'm guessing he felt the same and was just waiting for me to signal him to stop. I sighed and went back inside; moving out was inevitable I guess.

As I entered, Cassie had two glasses of champagne poured.

'It's a double celebration.' She grinned. 'You've moved in and I've met someone.'

I hope my face looked happy enough for her. I was happy for her but while I was in so much pain it was hard to get there.

'Who? What? How? And thanks,' I said, taking the champagne and clinking my glass against hers.

'To moving in, welcome,' she said, in a toast.

'To housemates and friends,' I agreed. We moved to the living area and I collapsed on the other end of her huge L-shaped couch.

'I met him twelve days ago, but who's counting. I just kept him to myself for the first week... you know how it is?' she asked.

Did I ever. If Tomás could stop coming into the office it would be easier to keep it to myself.

'I get it,' I said. 'So?'

'I met him at the commerce ball at college and then we hooked up again for an official date last week and it is going wonderfully well,' she gushed. 'So even though you've just moved in, you might have the place to yourself a few nights a week, if you know what I mean.'

I knew exactly what she meant. 'You're going to stay over at his place and have wild, passionate sex?' I said, bluntly.

'Got it in one! We did it on the weekend and it was good, so good...'

Kill me now, please, anyone.

'Anyway, his name is Rick – it's actually Patrick, but everyone calls him Rick – and he'll be here tomorrow night to pick me up; you can meet him then.'

I looked at Cassie and she was alive with excitement, probably the way I was last week in the glow of Tomás's potential love. With her glossy red hair and pale blue eyes, she was quite a catch and every bit as nice on the inside as she was on the outside.

'Good on you Cass, you're such a good catch and no doubt he knows it.'

She leaned over and squeezed my hand.

'Thanks, Ali. But he is the catch, trust me, he's gorgeous.'

I knew all about gorgeous. I was the expert on it; I had seen it first hand only two nights ago. Aaagh, move on, I scolded myself. Not every thought I have has to lead back to Tomás, or I'll be buried in them!

'So, what's he studying?' I turned my thoughts back to Cassie and her new guy.

She cleared her throat and looked a bit sheepish.

'Oh... he gate-crashed the commerce ball but isn't a student?' I asked. 'No big deal.'

'Um, not quite, he's a lecturer in the school of commerce,

but I'm not doing commerce so it's not as if I'm doing one of my teachers,' she said.

I laughed and teased her. 'Going out with the teacher, ooh...'

She smiled and bit her lip.

'Cass, even if you were in his class, so what? You're both grown up, this isn't high school. How exciting!' I passed my glass over so she topped us both up. 'To Cassie and Rick, and our new housemate status.'

'It's great to have you here at last, Ali.' She clinked my glass for our second toast and we swallowed bubbles – Cassie was on top of the world, I was in hell.

Another glass later I bade Cassie goodnight as I went to unpack and she went to call Rick. I entered my new room and closed the door... on the bright side, I could wallow without Dad scrutinizing me and worrying. I found my stereo, put it on softly, and began to sort my gear out. It was going to be good here, good in a weird way – I couldn't wait not to cook if I didn't want to, to just to buy Cup Noodles if I felt like it. No rush to get out of the bathroom since Cassie and I each had our own now, and I could come and go whenever I wanted… not that I couldn't before but Dad still clock watched and worried. Plus I would have a little bit of dating privacy if I dated again, ever.

I cleared the bed and lay down on top of it. Mia was going shopping with me on the weekend – it was an away game and she didn't have to be at the game and I didn't have to work – and we'd get serious about doing up my room with lamps, bedspread and curtains.

My phone rang and I groaned, then I noticed it was Dad.

I swiped and answered. 'Miss me already?' I asked.

Dad chuckled. 'Of course,' he said. 'Love, Tomás was just here looking for you.'

'Ah, right, sorry about that,' I said.

'That's perfectly alright. I told him that you had moved into your own place now but I didn't give him the address, I said that was up to you.'

'Thank you Dad, he didn't get angry about that did he?' I hated the thought of my father facing off a tall, fit guy like Tomás.

'No, not at all, he was very polite. He said he'd call you. Is everything all right with you and him?' Dad asked.

I didn't want to lie so I applied the side stroke swimming technique and paddled around the question.

'I just want a bit of space between work and home and dating. Don't want them all falling in on each other,' I said.

'Good thinking,' Dad said. 'All right, well leave you to it. Remember you can always come home.'

'Thank you, Dad. Love you.'

'Love you too,' he said and hung up.

Tomás, Tomás, Tomás, just be with your girlfriend and stop trying to see me. Where is she while he's on his bike running over to my place?

I closed my eyes and thought about Saturday night when Tomás and I played after hours at his place; me with my kitty ears on and Tomás with his magic tongue. It was so good and how did it get to be this bad only a few days later? How was he going to keep his worlds apart?

Then my phone rang again and my heart rate raced, only this time it was safe, it was Dane.

'Hi Dane,' I greeted him.

'Alice, miss me?' he asked. 'When's our next conference together?'

I laughed. 'Hey thanks again for the beautiful flowers, they are breathtaking and you shouldn't have.'

'The pleasure was mine,' he said.

'So, did I miss anything when I left early Saturday night?' I asked, regretting now that I had left the superhero-themed ball early to go to Tomás... even though he had lit up his whole house for me. Seriously, shut up!

'Hell yeah, it was wild,' Dane said.

'Really?'

'Really. You remember Kelly?' he asked me.

'Of course, she was a bit keen on you,' I teased him.

'I don't know about that,' he said modestly, 'but you know how she came dressed as Poison Ivy, who technically isn't a superhero but a villain but that's not important to the story... still with me?'

I laughed. Dane was just what I needed. Sexy, sweet and really single.

'I'm with you. So what happened to Kelly?'

'Well, she sort of became her costume... poison ivy. I don't know whether she had a peanut or shellfish allergy or something but not long after you left she broke out in these hives and we had to call an ambulance.'

'Good grief, is she okay?' I asked.

'She is now. They gave her a few shots of whatever they give you for that sort of thing and released her from the hospital the next morning,' Dane said.

'Did you send her flowers?' I teased.

'No, Alice,' he said and nothing else. It wasn't said harshly or negatively just solidly if that makes sense. 'But that's not all,' he continued.

'There's more?'

'Yep, you remember that lady who did the presentation on events for kids?' Dane asked.

'I do, I sat next to her for a while. She's very nice.'

'Well she was dressed in a Thor costume, a female version and I don't know how or why but she got into a fight with Supergirl and hit her with her fake hammer. Luckily it was only Styrofoam but then Supergirl threw her drink over Thor girl and it was on. It was insane. Wonder Woman broke it up.'

I was laughing as I pictured it in my head. 'Well, I expected that,' I said. 'Who else would have saved the day?'

Dane laughed. 'How has your second week on the job been so far?' he asked.

He was so lovely and sincere and such a good listener. We talked for about thirty minutes and then I was so tired, I had to wrap it up. I haven't slept much over the last three nights with the conference, a night at Tomás's, and then last night when I was crying over Tomás.

I thanked Dane for calling, hung up, and then I must have fallen asleep on top of the bed.

About an hour later the phone rang beside me, startling me awake. I grabbed it and answered – force of habit not wanting to wake Dad or Ryan, but now I was in my own room in my place and didn't have to worry about that.

I heard the person on the other end of the line draw a sharp breath. I quickly looked to the phone.

Fuck, fuck, fuck, I had answered a Tomás call. Should I hang up?

'Al…iss.' I heard him say. His voice was raw and husky.

I took a deep breath. 'Tomás. What do you want?'

He made a guttural sort of sound. 'I am desperate to see you.'

I didn't have anything to say… I couldn't think of anything. I wanted to see him more than I'd wanted anything in all my twenty-one years of life that I could recall, but I needed more pain like I needed a hole in the head… the hole I'd have after the lobotomy for agreeing to see him. Wow, another weird thought, sometimes I worried myself.

'I came around to see you today at work and home and you were gone,' he said.

'I went to a clinic with Ed, and I've moved… in with Cassie.'

There was a silence on the line.

'Who is she Tomás?' I asked. I bit my lip, waiting for the reply.

'She's my girlfriend but I need to explain it to you…' He rushed the words. 'She was, is, but…' He was talking quickly, his words tripping over his accent. 'But it's not what you think…'

'I think she's your girlfriend,' I said, and I hung up on Tomás. There was nothing more to be said.

Moments later he sent a message.

TOMÁS: Fuck Alice, hear me through, for us, pls.

ME: Tomás You have a girlfriend, you can't have two.

Technically, he could have as many as he liked I guessed, but he wasn't counting me amongst the number. What a dick, who did he think I was? Some virgin who can't get a date? Yeah, the virgin part was correct but that's where the similarities ended, buddy.

I was on fire now, I took a deep breath and put my phone on silent. I was sure I would sleep tonight, I was too exhausted not to and now I was cranky as well. It was kind of comforting to know that Tomás didn't know where I lived and I didn't have to keep my ear tuned for the purr of a motorbike engine. I just needed to sleep and not think about him for a little while.

Chapter 26

Saints' captain, Lucas Ainswright, was in the building. The girl wires were on the alert; the news traveled from Suzie at the reception – she should have been a code breaker for the government, she was right onto it dispersing the signal via the female office grapevine. By the time we got the message 'captain onboard', we had already seen him pull up in his Lamborghini – it was fortuitous having a view of the office parking lot from our window. He was here to see Shayne of course. They had a weekly catch up, but that didn't stop every girl in the office checking him out. Luckily Mia was a secure type of girl and Lucas only had eyes for her – and I wouldn't be telling her about the Lucas grapevine alert system.

This morning, in our team on our side of the office it was tense – it was monthly magazine deadline day for Sasha. She was in a state trying to get the copy off to the printer on time. Jim said it was like PMS time which was pretty brave of him especially since he had sold another two advertisements at the last moment, which meant Sasha had to go up an extra four pages in size and now had an extra two editorial pages to fill. Jim elected to keep right away from our partition area. Kay and I helped out with proofing and filler stories – I had already supplied my story and pics about Ed's clinic, but I drummed up another quarter-page story about the pending girls' lunch, and I selected some game day shots for Sasha to do a montage page.

I then got back to work on the Saints' Sisters lunch which was next week – yep, once every three months the Saints' female sponsors, fans and friends had a lunch event. It was girls only and tickets were seventy dollars each and included a two-course lunch, champagne on arrival, a lucky draw and two special guest speakers which were usually two of the Saints' players – there was safety in numbers. Our female MC, who was one of the local radio personalities, interviewed them and called for questions from the audience; I can just imagine. The cheerleaders usually kicked it off with a performance, one of the city stores put on a fashion parade and usually got quite a few sales from it, and it was a great day – supposedly – I hadn't been involved in one before but now I was organizing it!

I found all of my predecessor's notes and luckily the venue had already been booked for the four events of the year; one of the five-star hotels that were a Saints' sponsor. I updated the rundown for the day, spoke with the MC, checked on ticket sales, confirmed the social photographer was booked, checked with the choreographer and head cheerleader that they were good to do the opener, sorted out a luxury raffle prize of a pamper session for the winner and three friends, bought the raffle tickets, and all I had to do was to give a final rundown and a few briefing notes to our MC and guest speakers and meet with the hotel public relations person. The venue took the bookings directly – too easy. I found the hotel contact and emailed her to catch up tomorrow morning if possible to introduce myself and ensure I was doing everything I was supposed to do.

Then, I just had to hope and pray that we sold out and it went smoothly on the day. Having said that, I was saving my prayers for really important stuff, not Saints' Sisters' lunch days – more like world peace and Tomás telling me there had been a translation mix-up and this woman was his first cousin and had a clinging disorder. Yeah, back to work.

With only four Saints' Sisters lunches a year, eight players all up were allocated to the event and Jim said they had to be stars of the team, not rookies, or the girls wouldn't come and wouldn't pay and we wanted the dollars – it was a nice little earner for the club and good PR for the female membership drive. I found the list of player commitments in the folder. Lucas and Nik had appeared at the first one. That would have been fun – I could just imagine those two on stage together. I looked at the names confirmed against the next event and holy unlucky draw, yep, you guessed it – Tomás and The Russian. Great, just great.

This was so fucked. It was so fucked that there were no words to describe how fucked it was. Could I change it? I looked through the folder but it was way too late for that. The event was well-promoted and the ladies might not appreciate a late scratching. I checked out the invitation – it was cute, all in pink, and featured Tomás's and The Russian's names. Damn.

I had a thought... I wonder if this is why my predecessor left? Did she get too close to one of the players and then it was too hard for her to continue to do this job and see him? Hmm, Sasha would give me the lowdown, but not today on her deadline day – I glanced at her; I'm not sure she was breathing.

I drew a deep breath for the two of us and sat up straighter. Well, I wasn't going to leave the Saints because of Tommy boy. No way. I loved this job and he was a flash in the pan. He'd probably be signed to some other team – the Two-timing Twits – and be long gone while I was still building my career here. So we were going to keep this really professional and we were going to work together and be nice to each other. Right then, that was sorted. I just had to get Tomás on the same page.

And then I heard the low rumble of a motorbike and saw the black Ducati and its leather-clad rider pull into the Saints' parking lot. Could today get any better? I went through a thousand escape scenarios in my head. Nope, nothing, but I couldn't have Tomás dropping into my work trying to fix this. Unless he wasn't here to see me, but odds were he was. *Crap.* I grabbed my file on the Saints' Sisters lunch and luckily Sasha was so stressed that she didn't notice me leave the office or Tomás arrive. I looked in at the Saints' Security office next to mine and saw The Russian sitting back with his feet on the desk, watching last week's game replay. Ed was nowhere to be seen. I rapped lightly on the door.

The Russian looked up. 'Alice, come in. Flat out here but you never need an appointment,' he said in his unhurried way. He paused the game and took his feet off the desk. 'I'd offer you a tea or coffee but you know where the kitchen is.'

'Yeah, that would just be silly, thanks Russian,' I agreed with him. 'Besides I know you're very busy. I don't want you going to any trouble. Got a minute to talk about next week's Saints' Sisters lunch?'

'Sure, we've got to look after the girls,' he said with an interested grin on his face.

I wondered if that grin was wider since he had broken up with Leesa and was looking forward to being the center of attention at a lunch with well over three hundred women in attendance.

I closed the door and entered. Mission accomplished; when Tomás passed my desk, I would be AWOL again. I'm so clever sometimes I impress myself. I gave The Russian a five-minute overview of what time he'd be expected, what he would have to wear, and the sort of things he would be required to do. I checked he was cool to take questions and told him to talk with Lucas and Nik if he was worried because they did it last time.

'Do you feed us?' he asked.

'Hell yeah,' I said.

'Not girly sized serves,' he said.

'I'll make sure they're alpha size,' I assured him.

He nodded. 'I hope the girls notice Tomás next to me, you know... those Latin good looking types just tend to look insignificant next to a man of my size and stature. I've got three inches on him.' He tried not to smile delivering that line, but couldn't help himself.

I grinned and shook my head. 'Way too much info thanks, Russian.'

'Height, I'm talking height. He's about six or six-two, I'm six-five and pure muscle.'

'Oh, height,' I said, playing along with wide-eyed wonder. 'Oh, well, it's just his bad luck he drew you as his co-star. What can you do? It'll be character building for him.'

The Russian shook his head. 'Not fair to the rest of humanity.'

We both laughed and as I closed my file, signaling this meeting was well and truly over, there was a knock on the security office door.

'Come in,' The Russian bellowed. He turned to me, and added, 'rushed off my feet.'

The door opened and Tomás stood there. His eyes went straight to mine and if The Russian could read reactions, he would have blushed, if guys do blush. In one momentary stare, a collision of anger, lust, passion and fear traded between us. It was so real to me I could taste it.

'We were just talking about you.' The Russian indicated for him to come in. The small office was now crowded and Tomás stood blocking the doorway.

'Russian, Al...iss,' he greeted us both, glancing momentarily at The Russian before returning his gaze to me. 'So, why were you talking about me?'

'The Saints' Sisters lunch next week... it's you and me offered up as the entertainment,' The Russian said. 'I just hope you get a few questions.'

Tomás grinned and gave The Russian an expression that

said *you're totally screwed* and I think The Russian was, especially if Tomás was wearing that leather jacket.

'Anyway, got to go.' I rose and tried to move around Tomás who stood blocking the entrance. 'Thanks Russian, you're sorted then, and I'll email you the details Tomás to your club email.' I said my piece to Tomás making only minimal eye contact. See, this was going to be possible, we'd be fine working together and it would get easier.

Then all that went out the window as Tomás grabbed my arm and sent an electric charge through us both.

'Al...iss, I just need to see you for a minute,' he said.

'I'll be at my desk,' I said, pulling my arm away from his.

His eyes narrowed and he blocked the exit with a muscled arm that pulled his grey T-shirt tighter and showed his definition. If only he looked awful – it was so unfair.

'Just five minutes, alone,' he said.

'I can't right now, I'm at work Tomás unless this is a work matter.'

'Fuck, Al...iss,' he hissed under his breath. I could feel The Russian watching us with much interest. Tomás turned to The Russian.

'I know it's your office, Russian, but could you fuck off somewhere for five minutes?' he asked.

'No, he's busy, I've got a stack to do too,' I waved the folder at him, 'and it's magazine deadline day and...' my voice trailed off.

The Russian stood and held up his hands. 'All good, I've got to go see Johan anyway, and make a coffee since Alice wouldn't make me one.'

'Russian, I don't want to lose this job,' I said in a low voice as he passed me.

He nodded at me with a look that promised discretion and slapped Tomás on the back as he departed.

'Five minutes then,' he said for Tomás's benefit.

He moseyed on out in typical Russian fashion. The moment he was through the door, Tomás shut it, locked it and spun around to face me.

I was trapped and with him and I wanted him so desperately. He reached to hold me and I stepped back, bumping up against the desk. Damn these poky offices.

Tomás exhaled with frustration.

'You're being unreasonable, Al...iss, you could just hear me out,' he said, his eyes blazing.

I think my jaw dropped because I felt my mouth open.

I said in a low, dangerous voice, 'You spent Saturday night with your tongue all over me and I'm unreasonable for ignoring you when I see you with your girlfriend on Sunday?' I hissed the words at him and finished in a sort of hysterical high.

He grabbed at me again and pulled me to him. He put his hand behind my head and pressed his lips on mine. A guttural sound rose from his throat as if he needed this as much as I did. I hit his chest with both of my fists and he pulled tighter, pressing me against him, giving me no room to hit him or push him off.

He continued to press himself hard against me. He moved his mouth to my ear and whispered. 'Listen to me, just listen.'

He waited until I stopped fighting against him but didn't

release me. His cheek was pressed next to mine and he clutched me, continuing to whisper in my ear. 'Yes, she's my girlfriend but not for much longer... I'm working on...'

I gave him a good shove and pushed away from him. He regained his footing and dropped his hands to his hips. 'You're not working hard enough Tomás. You knew she was coming, so why start with me unless I was nothing more to you than a few nights' fun?'

He ran a hand through his hair, closed his eyes and drew a deep breath, reining in his temper. His eyes looked even darker when he opened them and re-fixed them on me.

'You are not that, never that,' he said between gritted teeth. 'Can you let me explain?'

'What's to say, really?'

'Who were those flowers from?' he asked.

It took me a few seconds to make the connection of what he was asking me.

'The flowers near your desk,' he clarified.

'Not from you,' I said.

'No. Who is he?'

'He is no-one. A nice guy I met at the conference and he sent me flowers, not that it is anything to do with you.'

'Hell, yes it is. You were in my bed on Saturday night and during the day you're chatting up some guy at the conference.' His dark eyes flared and his chest puffed like a caveman.

'Seriously? That is not the same. I sat next to a nice guy. We chatted, I did not flirt, I did not kiss him, or drape myself over him, or promise him anything. I left early and came to you, a big mistake. The next working day he sent flowers.

So not the same as you picking up your girlfriend from the airport, taking her out, being all over each other and... sharing your bed with her.' The last words I spoke brought tears to my eyes and I blinked them away self-consciously.

The door handle turned and finding it locked, Ed rapped on the door.

'Are you there, Russian?' Ed called.

I reached past Tomás, flicked the lock and opened the door.

'Hey Ed, he's in the kitchen. Good timing, thanks.' I strode out and tried to avoid looking at Ed, while I blinked to clear my eyes. I turned back just in time to see Tomás punch the wall. Ed quickly entered and closed the door. I heard their voices for a few minutes and then I heard The Russian enter. Boy therapy, whatever.

'Want to get some lunch? I need a break from proofreading,' Sasha asked, interrupting my thoughts as I dropped the folder back on my desk and sank into my chair.

'Absolutely.' I got back up so quickly that Sasha raced to keep up with me. 'Want anything, Kay?' I asked.

'No thanks love, I've brought a sandwich.'

I looked in on Jim's office but he was missing in action. I raced Sasha out to my car and we left. When we returned twenty minutes later with our lunch, Tomás's bike was gone. Seriously this could not continue or else I would have to hire The Russian and Ed as my personal security detail. Mm, that was a nice thought.

Chapter 27

Tomás kept away from me at work thanks to The Russian. I didn't want to drag The Russian in as a sort of love referee but I was hoping he would have a subtle word to his team's Latin American goalkeeper. The Russian called me into his office before he left for training that afternoon.

'Alice, you seemed to have stirred up the Latin lover,' he said in his matter-of-fact tone.

I sighed. I waved my hand around trying to find some words to explain it in ten words or so, but I had nothing. I shrugged.

'I know.' He nodded. 'You and I, we can't help but attract the opposite sex, it's a curse.' His lips twitched into a smile. I smiled and shook my head at him. He had a calming influence on me.

'His girlfriend is here from Buenos Aires, so he'll be just fine,' I said, assuring The Russian there was nothing to worry about.

The Russian frowned, confused. 'I think the *family friend* is going home mid next week from what Tomás tells me.'

'Really. Mm.' I stored that away to think more about it

later. 'I may need to hire you Russian, you and Ed to protect my turf in the office,' I suggested.

'Say no more,' he said. 'After the look you gave me earlier and that muffled sentence about not wanting to lose your job, I had a quiet word to Tomás. I suggested it might be best to phone or message you, and that he needed to give you some space to find your feet at work.'

I breathed a sigh of relief and looked gratefully at the six-foot-five wall.

'Perfect, thank you,' I said.

The Russian continued. 'I mentioned that you would like him a lot less if he was responsible for causing you trouble at work.'

I nodded. 'So true. Thank you, Russian, I appreciate it, and your brilliant skills at muffled sentence interpretation.'

'I have three sisters,' he explained. 'I can pretty much read any expression and I have learned some handy skills.'

'Oh?' I asked out of curiosity.

'Yes, like when it came to dealing with women, most things were usually my fault, the bathroom is out of bounds most of the time, no means no, maybe means no, yes could mean no as well.'

I grinned. 'Hence your success with females now.'

He nodded and looked pleased with himself.

'I owe you,' I said.

'Yes, and I'm collecting now,' he said, rising from his chair and grabbing his phone off his desk.

'Already?' I frowned.

'I'm putting it out there, Alice. If Tomás's game begins to decline because of girl trouble, regardless of how much

I might like the girl,' he said with a raised eyebrow, 'you're going to have to kiss-and-make-up and take one for the team.'

I opened my mouth to protest and The Russian held up his hand.

'Think about the good of the club, Alice. I'm not calling in that favor yet, but I'll let you know.'

I nodded and left his office so he could log out and head to training. I gave him a backward glance to make sure he was serious and he was. I wondered what it would be like to go out with The Russian.

Stop that and go back to your desk, I ordered myself.

Ah, men, seriously! Can't work with them, can't work without them.

*****

Tomás continued to send me a message every morning and night but had given up on begging to be heard. Now they were simple messages:

TOMÁS: Morning *Bella*, I hate the thought of a day not hearing from you

TOMÁS: Please wait for me Alice, sorting stuff out

TOMÁS: I want you. Don't give up on me

TOMÁS: Goodnight Cookie, thinking of you

And on it went. I felt sick every time the phone beeped with a message and I was sad and melancholy, but I didn't know what else to do – his girlfriend was here, staying at his place. I wasn't going to be the standby girl, as much as I wanted to be. So, what was there to say? I tried to be up and positive so no-one could tell that I just wanted to sit down and cry and tell everyone how miserable I was and get their perspectives.

I can't believe the misery wasn't coming out of my pores, that it couldn't be sniffed in the air. I tried to make nothing about me and divert every personal question that came my way – so exhausting but on the upside, it was a good people skill to practice.

Don't get me wrong, there were highs to the week as well; I met Cassie's Rick and he was lovely; they looked so happy together. I had hardly seen her since I moved in. I bought my first groceries which was kind of fun and on Wednesday night I caught up with Mia for dinner after hot yoga. Tonight, I had dinner with Dad and Ryan starting up our new tradition and Friday night, the team was flying out for an away game on Saturday afternoon and I had a date with Dane.

Chapter 28

Dane picked me up right at seven p.m. for drinks, dinner and dancing. I seemed to have this alliteration thing going with Dane – sexy, sweet, and single. My English teacher would be proud I'd even remembered what an alliteration was... I blamed Sasha Saxon from the Saints who started it. I wore the dress I bought for Lucas's pre-season party – a little red number with tassels that worked a treat when dancing. It hadn't got an airing since the party, so would be ideal for a first date.

I was kind of bummed out to meet Dane at this time in my life. If I had met him a month before Tomás or even several months after I was pretty sure I'd be falling at his feet, my tongue out, my V-card ready for punching, but I wasn't in the right space just now and I'd have to come clean with him early up so I didn't lead him on, then it was his choice to stay or play.

Cassie was heading out too but stuck around long enough to meet Dane; nosy cow, but I confess I would have done the same to her. She gave me the thumbs up and an encouraging raised eyebrows expression behind his back.

'We should get going then. Good to meet you, Cassie,' Dane said, being charming.

'And you Dane, hope we see more of you,' she said, with a smile in my direction. Sigh.

Dane looked better than I remembered, funny that. Clearly, I didn't fully notice him in my lustful Tomás phase. He wore a dark suit and crisp white shirt, open at the neck. He did look a bit like an older version of *One Direction*'s Harry. I had a bit of a thing for Harry even if I was about five years older than his average fans.

Cassie gave me some rude hand signals behind Dane's back which indicated what she thought I should be doing with Dane – so incorrigible – and I left her to get ready for her night with Rick. Outside, Dane unlocked his silver 4WD and opened the door for me.

'I might need a leg up,' I teased and Dane looked just a bit too enthusiastic to help. We headed out for drinks and it was nice to be beside him in the car. Nice. Ugh, what an awful word. Poor Kelly from the conference would have killed to be in my place and I was thinking how nice it was.

'Week two and still surviving the Saints?' Dane asked. He was good at detail.

'I'll be up for long-service soon,' I joked. 'It's a great job, and my boss Jim says I can create some of my unique events once I find my feet. I'd like to do a bit more with the kids' club and the clinics.'

'It's the future of the game,' Dane agreed.

'How was the week in film?' I asked him.

'Ah, busy – some big-budget films coming which mean big promotion budgets and that's very good for me.' He pulled into a parking spot in the city and we wandered to a bar not far from where he planned for us to grab a bite and party on. We found a table and Dane went to order. I noticed all the televisions were on sport and one of them featured interviews about the weekend's soccer games. Johan, the Saints' coach, was on the screen and then there were some flashbacks of last week's game including the supremely talented Tomás Carrera. The program moved on to another team and Dane returned with our drinks. There was no escape, I'm telling you, no escape!

Later that night or actually it was about two a.m. the next morning when Dane dropped me at the door, I didn't invite him in. It was only the first date and late enough.

'I had a great time, thank you,' I told him.

'Me too,' he said, not dropping his gaze. He moved in for the kiss... his hands found my hips and his lips found mine. Thank God that Tomás had left for an away game – I wouldn't put it past him to spring out from the shadows to reclaim his property.

It was a soft kiss before Dane moved away slightly and looked at me, almost as if he was seeking permission to proceed. I was pleased he didn't push himself up against me; I could already see his pants were tighter.

The kiss made me sure of one thing – I wanted to kiss Tomás. Damn, damn, so unfair.

'Dane,' I began, 'I just came out of something and you're gorgeous, but I don't want to leap straight in too fast. I want to be fair to both of us and if you want to run a mile now...'

He nodded and kissed me again. My body began to respond. Damn Tomás, I wished I hadn't met him. Dane's kiss ended with a tease of his tongue. Holy mother of kisses that was good and got my attention.

'I've got all the time in the world, Alice,' Dane said. Then he kissed my forehead and moved away. 'I'll call you tomorrow. Thanks for a great night.'

'Thank you,' I said feeling just a bit giddy. Dane stopped halfway down the stairs, turned and hurriedly came back. He kissed me again. An amazing kiss and this time I not only felt his erection against my leg, but my own body reacting. *Good grief, go already before I invite you inside.*

He pulled away, gave me a sexy grin and left. Mm, wonderful and weak-kneed was I.

Men. Thank God for them. Dane was wonderful medicine.

*****

It was Saturday midday and Mia took the avocado from my plate and I took the tomato from her salad. We sat in the food court in the mall with salads and a second-round of coffee.

'We've done well,' I said, looking at my shopping bags, 'consider the bedroom decorated and all within my budget.'

'When have you not shopped well?' Mia asked. 'You're the queen of shopping; I am but your humble follow-behind servant.'

'You lasted, thanks, I know it is not your thing.'

'The coffee helped.' She smiled. 'So...' she grabbed some lettuce on her fork, 'you've had a hot kiss from Dane and you've still got the hots for Tomás. What now?'

I groaned and sat back brandishing my fork mid-air. 'I don't know. I want Tomás but am I just being an idiot? Did Lucas say anything?'

Mia scoffed. 'You're kidding aren't you? Men are clueless when it comes to that sort of stuff. I'd be surprised if Lucas even knew Tomás had a visitor or that he was going out with you. I've kept it in the vault as you told me.'

'Thank you, I appreciate that. But Lucas knows Tomás and I started something,' I reminded Mia.

'Yeah, but anytime I mention you, all Lucas says is, 'she all right?' Guys, they're not big on detail.' Mia glanced at her watch. We were going back to her posh beach pad, well Lucas's place, to watch the game at two p.m. on his enormous television – that just reminded me of Tomás again for some reason, sigh. I still needed and wanted to watch the game, I was a Saints' employee and team player – watching Tomás as part of it was just unavoidable. After the game, I would go home and spend my night re-decorating my room, drinking wine and wallowing in the pathetic-ness of my indecision. Wow, that's poetic.

'I did get a bit of info from Laura, Buzz's partner,' Mia said, hesitantly.

'Buzz the defender,' I said, still learning my players. 'You didn't say anything to her did you?'

Mia gave me a look that made me feel guilty for doubting her skills.

'Come on, let's head home to watch the game, I'll tell you on the way,' she said.

I grabbed my bags, giving half to Mia and we left the

center. As we sat in Mia's BMW, a gift from Lucas, yeah wow, she went into detail.

'I had coffee with Laura the other day. We've kind of connected after a lunch bet I had with her and I think she's a bit lonely. She and Buzz only moved here for his contract and she doesn't know many people,' Mia explained. 'Anyway, Laura met Valentina at a couple of the games; she came a fair bit last season supposedly.'

Mia was killing me, get to the point already.

'They started talking about Tomás, and Valentina mentioned that he had had a girlfriend for years, and they'd been going out since the start of high school.

I felt that sharp pain in the chest again, even though Mia wasn't telling me anything new. She reached a hand over to squeeze mine.

'Laura said that the girlfriend wanted to move here with Tomás last year when he got signed but *he* didn't want her to,' Mia said. This was promising again.

'Hold that thought,' Mia said, as she turned into the driveway and parked the car in her side of the garage.

Lucas's house on the beach was truly amazing, I didn't envy Mia, I feared this. If it ended, how do you go backward? I knew I should think everything would go on happily ever after, but I'd lost my mother and I'd lost my potential new boyfriend, so I was a bit neurotic, or at least wary.

I moved my shopping bags from her car to my car which I had left at her place earlier, before following her inside to watch the game. Ten minutes later we sat on Lucas's huge leather couch and Mia put the game on. We got glimpses of the players and the football management team as they checked out the grounds and set up. It was still thirty minutes until it started and the commentary team was doing their analysis.

Mia continued where she let off. 'Valentina told Laura that Tomás's girlfriend was very upset about that, so they agreed that she would come over at the start of his second season when he would be well and truly established.'

'You would think Tomás would want her to come over and be with him,' I said, 'especially when it was all new, you know, to give him some stability.'

Mia shrugged. 'According to Laura, Valentina said he wanted to have the first year by himself just to concentrate on his football.'

I made an ungainly snorting sound. 'Maybe, but it sounds as though he wanted a year free of responsibility and to concentrate on tarting around. Not that there's anything wrong with that, he's young and gorgeous and he told me he's had a lot of responsibility all his life.'

'Exactly,' Mia said. 'Valentina told Laura the girlfriend was holding Tomás to their agreement, and here she is, I guess.'

I nodded. 'Well, that's insightful.'

'Is it?' Mia asked.

'Yeah. He told me it was his girlfriend but things had changed and that he had to do some sorting out of stuff.'

'Sounds to me as though it is over,' Mia said.

'I hope so, that's what I want to hear. But maybe now that she is here, he'll be taken by her again... you know it will rekindle or something. Regardless, he should have told me... how was he going to hide a girlfriend for a week?'

'It'd be hard to call it off,' Mia said. 'You know if you had to let someone go that you'd been with a long time and made promises to... you know how hard it was for Ben and me to break up.'

'I never knew if you were on or off,' I said.

'It might be easier for Tomás if he wanted out now that he's had a year's separation,' she said. 'Maybe that was his plan... maybe he hoped she would move on in that time as well.'

I did feel a bit more sympathetic now that I knew the difficult situation he was placed in and he had told me he wanted out of all the family responsibility. But he just had to man up. Then I remembered I was stalling Dane too...

'Are you okay?' Mia asked.

'Thanks for telling me that, it helps. Now you know why I'm not quite ready to move on with Dane just yet and I can't give up completely on Tomás.'

'It's worth hearing him out,' she said.

I shrugged. 'I don't know. The practical side of me is shitty with Tomás. Why not just say, 'hey it's over' and send her back? She's been here a week and she's still here and in his house. I bet she's in his bed.' I touched my chest at the thought. I just put a knife through my own heart.

Chapter 29

Tomás was not having a good game. I sat gripping Mia's pillow across my chest, burying my face in it and not looking but then having to look. Lucas, on the other hand, was having a great game and The Russian was pulling his weight too. It was nearing the end of the first half when one of the opposition's defenders charged at Tomás and then found himself charged with violent conduct in return by the referee – justice served. But not before Tomás decided he'd dish out his justice and went for him. Lucas was there in a flash, pulling Tomás away and he and Lucas had a few words in a bit of a fiery encounter which wasn't a clever move on Tomás's behalf either. So not good.

Then Johan pulled Tomás off the ground and substituted him for a brief time to let him cool off. The commentators were discussing why he was off form and the camera cut to him a few times as he sat on the bench unable to keep still; he looked angry, distracted, out of whack.

'The magic of Tomás Carrera is missing today,' one of the commentators said, and I watched as Tomás came back on and Lucas ran up to have a word to him, accompanying him back to the goal area. Tomás rubbed his side, the result of an enormous leap to ward off a ball followed by a crash to the ground. It was unbearable watching. The other team – the Salt Lake Spears – were always tough competitors and while the score was even, today Tomás had not played a major part in that.

'I know it is just a game,' Mia said, 'but it is so much more at this level.'

'I hear you,' I agreed. 'Tomás needs to chill a bit, he looks so wired.'

They played for another ten minutes or so before the siren went and the players left the field for half-time. Mia and I got up to make tea and then my phone rang. I fished for it in my bag hoping it wasn't Dane since I was in Tomás mode. I had to will Tomás to have a better second half and hope it reached him through the universe wires. I wondered if Julieta was watching too.

I didn't recognize the number but thumbed the screen to answer.

'Alice, it's Lucas.' I heard a slightly breathless voice down the line.

'Lucas?' I looked to Mia, confused. 'Are you looking for Mia?'

'No, you,' he said. 'I need you to talk to Tomás – he's super fucking aggressive and distracted and I don't know what's going on but The Russian said to tell you he's calling in the favor. Kiss and make-up, whatever. I'm putting him on.'

'Hold on, Lucas,' I said. 'You can't be serious?'

'Oh, I'm serious. He's garbage out there. Take one for the team, Alice and just do it,' he snapped.

I was angry, who did these guys think they were? I was prepared to do it for The Russian as agreed, but for fuck's sake, they're professionals – play the game and get over it.

'Don't bully me, Lucas,' I said and drew a deep breath.

Wow, I can't believe I said that to the Saints' most valuable asset, especially when I was working for the team too and Lucas could make big trouble for me. But there's work and there's after hours and I didn't like the way he was demanding it. I could see Mia in the background, biting her lower lip. This was the old Lucas that was such an asshole when she first met him.

I heard the cleats on Lucas's soccer boots tapping on a concrete floor as he paced impatiently. He took a deep breath.

'I'm sorry, Alice.' He started again and spoke politely. 'As a personal favor to me, as a friend, will you just have a word to him please?'

As a friend? Wow. I guess he was living with my best friend and was in my friend circle.

'Sure,' I said. Who could resist that?

I heard him breathe a sigh of relief. 'Thanks, Ali,' he said. 'Hang on, I'll get him.'

I heard Lucas's shoes clap their way up the corridor and he yelled out Tomás's name. There was the sound of more shoes clacking and I heard Lucas say, 'call for you.'

'What?' Tomás sounded confused and then his voice came on the line. 'Hello.'

'Tomás, it's Alice,' I said, breathing out.

'Al...iss, why are you calling me?' He still sounded confused.

'I'm not, you're calling me.'

'Oh, right.'

I pictured him standing there looking gorgeous in the Saints' shirt and shorts, sweaty and ruffled.

'Tomás, I need you to come and see me when you come back. I want us to talk.'

'Really?' His voice lifted, and he sounded happy. 'That's great Al...iss, great.'

'So you'll come over?' I asked, bringing it home. 'I'll send you my new address details.'

'I'll come straight from the plane on Sunday.'

'Mm, shower first,' I teased him and he laughed.

'Thanks, Al...iss,' he said. 'I need to see you badly.'

'I miss you,' I answered.

Then Lucas's voice came down the line. 'Thanks Ali, Tomás has to go. See you soon.' He hung up. I put my phone back in my bag.

'What the fuck was all that?' Mia asked, wide-eyed.

I shook my head. 'Half-time therapy I think.'

'Was Lucas being an ass?' She narrowed her eyes. The good thing about Mia was she didn't let him get away with much.

'Only for a moment, but he came around. It's all good. I think you might have worked wonders with him.' I told her the details.

'I'm glad you stood your ground and I'm glad he respected that,' she said. 'You know you've just invited Tomás around tomorrow when he gets home?'

I nodded. 'I have, haven't I?' I looked at the clock, and it was after three p.m. 'Is it cocktail hour yet?'

'Somewhere,' she agreed and grabbed two wine glasses.

The game started up again and Tomás was different, he had a spring in his step, as though the weight of responsibility and sadness had been lifted off his shoulders. I got it, I felt that too. My heart was feeling lighter, everything seemed a bit brighter, I even felt a bit hungry which I hadn't felt for almost a week since... you know.

Tomás had a blinder for the rest of the game. He prevented several opponents' goals and the commentators went berserk.

'The Carrera magic is back,' one of the commentators was saying. 'Don't know what the captain or coach threatened him with at half-time but they should bottle it.'

'The sweeper keeper is in his element... look at that.'

'He's the commander of the offense, marvelous work.'

'Where was he for the first half... did he have the wrong boots on or something? Because he's back now.'

'A miraculous save! He makes hard saves look easy.'

I breathed a sigh of relief and guiltily, I was beyond stoked that I could make a difference to his game. I never wanted to do anything that would make him less than perfect ever again.

*****

That night I cooked some Cup Noodles and drank some wine – my diet needed improving since leaving home, so I'd review that on Monday. I decorated my room and it looked fantastic, even if I say so myself. I chose a crystal drop lamp for the corner of the room and a cream color theme with gold trim. So classic, it just looked lush.

Dane rang and I let it go to voicemail; I felt terrible about that, but I just didn't know what to say at the moment and having a long chat tonight would only make us closer, I was sure. Then my phone pinged with a message from Tomás.

TOMÁS: I love that you called today

ME: Well done on a good game

TOMÁS: Only after I spoke to you. I need you, Alice

ME: I miss you Tomás, but we've got to sort some stuff out

TOMÁS: Agreed. I'm not giving up on us, for anything or anyone

ME: See you tomorrow

TOMÁS: We land at 5, I'll be there by 6.

ME: Sleep well. Ax

TOMÁS: I will now. Tx

I slept the best I had slept since the first day I set eyes on Tomás Carrera. My life was looking brighter. I just hoped that what Tomás could promise would be enough to get us over the line.

Chapter 30

By the time Tomás was due to arrive at my door I was a nervous wreck. I had changed several times and opted for a soft blue dress that went to my knees and slip-ons that I could easily slip off. I was lucky that Cassie wasn't due home until later tonight, so we'd have some time alone to talk. I clock-watched, estimating when he got on the plane, got off the plane, got on the bus to the clubhouse, got off the bus, got on his bike, got here to the address I had texted him this morning when he woke me early with a morning text. God, he was adorable, I could just kill him. Then not long before Tomás was due to arrive, Ryan rang to say that he'd lost his keys, he couldn't reach Dad who was on a date, and could I come 'home' and let him in.

Crap, shit, damn it. I looked at the clock. I'd make it there and back in time. I told Ryan I was on my way and I messaged Tomás to let him know I was doing a mercy dash and I wouldn't be long should he arrive and find me missing. I jumped in the car, raced over, let Ryan in, and gave him my house keys until he got another set cut, and raced back to my new apartment. I realized Ryan's interruption might be a good thing; I wasn't sitting at home waiting for the knock at the door now, I was racing to get back for it.

As I ran up the stairs to the front door of Cassie's and my place, Tomás sat sprawled in the stairway, his back against the wall, his eyes closed. I stopped and took him in – what a beautiful sight. He wore his jeans and a long-sleeved marble grey T-shirt. His leather jacket and helmet sat on the stairs below. He opened his eyes when he heard me and he gave me a slow and very sexy smile. I went up the stairs towards him but he didn't rise. He turned to face me and pulled me between his legs. He pressed his forehead against my stomach and wove his arms around my waist. It was so damn sexy and vulnerable.

I heard him exhale as if the troubles of the week were leaving him and I ran my hands through his hair, resting them on his shoulders. After a few moments, he looked up and I sidestepped him so he could rise. He stood, grabbed his gear off the step and came up behind me as I unlocked the front door and let us in. His eyes glanced around my new pad and he put his leather jacket and bike helmet down on a chair. Then he returned his focus to me, pulling me closer and leaning down to kiss me. I didn't want to start here; I wanted to get everything sorted out first, but I could feel him in every part of my being and I just wanted this for a moment. We hadn't said one word yet and maybe that was the ideal thing.

His tongue slipped into my mouth, gently testing me, and I met it with my own, inviting him to take more of me. Oh God I needed this so badly, and so did he – his grip tightened on me and he made a strangled sound in his throat. Relief coursed through me. When he pulled away, we stared at each other. My eyes were probably desperate and wary and his were pained and so dark and deep.

I cleared my throat. 'Why don't I make us some tea and we can talk?' I managed to say and he nodded.

I went to the kitchen and he sat at a stool opposite me across the island and watched my every move. Very disconcerting.

'Have you eaten? Are you hungry?' I asked as I placed two cups on the counter.

'Not yet,' he said, 'my stomach is a mess.'

'I know what you mean,' I agreed. I grabbed the milk from the fridge and I watched as Tomás moved to the lounge, turned on a lamp and turned off the overhead light. I met him there with our teas and placed them on the coasters on the coffee table. I sat in the middle on one side of Cassie's L-shaped couch. It was huge, damn her.

I watched his movements. His shoulders were slightly hunched and I could almost hear him thinking as he moved to sit nearer to me, leaning against the arm of the couch.

'Did you find this place easily enough?' I asked, making the small talk that I hated.

He nodded. 'I know this area a bit. We've trained at a pool not far from here.'

His arms reached for me, resting behind my butt as he slid me closer to him. My legs were entangled with his long legs, so I pulled them free and crossed mine in front, pulling my dress between my legs and sitting to face him.

He swallowed and began. 'Al...iss, please hear me out, just until I finish and then you can ask me anything or throw me out or keep me, with luck,' he said with the slightest hint of a smile. God, he was beautiful, did I mention that?

I nodded. 'I'll listen,' I promised him. My insides were flipping out with anxiety.

He looked away for a moment then back at me. 'I've chosen these words very carefully.'

Of course, Spanish was his mother tongue, so no wonder he was tripping up under pressure in the office the other day and I impatiently shut him down.

'Did you have a childhood sweetheart?' he asked me.

I nodded. 'Paul Murphy.' I said his name.

Tomás smiled. 'Where is he now?'

I shrugged. 'I don't know, it was just a silly school thing. We were always associated together and then we moved on.'

'Julieta and I are the same. We met in school and we were boyfriend and girlfriend all through high school. Everyone knew. She was a family friend and a church friend. It was just expected we would be married and produce beautiful *bebés*,' he said with his fluid accent.

He stopped to reach for my hands. 'But you know when we met I told you that I didn't want any responsibility?'

I nodded.

'Part of that was that I didn't want any relationship at all, even one from the past. I broke it off before I left home to come here, but she was very upset and asked me to wait and give us some time, that the break might be all we needed. I suggested a year and that we'd talk at the end of my first season. And so, I escaped here – I set up my family so they would not need anything and I had complete freedom from all responsibility. It was great.' He smiled. 'I am even more clear after a year that I do not want to marry Julieta or be in that relationship. I came here to start new and find myself… I guess that is how you would put it. Do you understand so far?'

'I do, but do you feel responsible for Julieta?' I asked.

He shook his head. 'No. My family was disappointed that I called it off. I think getting the contract and calling it off at the same time wasn't the cleverest thing, they thought me arrogant. But it had run its course sometime before. She would not be here now except it was a promise I made and I couldn't after all those years call the relationship off over the phone. She had the flight and told everyone long ago she was coming to talk about moving here. She wanted to see Valentina too and some other friends and family she had here. I was going to deal with it when she came in person, and then I met you. '

'So now that she is here, how do you feel?' I asked and held my breath. I only wanted one answer.

'I feel the same. I love Julieta like a sister, a friend, but I don't love her like a lover. It was such bad timing. I think of it like two waves coming to shore from different directions: Julieta arriving and just before that, meeting you; I didn't know how to manage it,' he said.

I watched him explaining and thought about his analogy. I understood it.

'Why could you not tell me about her coming and trust me?' I asked.

'I gave it some thought,' he said, honestly. 'But Al...iss, when I met you, I wasn't ready either. I was just playing casually...'

'Playing the field,' I said.

'Yes, and that required nothing that would distract me from the club and the game. Then I tried not to want you but that didn't work.'

I smiled. He shook his head when he said it, so cute.

'I made a decision to not contact you at all and I didn't for the first week, but then I couldn't stop myself because you were driving me crazy, and I sent you a message.'

'I remember,' I said.

'Then there was that college football player around you and I wanted to remove him. So I knew then I had to stop playing casually. And I asked you out and you chose me over him and then I still had the problem of Julieta arriving.'

I nodded, listening attentively. He was so sincere and his eyes were trying to read me as he told me how it unfolded. I believed every word.

'I thought if I told you, you would drop me and go back to college guy and if I didn't tell you, I might be able to just manage it so that Julieta returned home and was not in our lives at all. I wanted us to be about the future, not all that I've left behind. I'm sorry if that doesn't make sense.'

'I get the bigger picture now,' I said. 'But I was devastated, Tomás, when I saw you and her together at the jazz bar. How would you have felt if you saw me all over Finn?'

'I would have killed him,' he said, sincerely. 'Are you seeing the conference guy who sent those flowers?'

'I saw him Friday night, and we went dancing. Nothing happened. I didn't invite him in,' I said. I wanted to be completely honest. 'Even though you are still living with your girlfriend,' I reminded him.

Tomás rose and paced, and he looked pissed off.

'She's an ex-girlfriend. Did he kiss you?'

'Does it matter?'

'Hell yes, Al...iss,' he said, and spun around to face me.

'Have you slept with Julieta?' I asked. Then I covered my ears, rose quickly and went behind the couch. 'Don't answer that, because I'm not sure I could cope with the answer.'

He strode over and pulled me to him. 'I have told Julieta that we are over. She is staying in my house in the guest room until Wednesday when she flies back home. It hasn't been easy for her, I think she thought I would propose when she came over,' he said, with a sigh. 'It's an awful thing to hurt someone.'

I nodded. 'Did Valentina know you had tried to break up?'

'Of course. She thinks it is her business to know everything about me, she's my sister.' He smiled. 'Besides, she never thought we were good together.'

I took that all in. I was right about Valentina, she hadn't given me the tickets to the jazz club to hurt me. That was a relief, especially that I wouldn't be filling the shoes of someone she loved and wanted with her brother. I could feel my chest getting lighter.

Tomás cleared his throat. 'Will you forgive me, Cookie? Are we good?' he asked, his face a mask of worry.

I touched his face. 'We're good.'

His face lit up with a smile. 'Really?'

I nodded. 'Really.' I narrowed my eyes. 'As long as you really are ready to stop playing casually and you have your guest in the guest room?' I teased him, using his expressions.

'I want only you Al...iss.' He leaned on the back of the couch and pulled me between his legs.

'But...' I said.

Tomás raised an eyebrow. 'Yes?' He slipped his hands under my dress and without even thinking I pushed him back. He fell back onto the couch taking me with him. He didn't let me go, protecting me from the fall as I landed on top of him.

'That works for me,' he teased as I stumbled up to straddle him.

'My but...' I said.

'I know. I love your butt. I've seen it up close.'

'No, I mean, the 'but' I was going to add...'

He put his hands on my hips and positioned me on the hard bulge in his pants. He reached around, grabbed a cushion and stuck it behind his head, his long legs extended down the length of the couch. He looked as if he was settled for the night.

'Go ahead,' he encouraged me. 'What is your 'but'....' He watched me and looked so kissable.

I drew a deep breath and tried to stop thinking about his body; very hard given the way in which he was pressing against me. I kept talking. 'But... I don't want us to start again until Julieta has gone home. You can't have us both Tomás. When she is gone, definitely gone, then I want to have you and have you inside me.'

My words had an instant effect on him; a soft growl emanated from his throat and his eyes drank me in.

'What about the event guy? Will you see him again?'

'No. Not if we agree tonight that we will start on Wednesday. I will only have eyes for you Tomás.'

'You won't let him touch you?' he asked again.

I shook my head. 'I won't let him touch me.'

'No one has touched you? You are still my virgin?' he asked, his fingers dancing around the borders of my dress.

I nodded. 'I'm stuck with only qualifications in hand and tongue class.'

He laughed and then sat up, holding me tight, as he swung his legs forward onto the floor, still holding me as I sat in his lap on the couch. He leaned back and studied me.

'I want to have you Al...iss, I want to be the first to touch you and be inside you and the only man to satisfy you. Okay?'

'Yes.' I nodded, unable to get more words out than that and then Tomás pulled me close to his chest and he kissed me with all the passion and healing powers of a true make-up kiss. Relief flooded us both. I was so in love with this man and one day soon I would tell him.

The deeper he kissed me the harder he seemed to become and the more I wanted him. His hand slipped beneath my dress again and I pulled it out.

'No Tomás,' I said, breathlessly between kissing him. 'You still have a woman living with you.'

He felt hard and urgent against me and my hips betrayed me, swaying with him.

'Touch me, Al...iss,' he begged.

'No. Wednesday we begin.'

He groaned and our closeness increased the need in us both. I wanted to move away but I wanted him too. I wanted to hold on to my principles but what a price to pay – I must be crazy. He began to kiss me more feverishly and I groaned his name. I don't think I said stop, just his name over and over as he kissed down my neck and found his way to my bra line.

'Tomás...' I wriggled. I needed to be strong on this, or I would hate myself later and he'd go home to her.

'I won't touch you,' he said. 'Wednesday, I will have you, but my hands and tongue want to touch you tonight. Like our first two classes.'

I conceded we had done that before but... it was crossing the line of my directive. I was so weak. He moved me from his lap and lowered me onto the couch on my back. I pulled my dress down and he lowered himself on top of me, holding his weight above me. Probably safer I thought since he couldn't grope my ass in this position, although he was at eye level with my breasts. I breathed in as the new angle allowed him to rub against me, and it felt so good. Each orchestrated movement of his hips, each flex of his arms as he held his weight above me, turned me on. The friction he caused was not good, not good at all for abstinence.

I wrapped my legs around him – they just had a mind of their own – and I could feel his hardness against me. Oh God, we were like teenagers in a car at the drive-in. I didn't need to undress, I was going to have an orgasm from Tomás Carrera pressing against me. There was something so desperate and needy about that but I couldn't stop him. His lips found mine again and he kissed me roughly as if he was getting his fill for the days he missed and bruising my lips so that no-one else could touch me. My nails dug into the T-shirt on his back and he moaned my name. I might have gripped his butt in the moment, I can't be sure.

I wanted him to stop but I didn't if that makes any sense. I gasped. I couldn't believe it, the friction, the feeling was unbelievable and I arched my back. For God's sake, I was going to come just from having him on top of me, rubbing and pressing against me. I was desperate for his touch.

'Tomás, oh my God,' I panted.

'It's okay, *Bella*,' he whispered in my ear, holding me and then I came with a needy cry, my body shuddering. His lips covered mine, swallowing my cries of relief and I then felt his own body react – his shoulder muscles tensed, he buried his face in my neck and his breath escaped between clenched teeth.

His body shuddered and moments later, he collapsed on top of me, keeping his face buried in my hair.

'Holy Mother of God,' he said, panting beside me.

I started to laugh and he looked at me and grinned. He raised himself on one arm and licked his lower lip. So sexy.

'Well technically Al…iss, I didn't touch you.' He pointed out the obvious.

'You've just given me a no-hands, no-tongue orgasm. We didn't have that lesson.'

'No,' he agreed. 'I was playing catch-up.'

'I've never had a teacher like you,' I teased him. I ran my hand through his hair and he met my gaze. He moved up the couch a little, pulled me hard against him, and kissed me very slowly as though sealing our agreement.

'I want to stay the night with you,' he said.

'No. You've already crossed the boundaries of our agreement on a technicality.'

'It was only a minor penalty,' he said.

I shook my head. 'I'm red carding you.'

He winced and moved slightly. 'I haven't done that since I was a teenager.'

I grinned, pleased it was with me and was going to be just that bit uncomfortable for him. Is that wrong?

'Do you want to clean up here?' I asked.

'If I go have a shower, I'm getting into your bed and staying,' he warned me.

'Then you can't clean up here,' I confirmed. I was standing my ground; I wouldn't let him stay the night. I meant what I said – we weren't official until he had sent Julieta home for good. I wasn't his good-time girl.

For the next hour or more, we talked, shared a drink, I fed him some cereal – I would have cooked but he didn't want to waste time in the kitchen – and he lay in my lap as I stroked his hair. He closed his eyes looking happy. I remembered I had to text Mia before it got too late to tell her I was okay. I looked down at Tomás and he was asleep. I guess it had been a long day for him. Cassie's big L-shaped couch was perfect for tall soccer players as luck would have it.

I sneaked out from under Tomás. He was giving me a dead leg, and I gently pushed a pillow under his head. He moved onto his side, crossing his arms over his chest, but didn't wake. I stood back and looked at him; this was my Tomás and he was divine. As I moved through the lounge I heard Cassie's key in the door and I raced over to open it for her.

'Shh,' I warned with my finger to my lips as she came in. I pointed to the couch and she grinned and squeezed my arm. We moved to the kitchen island where we could see Tomás and talk.

'How was your night?' I asked in a quiet voice.

'So wonderful,' she said. 'I didn't stay because Rick has his mother visiting for the week. His mom is in the guest wing so we're pretending we don't sleep together but I'm so frustrated I may have to visit his office at college tomorrow.' Cassie rolled her eyes.

'That's cool, you should do that,' I agreed.

'I know. Turns me on thinking about it.' She looked to Tomás. 'Is it sorted?'

I nodded. 'It's over with his old girlfriend and she leaves on Wednesday. He just couldn't call it off over the phone. They'd been together a long time, and he had promised her the trip – there's a lot of history there. But it's over, and from Wednesday, we're on.'

She put her arm around my shoulders and squeezed. 'I'm so relieved for you. Why wait until Wednesday?' she asked in a hushed voice with a glance to the couch.

'My rule,' I said. 'I want to be sure there are only two of us in the relationship.'

She nodded. 'Good thinking… amazing willpower.'

'I know,' I said and sighed.

We looked at Tomás as he slept.

'That couch is huge,' I said. 'Good for sleeping but not so good for cuddling.'

Cassie grinned. 'It was a leftover from one of my parents' investment places, so I grabbed it. You can sit on one side by yourself while the other half of the 'L' fits four people with a game console. I know, I've test-driven it.'

Tomás turned, groaned and winced – and we watched, fascinated. I'm guessing the wince was from sore muscles postgame and not the uncomfortable mess we just created.

'He is very pretty, isn't he?' Cassie said.

'That he is,' I agreed.

Tomás's phone rang and he jolted awake and sat upright. He ran a hand over his face as he looked around trying momentarily to work out where he was. He saw me and smiled before grabbing for his phone, swinging his legs around and sitting upright. He answered and spoke quickly in Spanish.

'Sexy,' Cassie said.

'Hell yeah,' I agreed.

He hung up and pushed himself up off the couch.

'Tomás, this is my friend and housemate, Cassie,' I said and introduced them.

He took her hand in his and greeted her, then he returned his gaze to me. He ran his hand through his hair.

'Ah, sorry to fall asleep on your couch,' he said, looking sheepish.

'Best couch ornament I've ever had,' Cassie said, and I nudged her. She laughed.

'Thanks,' he said, looking a little embarrassed. 'Well, I'd better go. Al...iss won't have me until Wednesday,' he said, looking to Cassie for sympathy.

'Good for you Al...iss,' she said, imitating his pronunciation of my name.

Tomás grinned and shook his head. 'Girl power, I see,

That's fine,' he grinned. 'Goodnight Cassie, goodnight *Bella.*'
He reached for his things.

'I'll walk you to your bike,' I said and followed him as he
grabbed his jacket and helmet. We walked downstairs and
he put on his jacket and straddled his bike. I shivered in the
night air and he pulled me closer, pushing me against his
chest and wrapping the folds of his jacket around us both.

'I know we haven't made love yet, Cookie,' he nudged my
neck with his nose and kissed me lightly, 'and we will... it's
the next step in our learning curve...'

'I can't wait,' I said, my eyes alive with anticipation.

'But you will wait for me? We agree now that we are a
couple?' he asked.

A couple. I drank those words in like they were water and
I was dying of thirst in the desert... such wonderful words.
'I will definitely wait for you,' I said, and couldn't help but
beam at him.

Matching my smile, he gave me a kiss that would have
felled nations.

'I want you to know something before I make love to
you,' he said, 'but I'll tell you again before then.'

'What's that?' I asked and bit my lip. I had the motherlode
of confessions tonight – I was kind of up on my quota
without hearing any more.

'I love you, Al...iss,' he said.

I inhaled sharply. I wasn't expecting that, not for a minute,
and before I could respond he released me, started the bike,
kissed me again and slipping his helmet on, sped away.

Chapter 31

Next morning, Monday, and Tomás loves me, sorry I don't know how that slipped in. I sent a message to Jim and Sasha to let them know I was whipping by the hotel before work to check all was on track for the Saints' Sisters luncheon later today. When I got in after nine, they were all hard at it and basking in the glory of the Saints' weekend win.

Sasha Saxon from the Saints squealed as I walked into our office area wearing a Sasha Saxon original. I did a pirouette for her and Kay.

'It's by Sasha Saxon,' I said, showing off the fitted designer original dress. 'Ladies, you're looking at a long line tuxedo dress in passion red, a blend of elastane and polyester to show off all the right curves, fully lined with button front closure.'

Kay laughed at my fashion speak and catwalk impersonation, while Sasha was jumping on the spot clapping her hands.

'Oh my God, you are the best. I didn't know you had bought that.' Her eyes narrowed. 'I mail out all orders and I didn't mail that to you.'

'No, you mailed it to my friend Miranda who I paid to buy it for me so you wouldn't know. And I'm going to wear it to the lunch today so that when all the girls ask about my outfit – and they will,' I said, 'I can tell them where to get it.'

'You look a million dollars,' Kay agreed, beaming at us. 'You've got talent Sasha, a real talent.'

'Thanks Kay, and thank you Alice, I mean it, thanks a lot,' Sasha said and ran over to hug me just as The Russian walked past.

'You wait long enough, your fantasies come true,' he said, looking at Sasha and me embracing. We both gave him a look – Sasha's look said *you are sick*, my look said *What? Oh, ewww!*

'Great game hey Russian?' I grinned at him, even though he dobbed me in to Lucas and called in his favor.

'Well done Alice, you played very well too.' He winked at me and I'm sure I went three different shades of red.

I cleared my throat. 'Um, so you'll be in your Saints' suit and at the luncheon by noon Mr. Star Guest?'

'Yes, bossy. I'll be picking up Tomás so he doesn't arrive ruffled on his motorbike and we'll be there.'

'Thanks.' I nodded. I was a little anxious about lunch. The Russian and Tomás were both quiet personalities and I hoped the interviews would be a little bit of fun and lively. Loretta, our master of ceremonies, had her work cut out. Failing that, let's hope the champagne was flowing, the girls tipsy and no-one cared if the boys were quiet since they were such good eye candy – much better plan.

I downloaded the weekend game photos from our

photographer's server and updated all the Saints' social media channels and website. Then Kay and I headed off to the hotel just after ten-thirty to set up the registration table and name tags. Sasha was coming later and Jim would drop in but he wasn't allowed to stay because it was girls only. I think he was relieved.

I couldn't wait to see Tomás, especially in the navy suit that was the Saints' uniform. I sent him a message as soon as I woke up, and I woke up the happiest I've ever been in my entire life. This love thing is so complex.

ME: Breathless this morning, can't stop thinking about you

TOMÁS: *Bella*, I'm the happiest man on the planet. On Wed I will be uncontrollable

ME: Can't wait. See you at noon

TOMÁS: Nervous about the pack of women, going to hide behind you

ME: I'll protect you

TOMÁS: I meant what I said when I left

ME: I'm counting on it

I didn't want to tell Tomás I loved him too until I saw him in person. Telling him by text or phone for the first time wouldn't do.

I brought my attention back to the day and ensured the name tags were ready and checked the room which was a mixture of Saints' colors and pink; not that they went well together but what can you do? Then I spotted Loretta from Kiss FM radio station walking towards me. Bless her for being early. She kissed me on the cheek as if we were old friends. She was an attractive woman, a bit taller than me, blonde with very green eyes and probably in her early thirties.

'So no scratchings?' she asked me looking at the rundown.

'Nope, all going to plan,' I assured her.

'The players, today's talent for the interviews, can they talk?'

'The Russian and Tomás... they'll be fine. They are not big mouths, but they can answer a question.'

'Single?'

I grinned at her. 'I think The Russian is, but I'm pretty sure Tomás is taken.'

She looked disappointed. There was going to be three hundred women looking at Tomás today, and I would just have to deal with it. Let's hope he didn't look back.

The ladies starting rolling in right on time and the room sounded as if a flock of birds had landed with all the chatter and clinking glasses. The coach's wife, Elizabeth, arrived with a friend and we had a brief chat and I could see some of our major sponsors in attendance – a good showing. I also met Maggie, Jim my boss's wife. She was a bit like him, small and wiry only she was a little nervy with plenty of energy. She was there with a lady she introduced as Anne, the wife of our office accountant Derek.

'We always worry that the office girls are going to steal our husbands,' Maggie confessed to me sort-of-jokingly.

I smiled and eased both of their minds.

'Maggie, Anne, you couldn't be more wrong. If I wanted to save my marriage, I'd love my husband working at the Saints,' I told them.

They both frowned at me, confused, so I elaborated. 'The office girls are surrounded by hot, fit, players, all day, every day, coming and going. My office is right next door to The Russian and Ed. Even the coaching staff in the office is made up of former players. So, not to say that Jim and Derek aren't lovely men, but I promise you there are lots to distract the office girls.'

Both women chuckled and they brightened considerably as Maggie squeezed my arm and they left to find their table. Yep, Jim would get me for that but the sisterhood is important.

Then Valentina entered. I almost choked on a gulp of air. I grabbed the guest RSVP list. I didn't see her name on it, so maybe it was booked in the name of her guest. She hadn't seen me yet and I hesitantly glanced up praying and offering up a thousand Hail Marys that Julieta hadn't accompanied her, but really, what were the odds? Of course she'd be there. Valentina turned and then I saw her guest, an older lady I didn't know. Thank you, God, thank you, I breathed. Valentina saw me, waved and came over, kissing me on both cheeks.

'Don't you look beautiful, Alice,' she said.

'Thank you. You were wonderful by the way. I came to the jazz bar,' I explained.

'I saw you but you didn't stay to say hello. I haven't seen much of you of late Alice, you've been most remiss,' she scolded me, which kind of convinced me she was clueless as to what was going on in her brother's life despite what he said. She moved her guest, the older lady, forward to introduce her.

'This is my friend, Michelle,' she said. Michelle offered her hand, and we shook.

'Alice is a friend of Tomás's, and...' she read my name tag, 'the Saints' Event Coordinator.'

I nodded, welcomed her friend and helped them look for their name tags. Our receptionist Suzie had typed them up otherwise I would have spotted Valentina's right away and known she was coming.

'This is my first Saints' Sisters lunch,' she told me. 'With Tomás as a guest of honor, I couldn't resist.'

'It's my first too,' I confessed. 'Let's just hope it goes to plan.' She gave me an encouraging pat on the shoulder.

Then I saw Tomás and The Russian arrive; wow, what a sight – two tall, handsome, fit men in dark suits and ties. How I would love to have Tomás on top of me in that suit. Sigh. Right, try not to glaze over and remember you're working, I told myself. Tomás looked a little pained to be there and his eyes searched the room. When his gaze landed on mine, his face relaxed. He nudged The Russian and they headed towards where Kay and I stood at the reception table. He went to kiss me hello and The Russian stopped him.

'Ah yes, hello Al...iss,' he said, then noticed his sister. 'Hi Tina, Michelle,' He gave them both a kiss.

I introduce The Russian to Michelle and to Valentina, not sure if they'd met before, but whatever, and then suggested they all find their seats. Tomás lingered behind and whispered in my ear.

'*Bella*, that red dress and those four buttons, if I undid those...'

I looked up and he was yanked away by The Russian. He

shrugged as he was led off and I couldn't help but laugh. Well done Russian, a man on a mission to uphold the professionalism of the lunch, damn him.

The event kicked off with Loretta welcoming everyone and sharing some funny stories about her life on radio and her love of soccer. During this the entree was served, there was a raffle and our resident D.J. for the lunch played some good tunes. I didn't get to sit down for long and I placed myself at the worst table near the door, so I could keep jumping up and down. Tomás and The Russian were on the best table at the front with Loretta and some of our top female sponsors and of course, Elizabeth, the coach's wife who hosted the table for us.

I felt my phone buzz with a message and grabbed it. I hoped there wasn't a drama with the catering or at the office. I smiled as I saw the message from Tomás.

TOMÁS: Need to kiss you immediately

I looked at his table and found him watching me. I gave him a smile that I hoped read all my lustful thoughts. I sent a teasing reply.

ME: Behave and be a good star guest

Before he could message back, Loretta took to the stage again, this time to introduce our 'talent' and I held my breath hoping the boys were at least a little entertaining and gave the girls a bit of value for money, although I think the chance for lunch out and champagne seemed to get them across the line. Loretta called them up and gave Tomás and The Russian a microphone each; she stood between them on the stage. I could see Tomás searching for me again and he found me in the corner near the stage. I gave him an encouraging smile and he didn't reciprocate. He was more comfortable on the sports ground.

Loretta began. 'Ladies, I would like to introduce you to two of the hotties... um, I mean talented professional players of the Saints team...'

The girls broke up laughing and cheering.

'... Tomás Carrera and The Russian, who must have a first name, but I forgot to ask, and what a great game they both had on the weekend and a big win for the Saints.'

The room erupted in cheers. Loretta did a general interview with them both about how long they had been with the Saints, what they loved about the game, their biggest challenges, and their training schedule. She made both of them share their favorite love songs and favorite romantic movies which got a lot of laughs, especially when The Russian said '*Alien*'.

Throughout, the two men rolled their eyes and carried on, but secretly loved it by the look of them. Such bigheads. Then bravely, she opened it up to questions from the floor – three hundred women on the bubbles... good grief. I moved into the crowd with the spare microphone – my job was to head to whomever Loretta selected and give her the microphone. She picked someone on the complete opposite side of the room to me and I gave her the look. Again the girls laughed as Loretta commented on my journey across the room.

'Alice, the Saints' Events Coordinator is making her way across the room... she'll be there soon... don't forget that question... yes she should have worn her sneakers,' she said.

I grinned, playing along with Loretta, and finally getting to the woman with her hand raised. I gave her the microphone.

'What's your favorite position?' she asked.

The room erupted in laughter and The Russian and Tomás took it in good grace. Loretta nodded to Tomás.

'Well I play goalkeeper,' he said, with his sexy accent, 'and I like that position because it can make or break the game.'

'So,' Loretta frowned, 'it's a position you have to stay on top of to be good at?'

The girls in the audience tittered again.

Tomás nodded. 'Yes although I'm not always on top of it, my first half wasn't good at the weekend.'

Loretta's expression was definitely in the gutter even if Tomás was unaware of the innuendo with the translation.

The Russian interrupted. 'I think what Tomás is trying to say is that we have to maintain our fitness and constantly improve our skills to remain on top.'

'Yes, thank you, Russian, that's what I would have said except you did,' Tomás agreed and the girls smiled, watching him with adoring glances as if they all wanted to help him with his translation. Good grief.

'What position do you play, Russian?' Loretta asked.

'Forward. But you know that Loretta.' He turned the tables back on her.

'Yes, I do,' she agreed. 'Next question.' The hands shot up and she picked a lady on the opposite side of the room again and everyone laughed as I made a show of pulling off my heels and hurrying over with the microphone.

Loretta continued, 'That's a stylish outfit you're wearing Alice. A label?'

'Yes,' I said speaking into the microphone, 'an original Sasha Saxon, available at sashasaxon-dot-com,' I said, and, spotting Sasha, wrinkled my nose at her. I reached the young woman with black-rimmed glasses who was next to ask a question and handed her the microphone.

'Do you both get homesick sometimes?' she asked.

The Russian started first this time. 'Well I'm not actually from Russia, I'm from Boston.'

Several cheers went up in the audience and Loretta added, 'Well we have some Bostonians in the room.'

'That's the classy folk,' The Russian added and they cheered again. 'I would like to be homesick but my family moved here.' The ladies all laughed and I started to relax a little. They were both dry and funny, and it was going to be okay.

'And Tomás, where is your hometown?' Loretta asked.

'Buenos Aires,' he said, and I heard the collective sigh as the words rolled off his tongue in his sexy accent. That tongue that I was in love with and that would be all over me on Wednesday. I needed a glass of cold water immediately.

'Do you get homesick?' Loretta asked again.

'No,' he said flatly and didn't elaborate. Everyone laughed at his direct answer. Then he continued. 'My sister Valentina is my housemate, so I have some family here. She's here today.'

'Stand up, Valentina, where are you?' Loretta called.

Valentina stood up and gave a wave, and everyone cheered.

Tomás continued, 'She's a very good jazz singer and performs every Saturday and Sunday night from six p.m. at the *Buzz Club*. There's a free plug Tina, you can cook me dinner for that.'

The room broke up again.

'So do you two do duets?' Loretta asked.

Tomás shook his head. 'I don't sing. But The Russian does.'

Every eye in the house turned to The Russian. I had forgotten until now that he did a version of *Sweet Child of Mine* at Lucas's pre-season party and did as good a job as Axel, well almost. No-one can do Axel better than Axel and those dance moves, yeah.

Loretta worked the audience up. 'So could we get a duet then Valentina and Russian?'

The crowd starting clapping and The Russian held up his hand and shut it down with a firm head shake.

'Can't see any electric guitar here, Loretta and that's the only way I'll perform, I only do rock.'

Loretta looked forlornly at the D.J. who shook his head. 'Right then, stored away for next time,' she said. 'Another question.' This time she picked someone nearby, in the middle of the room.

I gave the microphone to a woman who looked like a personal trainer. She seemed super fit and her question confirmed it.

'What's your favorite workout?' she asked.

Loretta nodded to Tomás.

'I like to swim but the coach, Johan, likes us to run.' He glanced to the coach's wife, Elizabeth, as he said this and they exchanged knowing smiles. 'So I'm running all the time, more than I've run in my entire life. He even makes us run to the pool.'

Elizabeth nodded in understanding, and the ladies laughed again. He was so endearing and everything he said with his sexy accent and delivered with his boyish good looks just had them eating out of his hand.

'And Russian?' Loretta turned to him.

'I like weights,' he told the gym bunny. 'I'm not into speed, as you can tell from my svelte shape.' Laughter erupted around the room as everyone studied The Russian wall who was anything but svelte.

My first lunch was going to be a hit, thank you, boys.

The Russian continued and addressed the lady who asked the question. 'I bench press around 320 pounds,' he said, and she looked impressed. Most of us had no idea if that was good or not but by her reaction, I'm guessing it was good.

'The last question,' Loretta said, looking around the room, 'and let's make it a good one.'

'A good one near me,' I said into the microphone and got a round of laughs.

She teased as she skimmed over the twenty or more hands that were in the air and settled on a hand from the back row. I took off with the microphone and passed it to a lady who looked as if she had way too much plastic surgery and was barely forty.

She had a husky voice and I knew she was trying to be sexy.

'I have a question for Tomás,' she said. 'The tango has its origins in Buenos Aires. Do you tango?'

The room erupted in whistles and cheering and Tomás looked as if he was sizing up where the quickest exit was located. He smiled and shook his head slightly.

'Tomás, you must have learned at school at least? It's the national dance, isn't it? Do you tango?' Loretta pushed him.

'Ah, I guess every South American schoolboy learns to tango.' He looked towards me begging me to rescue him and wrap it up. I gave him a smile that said 'bring it on'. I'd pay for that later no doubt.

The D.J. began with some perfect slow tango music and the girls clapped and started saying 'tango, tango, tango...'

Loretta held up her hand. 'We have to find Tomás a partner.'

He smiled and started to look pretty satisfied that he'd be safe now. The Russian took Tomás's microphone from him, freeing him up, but Tomás put his hands in his suit pants' pockets and rocked, expecting no-one would know how to tango to partner him. Loretta was smarter.

'Valentina, you must be able to tango, yes?'

'Yes.' She nodded and stood.

Tomás gave her a pained expression but folded to the crowd pressure. He took the couple of stairs down from the stage and glanced at me with a look that I couldn't read but I think it was *thanks for getting me into this!* – I would have to remind him it was all set up by my predecessor and who was I to stop the flow of a good show? He stopped near his sister, slipping off his suit jacket to a fresh round of whistles and catcalls, and placed it over the back of the chair. I swear he looked embarrassed – who would have thought.

Loretta introduced them. 'Ladies and the few gentlemen present, allow me to introduce the tango with Tomás and Valentina Carrera!' The audience cheered and then a hush fell over the room while the music began and we all imagined ourselves in the arms of Tomás.

He led his sister to the floor, raised his left hand, and placed his other hand on her back. Valentina put her hand in his and mirrored him, putting her hand on the center of his back. They stood tall, such beautiful creatures, and I held my breath watching the tilt of his jaw and his power over Valentina's stance.

On the beat, he moved forward with his left leg, slow, slow, quick, quick, slow and repeated it. They were so masterful in their walk together that I'm sure they must have danced together before, even if Valentina was the baby of the family and it might have only been at family weddings. It was such a sensual ballroom dance, emphasizing the long lines of their legs and the power of his arms. His butt looked fantastic in those suit pants, highlighted by the stretched moves of the tango, plus his masterful turns and power over her movements were so sexual. Tomás seemed to know where the music was taking him; he led Valentina around the floor so effortlessly, slightly frowning as he concentrated and using his strength to support her elongated movements. They moved as one in the high-speed sequences, and it was breathtaking.

Thank God Valentina was his sister because if my man – this tall, dark, handsome creature – was holding Julieta or any other beautiful woman close like this, dancing this intimate dance, it would have killed me. The audience, like me, was enthralled. There wasn't a dry panty in the house I'm sure.

As the dance came to an end with Tomás so completely in control and leading with every movement, I think I might have orgasmed and I don't think I was the only one. They finished with flourish and everyone rose to their feet and cheered. I wasn't the only one fanning myself. After today, Tomás Carrera had three hundred new followers in his fan club and this lunch would be a very hard act to follow. I pitied the next two Saints players to attend.

The audience roared for an encore but Tomás apologetically shook his head and led Valentina back to her seat. Grabbing his jacket and then The Russian by the arm, he excused himself to Loretta and the audience: 'Sorry, we have to go to training,' he explained.

Loretta called for another round of applause for the two Saints players and the roar must have disrupted traffic it was so loud.

Backing out of the room, Tomás glanced in my direction with a look that promised much more to come. Along with The Russian, he disappeared around the corner of the ballroom and out through the doors. Luckily dessert was served – we all needed some chocolate after that.

Chapter 32

I was walking in the door of my new abode after a long and really good day – the lunch went so well and I was getting more confident in the job every day – when my phone beeped with a message. I greeted Cassie who was sitting on the couch with her iPad and went to take off my Sasha Saxon original and change into jeans and a sweatshirt. I felt so high; love was amazing – I couldn't believe only a few days ago I was at rock bottom. Then I remembered I still had to deal with Dane and break the news to him. He had called and left a message today. Sigh.

I grabbed my phone and saw the message was from Dane, damn, just get it over with. I lay on the bed and called him.

'Hi gorgeous, how are you?' Dane said, answering the phone on the second ring.

'I'm good, and you?'

'Missing you,' he said.

Crap.

'I want to see you, so when can we catch up?' he continued.

'Dane, about that...'

There was a noticeable change in the phone atmosphere and I swallowed before continuing.

'This isn't the part where you say it's not me, it's you, is it?' he asked with hesitation in his voice.

'No,' I said, 'it's definitely you not me,' I teased and he laughed. But I kept going. 'You are gorgeous and fun and sincere and...'

'And you are working things out with that other guy aren't you?' he finished my sentence.

'I think we might be. I'm sorry that I went out with you on Friday... I should have waited longer to see.'

'I'm not sorry,' he said. 'I had a great time.'

'Dane, you're making this so much harder because you're so lovely.' I sighed. 'Can't you just call me a cow or be super angry at me?'

'I'm super angry at *him* for sticking around but I guess he knows he's onto a good thing. I'm super jealous too, but he better treat you right because I'll be waiting in the wings ready to move in,' he said, his voice lowered.

'And I would love that chance,' I said, 'but you and I both know that you won't be single for longer than a minute so consider us ships passing in the night.'

'I'm not the *Titanic* Alice, so don't sink me yet. Can we stay friends and I mean friends? I won't cross the line.'

'Yeah,' I brightened, 'I would really like that, really like it.'

'Good.' I heard relief in his voice too. 'So you could come to some of our movie preview nights just as friends, and bring your friends.'

'That could work,' I agreed. 'Thank you, Dane.'

'Hey, it's all good. See you soon then.'

'Yep, for sure.'

I hung up and breathed again, that was a shit job but it was done. He was so nice. What were the odds of meeting two great guys in the same week? The universe worked in mysterious ways. I finished getting changed and went out to catch up with Cassie.

'Diaries,' she said.

'Sorry?' I was confused.

'We need to coordinate our diaries. Now that we both have boyfriends, we can work out a system of who wants the place to herself and when.'

'Oh right, sure, but I don't think I'm going to be at Tomás's place a lot initially,' I said.

'That's fine because Rick has a great place and we'd both probably rather crash there anyway. You won't be pissed if I'm not home much will you?' she asked.

'Not for a moment.'

'That's a relief because my former housemate wanted company all the time. I swear she followed me into the shower one day.' Cassie rolled her eyes.

I laughed. 'No, I'm good in my own space. But this Wednesday night, I might be going to Tomás's,' I said.

'I'm going to Rick's place. His mother leaves on Tuesday thank the Lord.' Cassie chewed on the end of a pen. 'If you and I are coming and going with work, college, and boyfriends, maybe we should get a third housemate so someone is here,' she suggested. 'It would cut our rent down too.'

'It's not a bad idea,' I agreed. 'I'm happy to pay less. A guy, maybe?'

'Perfect. A guy who can cook, like a chef would be good. Or a flight attendant who is away a lot or a male nurse who does shift work, so between the three of us, there's always someone coming and going but we're not living in each other's pockets. We'd have some fun, too, with a full house.'

'Absolutely. Maybe a player who is at training a lot and away every third weekend at away games,' I suggested.

We both brightened at the thought.

'Brilliant,' Cassie agreed.

'I'll keep my ear to the ground,' I said. 'But there are only two bathrooms... I don't want boy germs.'

She wrinkled her nose. 'Me either. You and I could share and give him the ensuite room.'

'Done,' I agreed. 'Leave it with me.'

My phone beeped with a message and it was just the man I wanted to hear from – my Tomás, part-time tango dancer and full-time soccer star. He must have been finished at training.

TOMÁS: I need to see you tonight

ME: You still have a guest

TOMÁS: I don't care, I need to see you

ME: You saw me today sexy tango guy. See you Wed. Only 2 more days

TOMÁS: Just 5 mins, come for a ride on my bike

ME: Mm, super tempting and I get to wrap my arms around you. Bike ride only?

TOMÁS: Promise

ME: No repeat of last night

TOMÁS: If you insist. Your place at 7

ME: You will bring me back home?

TOMÁS: Of course Bella, I'll do my best
ME: Promise
TOMÁS: Ok, promise

✳✳✳✳✳

Tomás must have come straight from training as fifteen minutes later I heard his bike out the front, and with a wave to Cassie, I bolted down the stairs to meet him. He always looked so sexy straddling that bike. He alighted, pulled his helmet off, and grabbed me in a passionate kiss before I had time to speak.

'Better,' he said, pulling away. He handed me the helmet and I put it on. He lifted the bike seat and pulled out a jacket. 'I have a present for you.' He rushed the next words before I could protest. 'It's a safety gift, for traveling so I want you to accept it, please.' He handed me a soft black leather jacket. 'I'll make a bike babe of you yet.'

'Wow, thank you Tomás, when did you have time to get this?' I asked, delighted, and slipping my arms into it.

'This morning,' he said. 'Very cute, just right,' he said pulling it tight around me.

'Thank you, I love it, it's beautiful.'

'So you'll accept this? Should we have an accident, it's much safer riding in a strong jacket like this.'

I smiled. 'It's very thoughtful and since it is a practical, safety gift, I'd be delighted to accept it. Thank you.' I smiled at him.

'You're welcome.'

246

'You know you were the star of the Saints' Sisters' lunch, you sexy thing,' I teased him.

'Let's not talk about it.' He swung his leg over the bike and I studied him.

I stood beside him on the bike. 'You were great, you know that don't you?' I frowned at him.

He shrugged. 'I don't like being pressured into doing things, like an ambush.'

I bit my lip, wondering where this was coming from. 'Did you really not enjoy it? It was fun and you made a lot of people happy.'

'I would do it for you Al...iss, but... it doesn't matter, climb on board,' he said, 'and secure your helmet.'

Mm, odd. I jumped on behind him and wrapped my arms around his waist as he started the bike. God, it felt so good. He put his helmet on and we pulled away from the curb. We drove for a while along the beach, through the city, and it was amazing. Eventually, we went to his favorite quiet spot on the beach and he parked the bike and helped me off. We walked down to the sand.

'Can we sit for a while?' he asked.

'Sure, but if Julieta is going home Wednesday, shouldn't you be home doing some last-minute socializing?' I asked, not wanting him to but not understanding why he wasn't.

He shook his head. 'She's away for the night staying with her aunt. She'll be back tomorrow, so we'll do dinner with Valentina tomorrow night and I'll take her to the airport Wednesday morning.'

I nodded, taking it all in and knowing tomorrow night would be tough for me thinking of the three of them together.

He sat on the sand and raised his arms to me, lowering me down between his legs. Tomás wrapped his arms around me and we sat in the warmth of the night, watching the pull of the ocean and listening to the quiet and the waves breaking at his favorite get-away place. If we could just stay here, like this for the rest of our lives, it would be perfect.

'Tomás…'

'Yes?'

I turned slightly to face him, digging my legs under his.

'I don't understand what you said earlier, about the ambush… you looked so great today, why does it bother you?'

He sighed. 'I'm not like Lucas or The Russian or even Nik. I'm a bit like Ed. We don't like the limelight.'

'But you're in it so much,' I said. 'Your picture is everywhere and you've got sponsorship contracts where you appear wearing brand gear and watches.' I thought of the gorgeous shot I saw of him wearing a designer watch. 'There's footage of you all over YouTube.'

He nodded. 'But that's for sport. I'm comfortable with that, I know it and the model shots, I agree to do those with a photographer, not an audience. But I don't like being singled out as the center of attention in a crowd.'

'I get it,' I said, 'and it won't happen too often but I guess it is part of what you have to do now as a signed player.'

He sighed and nodded his agreement. 'True, but I don't have to like it,' he said, softly. 'Unless…'

'Mm?' I prodded him.

'You wanted to shoot a sexy Saints' calendar… maybe you could find a month for me – I could be Mr November

– and we could try all these different poses and positions in private to pick one for the shoot?'

I laughed. 'You're a nutter,' I teased him. 'But hell you were sexy doing that tango, I think I orgasmed when you were on the dance floor.'

His lips reluctantly twitched into a smile and he looked directly at me. 'Well, that makes it all worthwhile. I wish I'd known that earlier; it gives me a hard-on thinking of you turned on for me.'

'I can't wait for Wednesday,' I said, running a finger along the stubble on his chin line. 'I want to tell you something…' I said, getting Tomás's attention.

'What's that?' he asked.

'I want to say what you said to me, because I feel the same, but I can't say it until you are one hundred percent mine,' I said looking into his eyes.

A look of relief and sheer happiness crossed his face.

'But you feel that way, Al…iss?' he said, his face all smiles.

'Yes, I do.' I grinned.

He lowered his lips to mine then groaned and pulled away.

'You don't think we could just…' he began.

'No,' I said. I was sticking to my guns even if it killed me. I was going to be the only woman in Tomás Carreras's life and I wasn't going to go the whole way with him and send him home to his girlfriend/ex-girlfriend.

'You're seriously not going to let me touch you or stay or…'

I shook my head. 'It's not easy for me either let me tell you.'

'Fucking hurry up, Wednesday,' he muttered.

I grinned and he went mad at me.

'Stop teasing me Al...iss.' His eyes narrowed.

'What? Me?' I said, wide-eyed. 'You wanted to go for a ride on the bike, that was your idea.'

'Mm,' he grunted.

'You stopped here and wanted to sit on the beach.'

'Right,' he conceded. 'Yeah well, you look too damn cute.'

'Sorry,' I said and giggled.

He pulled me onto his lap and his tongue slipped into my mouth. He pushed against me and I felt the hardness of his erection. I felt just as needy. God, I loved this man.

Chapter 33

When I arrived at work on Tuesday morning I was accosted by both Jim and The Russian... this looked like trouble. Sasha, Kay and I looked up as the two of them walked into our area and stood with their arms folded across their chests. It looked pretty funny – The Russian wall and next to him, Jim, who was thin and five-foot-eight on a good day. I started to laugh.

'Very good job yesterday, Alice, ladies,' Jim said.

'Thanks boss, it was a good team effort.' I wondered if this was about me telling his wife that Jim was completely off the radar for all the office girls, men have delicate egos after all. 'But, I'm sensing something is wrong...'

Kay started giggling at the sight of them.

The Russian nodded. 'I was upstaged by *Tango*, Alice, that doesn't usually happen. I'm usually the star,' he teased with just the hint of humor twitching on his lips.

'You're calling him *Tango* now?' I winced, knowing he would hate that.

'Yep, new official nickname,' The Russian confirmed.

I sighed. 'Well Russian, if you had done the solo, if you

had done your *Sweet Child of Mine* number or similar as we begged you to, the audience would have been saying Tomás who? It was generous of you not to blow him out of the water.'

The Russian took this onboard and nodded. He was happy to play the martyr.

'I'm that kind of a guy, Alice.'

Sasha laughed and he gave her a stern look. She tried to turn it into a fake cough as I hid my smile. I looked at Jim.

'And Jim? An issue?' I asked. I was ready for this one. I was going to appeal to saving his marriage or something like that when he surprised me.

'Maggie, the wife...'

'Oh we met her, she's lovely,' I said and Sasha and Kay nodded their agreement.

'She might well be, but now she wants to go and have tango lessons.'

My mouth fell open. I didn't see that coming and I burst out laughing. Everyone joined me.

'Haha, yes, very funny,' he said and rolled his eyes.

We heard the coffee van arriving. 'Gee, well given you two were so wronged, I guess it is my shout for coffee,' I said.

The Russian looked at Jim. 'That should go some way to restoring things,' he said.

Jim nodded. I took their orders and checked if Ed, Kay and Sasha wanted one. A small price to pay for how lucky I was to work with them and have this job.

*****

When I dropped the coffee into The Russian I flagged that Cassie and I were looking for a male housemate for our three-bedroom apartment. The new tenant would have the room with the ensuite and I mentioned the price. We were charging them a bit more since they had their own bathroom. The Russian said he'd pass the word around and I mentioned it had to be someone who was away a lot preferably.

Word spread fast because just before training that afternoon around three o'clock, Nik – the Kaiser – made an appearance in our office. He dropped down into the chair at the front of my desk and again, Sasha and Kay's mouths fell open. He was exactly as Mia described him, gorgeous in all his German glory – six-foot-plus more, very blond-white hair cut very short, and the bluest of eyes. He was a perfect German specimen.

'Alice, we met at Lucas's pre-season party. I think we had a dance?' He frowned.

'Nik! We did!' I exclaimed. 'Have you met Sasha and Kay?'

Nik rose again and his eyes widened at Sasha – equally blonde and very alternative.

'Sah…sha and I have spoken many times on the phone organizing media interviews,' he said. As he moved over to shake her hand, an electric shock tingled their hands and they both pulled back.

'Ouch.' Sasha shook her hand and studied him.

'Sorry, that was quite a zap.' He smiled, and Kay and I exchanged looks. Mm. That's all I have to say on that but I'd be watching Sasha... quite a charged introduction.

He greeted Kay and shook hands with her, with no zap, and he sat back down in front of my desk, now and then glancing over at Sasha and I noticed she was trying hard not to glance at him. Mm, interesting.

'You are looking for a housemate?' he asked. 'I've got to be out of my place in a week but I just want somewhere to crash. I don't have much and I'm not home much.'

'Neither are we,' I said. 'Want to come over and meet Cassie and check it out?'

'Yeah, after training work for you? Say at six o'clock.'

'Great.' I gave him the address and he thanked me. We all watched as he left, Sasha stretching her neck around the corner just that little bit further to check out his nice tight butt.

'The Germans have made many great things,' I said, teasing her.

'Yes the BMW,' she said, her face a mask of appreciation.

'The airbag I believe,' I added.

'The helicopter,' Kay added.

'Really?' I said, impressed. 'A very talented people.'

I quickly messaged Cassie to make sure she could be there at six and got the affirmative back from her. Never a dull moment.

*****

Nik arrived a little after six as training ran overtime. I let him in, introduced him to Cassie, and noticed that she admired his form as well. God, we were hopeless. She showed him around.

254

'Alice and I will share this bathroom and you can have the main room with the ensuite but we're charging you a little more for it and you can't use our bathroom, no boy germs,' she explained.

He grinned and nodded. He walked into the room, which currently had Cassie's stuff in it, and through to the ensuite.

'Yeah this is fine,' he said. 'Bigger than what I'm currently in and half the price.'

Cassie frowned. 'Bummer, we should have charged more,' she teased.

'There's only one garage, but if you've got a really expensive car you can take it,' I started to say and Nik cut me off.

'That's okay, my car is used to being outside, it's just a SUV.'

'Is it for work as well or are you a full-time player, so to speak?' Cassie asked.

Nik smiled. 'I'm full-time, but I like a car that fits my surfboard in the back,' Nik said.

'Right. Well want a juice, tea, beer, or wine and we can all throw in our terms and conditions?' I suggested.

'Yeah, I'll have a beer if you girls are going to join me?'

'Definitely,' Cassie said and grabbed a beer for herself and Nik while I helped myself to a glass of wine. We made ourselves comfortable on the large L-seater.

'Shall I start?' Cassie asked and we nodded.

'No parties unless we all agree to hold one,' she said.

'No relatives staying unless we all approve,' I added.

'No girl underwear and washing hanging around,' Nik said.

We both looked at him; that was a new one.

'Fair enough,' Cassie said. 'No eating from each other's shelves in the cupboard and fridge unless it's a communal shop or you're invited. By the way Ali, sorry, I had to eat some of your chocolate.' She looked sheepish.

'Had to! I get it,' I said and grinned. 'I've got nothing else unless we should discuss cleaning?'

'I'll get the cleaning,' Nik said. We looked at him as though he had just offered to buy us both Mercedes and pay off our college degrees. He shrugged. 'I have a cleaning lady that comes once a week now. She's cheap enough, so I'll just give her this address and if you have a spare set of keys, she can clean here every Wednesday instead. Okay?'

'Hell yes,' Cassie said.

'But we should put in,' I said, feeling guilty.

Nik shook his head. 'It's all good. I suspect I earn a little more than you two and the rent here is less than I'm paying now. I've got it covered.'

'You're the best.' Cassie grinned and turned to me. 'A man who comes with cleaning!'

I heard the sound of a motorbike pull up out the front. It couldn't be – Tomás was supposed to be at the farewell dinner for Julieta tonight with Valentina and I was doing my best not to think about it. Moments later I heard a knock at the door. I jumped up to get it and left Nik and Cassie to finish discussing payment and the move-in date.

I opened the door and Tomás stood in the doorway, his leather jacket in his hand and helmet in the other.

'Hello *Bella*,' he said and leaned in to kiss me.

'Hi.' I kissed him back and then frowned. 'Why are you here?'

He looked me over. 'I like these jeans and knit on you. I don't think I've ever seen you in jeans. Now can you take them off?' he teased.

'No.' I smiled and bit my lip. 'Come in.'

'Hey Cass...ee, Kaiser,' he said greeting the two couch dwellers.

'Hey *Tango*, I didn't know you two were together,' Nik said, looking surprised and glancing at both of us.

'Yeah, we are,' Tomás said. 'So I heard from Russian that you might be moving in?' He studied Nik while I studied Tomás. He was getting very territorial.

'Later this week,' Nik said.

'So, which room will be yours?' Tomás asked. I saw Cassie trying not to smile.

'Ah the main room,' Nik said, 'with the ensuite. Why, did you want to move in?'

'No.' Tomás looked to me. 'I'm just checking up on Al...iss.'

'Did you want a drink?' I asked.

'No, I have to get home for the ... thing.' He shrugged.

'Right, the thing,' I agreed. I could feel Nik and Cassie watching us.

'So will you still be in the same bedroom?' he asked me.

I frowned. 'Yes ... and Cassie and I have declared that a girl bathroom.' I pointed to the main bathroom, subtly assuring Tomás I wouldn't be naked anywhere near Nik.

'So we were just discussing where we would hang our washing and underwear,' Nik said and gave me a cheeky grin.

I felt Tomás bristle beside me.

'You're a stirrer, Nik,' Cassie laughed. She turned to Tomás whose eyes had narrowed. 'He's just being silly, ignore him.'

'So Niklas…' Tomás used Nik's full name as though Nik was in trouble. '... you won't be going anywhere near that bedroom or bathroom will you? Otherwise, I'll have to deal with you!' He teased with a hint of seriousness.

I'd never seen him like this, he was super possessively weird and I had to stop myself from giggling.

Nik stood and came over to the kitchen near us. 'Nowhere near it at all brother,' he said, assuring him.

'Good.' Tomás nodded, satisfied.

'Unless there is a scream or something and I have to investigate,' Nik clarified.

'You are a stirrer, stop it,' I said, and hit Nik on the arm, and nearly broke my hand – the man was all muscle. 'Did you want to mark your scent around my room?' I asked Tomás and I heard Cassie giggle behind me. Nik crossed his arms and grinned.

'Yes, that would be good, the way I did around your office,' Tomás said, but I wasn't sure if he was joking. He bent slightly, put one arm under my butt, and picked me up, pressing me to his chest, my face was even with his. 'Come and see me off.' He gave me a quick kiss and turned towards the door, still carrying his helmet and jacket and now me. 'Bye Cass...ee ... Kaiser.'

'Bye *Tango*, see you at training tomorrow,' Nik called.

Tomás grunted a reply – I don't think he was keen on his new nickname. We exited down the stairs but he stopped when I began kissing him over his face. I teased him with my tongue and then pulled away.

'Sorry, but you have 'a thing' to go to,' I said.

He continued down the stairs and put me down next to his motorbike.

'Now look what you've done, Al...iss.'

'What, this?' I ran my hand down the front of his jeans and across his hardness.

He moaned and threw a leg over his bike and adjusted himself.

'That's going to be a shit trip home now.' He shuffled, trying to get comfortable.

I grinned. 'Well, have a good night, but not too good.'

He put his jacket on and pulled me close again.

'Don't worry.'

I nodded. 'It's not easy.'

'I know. For anyone.'

He kissed me, slipped the helmet on, readjusted himself with a wince, and gave me a look through the visor which said *super uncomfortable*. And then he was gone to have the last night with her and I had to survive it. I felt very sad for Julieta who would never be his again after tonight.

Chapter 34

I had a fitful night, thinking of Tomás with Julieta and then the next morning before work I went to my hot yoga class since I was awake so early. When the class finished at seven-thirty, I knew she was boarding and when I left the apartment at eight-fifteen a.m. to go to work, I knew she was gone, well I desperately hoped she was gone. I debated whether to message Tomás to check he was okay or whether to leave it for him to do so. I knew he would be in some pain seeing her off – it was the end of an era, the end of a long love and even though he hadn't had much contact with her for the past year, she would be emotional.

I was the first at the office; I even beat Jim in this morning. I decided on a message for Tomás; something that didn't question his actions, or expect any reply, just a statement that affirmed I was there for him. I wasn't going to do this by text or phone, but I felt it was needed.

I messaged him: 'I love you.'

*****

Tomás replied almost immediately. I think my message might have been what he needed to hear. His response was so sweet.

TOMÁS: I love you, A. I need to hold you. Need you tonight.

Even though there was no training tonight for the team, Tomás messaged he was going to do a few weights in the afternoon with one of the players I didn't know very well yet – the midfielder Josh. He'd mentioned Josh a few times so I suspected they were buddies.

It was a home game weekend so at work, I was busy enough confirming all the usual things – the game photographer, kids' entertainment, post-game band to try and keep a few people at the ground so everyone didn't try and leave at the same time making for a huge traffic jam, kids' soccer display at half-time and the Saints' mascot – the poor sucker who wore the Saints' suit which was a Saint Bernard dog costume in the team's jersey.

I clock-watched and planned all day. Tonight, I was going to wear a dress for quick access – a pale cream dress that zipped at the back all the way down to my butt and had a flowing skirt. It had three-quarter sleeves and beneath it, I had a cream lingerie set I bought just for the occasion. The dress was demure, the lingerie wasn't – it was a lace see-through underwire bra with matching cream lace thong. God thongs are uncomfortable, seriously, would I ever get used to having something stuck between my butt cheeks? Anyway, I was happy with the selection. I didn't want to look too virginal but I didn't want to look like a tramp either... such a fine line!

Luckily Jim left early at four p.m. to go to a marketing networking meeting which meant Kay, Sasha and I could bolt from the office right on five p.m., and we did. I went home and I had ninety minutes until I was due at Tomás's place at six-thirty. I could barely breathe for the anticipation. Cassie was there when I arrived but she was heading to Rick's for the night and I was heading to Tomás's place. Nik wasn't moving in until later in the week, but if he had already, he'd have the place to himself. This threesome, so to speak, was going to work out well. I wondered what kind of girls Nik was going to bring home... I was guessing he was into girls. Mm, good thought, not that I mind having more guys around the place.

Cassie left pretty much right away and I decided to have a bath and pluck and shave every hair that needed to be removed from my body. By the time I left at six-fifteen p.m. to head to Tomás's large house, I was so clean you could eat from me – and if that was part of the plan, consider me served.

*****

Valentina's car was not there when I arrived but Tomás's bike was and his level of the house was softly lit. As I pulled up, I saw the front door open and he headed down the driveway in jeans and a soft black knit top. .He looked so sexy. Tomás arrived at my car, opening the door for me. As I stepped out of the car, he picked me up, whirled me around and put me down before kissing me. Wow, would life always be this good?

'I needed that.' He exhaled, holding me.

'And here I am to meet that need,' I teased him.

Tomás released me and after that greeting, I had to stabilize myself against the car for a moment. He opened my car's back door and grabbed my overnight bag. I grabbed tomorrow's workwear that was hanging from the back hook.

I followed him in and up the stairs. He took my items, hung them up and put my bag in the bathroom, and then he pulled me down the hallway to his bedroom. He opened the door and it was beautiful. I gasped on seeing it – softly lit by candlelight, warm and scented. He must have engaged Valentina's help or a sales' assistant because the stripes and bold designs were gone and instead the room was white – a white tulle canopy over his black iron four-poster bed, white roses and they were real, white candles, a white bed quilt, and sheets, half a dozen plush white cushions and pillows. I wanted to run and jump on the bed like a kid. I walked around the room, taking it all in and finally rested my gaze upon him.

'Tomás, it is wonderful, so romantic,' I gushed.

He smiled, delighted at my reaction, and closed the bedroom door. He held out his hand to me and I took it and then he led me to the edge of the bed, where he sat and pulled me between his legs. He looked up at me.

'Al...iss, I want to know that you are ready for me to take your virginity tonight,' he asked, looking so sincere and beautiful.

I nodded. 'I desperately want you to be inside me. I have been waiting for this day,' I assured him.

His lips twitched in a smile. He continued to rest his hands on my hips.

'I am not going to give you champagne or dine you Al... iss, until later, after we are exhausted in bed. Tonight, our lovemaking is the entree, main course, and dessert. Okay?'

I nodded and inhaled sharply in anticipation, trying to take in everything, trying to remember every moment. How many women have lost their virginity like this? I was so grateful to Tomás for making me feel like the most amazing and beautiful woman on the planet.

'If you don't like anything, you just say so,' he continued, 'but after tonight, we will keep practicing all the very many positions and other things...' he said, with a wicked grin.

I nodded again. I wasn't sure I was capable of words, but my eyes just drank him in and I felt hazy with lust for him.

He remained seated, my breasts at his eye level. Then he took off his own knit jumper first and then his white T-shirt underneath it. He sat in his jeans, his desire so obvious and his body so toned and golden. Then he reached under my dress and worked his way up my legs, sending my body into a total spin. There is no way I would be able to stand for long, no way.

Tomás removed his hands from up my skirt and reached behind me with his long, muscled arms. He unzipped my dress, peeled it off slowly and inhaled as he undressed me. I stepped out of it as he placed it over the end of the bed.

'So beautiful,' he said looking at my lingerie. And then he rose, turned me around and lowered me to the bed. I lay in the white canopy of his room with the soft flicker of the candles and watched as he undid his jeans and slipped them off. He then slipped off his white boxer-briefs and my eyes widened at the full picture. I desperately wanted to feel Tomás inside me but I also secretly feared he would tear me; I couldn't imagine how he would fit.

He lowered himself on top of me and with a look that said trust me, he began to own me. It was heaven. I had no benchmark for when you should come or how long to hang on or even if I could last. I knew my breathing was fast and a thousand thoughts were going through my head.

'Al...iss,' I heard Tomás whisper.

'Yes?'

He stopped touching me and moved up to lie beside me and look into my eyes. 'Tonight is about pleasure and fun. I love you,' he said.

I smiled and tears welled in my eyes.

'You can't do anything wrong, you just can't. And we have plenty of time to practice and explore ... that's the fun part. Okay?' he assured me.

I nodded.

'You are very unrelaxed, so take a deep breath for me,' he said. With a slightly concerned glance, and a smile to assure me this was worth the wait he gently began again.

He was masterful; I arched with pleasure and groaned which seemed to make Tomás very pleased as well. His large and very capable hands firmly held my hips and then he spoke again.

'Even though you are well lubricated, it's your first time, so you're going to be very tight. We're going to go slowly, yes?'

'Yes.' I nodded, happy to obey the teacher. 'No more teasing Tomás, I'm too wound up. Please come inside me, I want to feel what that is like.'

'Such an impatient student,' he said, smiling. He reached for a condom that was next to the bed. He tore the wrapper off the condom and slid it on. I watched, fascinated, as it covered his size.

He pulled himself over the top of me, cupping the side of my face in one hand and looking down at me. His dark eyes were so honest and beautiful and he tried to read me.

'Ready?' he asked.

'Yes, please,' I said, and he smiled and shook his head slightly at me.

Tomás reached down and navigated himself between my legs and pushed in just a bit. I felt my body brace as if it was resisting his entry. My fingers dug into his back as he pushed a little more, then pulled out and pushed a little more and pulled back again. He was right, it was intense and it hurt.

I gritted my teeth and closed my eyes as he moved a little farther each time.

'Al...iss, look at me,' Tomás said and I opened my eyes. I'm sure they were swimming, trying to focus on him. It was a fine line between pleasure and pain.

'Don't push in too fast will you?' I asked, a little panicked. I had read in books of guys that push in hard all at once, and I was scared he would tear something. The tightness was amazing.

'Shh, never, I won't do that,' he assured me, 'nice and slowly. But you need to relax a little, okay? You're anxious and it is making it harder for you.'

I nodded. 'Relax, right,' I said and breathed in and out.

'Can you feel me?'

I think my laugh was a little hysterical when I answered, 'Yes!' I made him laugh. 'I feel as though I'm joined to you. It's amazing.'

'It's good?' he asked.

'It's ... amazing,' I said again, struggling to find words. 'Like we are one. I can feel you everywhere,' I said, my nails still digging into him. 'What's it feel like for you?' I asked him.

'Amazing, I can feel you all around me.' Tomás closed his eyes for a minute and breathed slowly. He opened them a minute later and looked at me, all the time holding his weight above me in his arms. He kept going slowly, patiently, calmly.

'Last bit, ready?' he asked.

I nodded and felt him go the final gentle push and then we were one, he was completely inside me. I held my breath. Tomás was in me, completely in me. I had lost my virginity to Tomás Carrera, my gorgeous lover.

He was studying me. 'I have deflowered you, Al...iss,' he teased, giving me a sexy grin.

'Thank God it was you,' I said, and he touched my face tenderly.

'We're going to have some motion now, so let me know if it hurts too much, otherwise, enjoy the ride,' he said and started to move in and out of me with a pace that was gaining in rhythm.

His masculine body was all around me and inside me, I felt completely cocooned by him and inhaled his scent.

I moaned with the shivers it sent through my body. My hands were moving over his arms and his shoulders but it was hard to focus on what I was doing with my hands, as he moved. If he stopped now, I know I would die.

'I'm not going to last, Tomás,' I said, almost panting. I was scared to come too early but I felt I had no control. He made a strained noise as if he was only just keeping it together, and closed his eyes. I touched him lower and he grabbed my hand away as though I had done something wrong.

'I am so close, I have to get some control here,' he explained and bit his lower lip. 'You are like a vice around me Al...iss.' And then he stepped it up and I cried out with the intensity of the sudden pace and electricity running through us.

We were both so needy that I wanted it all now, immediately and as he brought me to the point of no return, I arched and came officially for the first time with a man inside me and not just any man. Tomás crushed me against him and released himself. I felt the hum in his chest and the moan on his breath. We were both panting as if it was the end of a marathon and when we had nothing left, Tomás's muscles started to relax. He didn't release me but lowered himself, turning me slightly to sidle up next to me, still inside me.

He opened his eyes and really looked at me. I knew I had tears in my eyes and I saw him frown, confused. I cleared my throat to speak.

'I'm not hurt, I'm in love,' I whispered and he smiled and breathed out a sigh of relief.

We didn't move for a short while, until eventually he

pulled out of me, turned to remove the condom and headed to his bathroom to dispose of it. I watched him in all his naked beauty walk across the room and then back to me – every muscle and sinew defined. He lowered himself to lay next to me and pulled me into the cradle of his arms.

He gently ran his fingers over me. 'Sore?'

'A little,' I confessed.

'I love you, Al...iss,' he whispered.

'I love you, Tomás. Thank you for taking my virginity.'

'Thank you for giving it to me. The pleasure was all mine.'

'No, trust me, it was mine.' I smiled.

'No *Bella*, I insist, it was all mine.'

I grinned. 'Tomás my teacher, trust me, the pleasure was...'

And he laughed and kissed me, taking the words right out of my mouth.

Chapter 35

Saturday and a game day at home... how I loved them. I loved being part of the organization, part of the game-day atmosphere, being at the game and being with Tomás. It didn't get any better. I loved it when the Saints ran on the field, especially Tomás, and I loved watching him as he managed the goalkeeper's area so masterfully. It was foreplay on a major scale. I was officially staff and a WAG so it was a strange line as some of the WAGs were a bit standoffish with the female staff and vice versa. Whatever, I had Mia with me on game days anyway and I found everyone had been really nice to me so far.

This weekend we were playing the Warriors – a team from Washington D.C. – well not me personally, the team was playing them, but I was well and truly there in spirit. We had beaten the Warriors once and lost to them once so it was a bit of a grudge game. On Saturday morning Tomás left for the club early and I went home to my place to shower and change. When I got there, Nik had gone too and headed to the ground, so Cassie and I sneaked a look at his room – he was right, he had nothing. He must have arrived with a suitcase of clothes and that's it. Good thing it was furnished thanks to Cassie's folks. We hadn't all been home one night together yet, but I was kind of looking forward to that.

I had a bit of discomfort walking for a few days after giving up the big V, as if I had been horse riding for hours and I guess I had been – riding a tall, dark, Latin stallion called Tomás, that night and the next morning. Tonight we would play again, and it would be even sweeter if the Saints could win so we could be on a game-high in the bedroom too. I couldn't believe that I looked the same the next day after losing my virginity. I know that probably sounds lame, but every mother-figure I knew from home to school made such a big deal of 'giving' it up, yet life went on the next day.

Arriving at work, I checked that all of my event contacts and charges were doing what they were supposed to do, then checked in with Jim, Kay and Sasha. Everything was under control, or so I thought until I got called to the entertainment change rooms – my Saint Bernard dog mascot was feeling unwell and she had to go home. *No!* Mascot girl gave me an apologetic look before leaving, but what do you do?

I rang the backup Saint Bernard dog costume wearer, yeah we had a few – one guy, two girls – and he was on his way, coming to the game anyway and happy to earn a few dollars. So there was just the small problem of the Saint Bernard mascot appearance in the kids' area in fifteen minutes. Well, looked as if it was me. Sasha doubled over laughing as she walked in on me putting on the suit.

'What the...?' She tossed her head back and laughed again.

'I've got a sick dog, and another is on the way,' I explained, 'and the kids are expecting the Saints' mascot to appear in fifteen minutes.'

She laughed again. 'I'll escort you, I'm not needed in the media box yet. You'll fall over your feet otherwise if you are not used to wearing it.'

Sasha was right. The Saint Bernard dog suit was super padded, probably to protect the wearer from the hugging kids and the little shits who decided to tackle the dog, and the head was so huge it took some balance to put one foot in front of the other. I positioned the head so I could see out and turned to face Sasha who still thought it was funny.

'What? Haven't you seen an event girl in a dog suit before?' I shook my dog head.

'Hell yeah,' she laughed. 'But I keep picturing you wearing it into the bedroom. Puts a whole new slant on doggy position.'

I laughed. Would Tomás find me sexy in doggy position? Hmm, I wonder if he'd like to do the mascot.

'You're sick, Sasha,' I told her and poked her with my large dog costume hand. 'Come on, clean it up, I've got kids to pat on the head.'

She led me to the kids' play area and they all cheered and ran towards me. Good grief, it's scary seeing about two dozen kids running towards you. I almost toppled over but luckily most of them were hugging not tackling me over. Of course there's always one kid who is obnoxious and today was no exception. I kicked the soccer ball as best as I could coordinate my foot and the costume and danced around like an idiot, whatever. I only had to last fifteen minutes and then it was job done.

'I'll be back for you in five minutes,' Sasha said, 'just got to take this call – try to stay upright.' I saw her move to the playground boundary and I tried to balance in the suit. I neared the swings just in time to overhear several women talking as they watched their kids play. I wasn't sure if they were WAGS or members or groupies, I couldn't turn around far enough in the suit to see and the dog head had no peripheral vision of course – damn it. But on hearing Tomás's name mentioned, my dog ears instantly tuned in.

'Wasn't he gorgeous doing that tango?' said Voice-1.

'Oh my yes, I almost had to finish the job under the table myself,' Voice-2 said, obviously trying to be discreet with kids around. I knew what she meant even though it was hard to hear them all talking about and lusting over my Tomás. Their voices mixed in together but I think there were at least four women there.

'I caught up with Valentina at the lunch,' one of them continued, 'and she said he had broken up with his girlfriend from home and she was heading back there alone.'

'She's gone, went on Wednesday. I can't believe she waited a year to come over anyway. Did she think he was going to be loyal?'

'Can't blame him for wanting some breathing space though. A new club, new pressures, that sort of thing.'

'I heard he's in love with a girl from the office.'

I wanted to pull my costume head off and yell, 'He is and I'm in love with him, life is so good' but I didn't want to give the kids a shock and send them all into therapy.

'Lucky her,' one of the women said. 'Well it will be interesting; he's been on the scene for a while, what will his fangirls do?'

Another laughed. 'I guess they'll move onto Russian. Leesa's gone you know.'

'What was that about?' I recognized Voice-1 asking the question and I moved away. I danced with a few kids, chased one away that kicked me in the shins, the little shit, and waved to the kids as I made it to the exit. Sasha grabbed my furry costumed arm at the gate. We headed to the dressing room, continuing to wave and pose for photos all the way back.

I couldn't believe I'd caught that snatch of conversation. We went inside, I pulled the head off and breathed – it was so hot in there. My hair was now a mess but at least it had volume. I thanked Sasha and we parted; she headed for the media box and I headed up to sit with Mia. The game was about to begin and I was the girl from the office that Tomás was in love with. I'm sure it was impossible to be any happier.

Chapter 36

It had been a great game and the Saints continued their winning streak. For the first time, we were all home together – Cassie, Nik, and me – plus Tomás. He stretched his long legs out in front of him on the L-shaped couch.

'I am so stiff,' he moaned.

'For God's sake *Tango*, keep your erection updates to yourself,' Nik ragged him.

Tomás gave him a wry look.

'I could rub you if you like?' I offered and Tomás brightened. This time Nik groaned.

'Well that's hardly fair is it?' big, tall, German Nik complained. 'Lucas has a live-in PT, you have a girlfriend who is prepared to give you post-game rubs, what do I have?'

'Well, pizzas on the way,' Cassie said, appearing from the kitchen with a bowl of pretzels and some more beers. 'Shove over.'

She pushed between Nik and me and took up the consoles on the couch. 'Come on Nik, show me what you are made of,' she challenged him and he grabbed for the console nearest him to start the game.

'You should know better than to challenge a game warrior at his own game,' Nik growled at her. 'Be afraid, be very afraid.'

'C'mon Cookie, show me your technique,' Tomás said, and ran a hand down my back, making me shiver.

'Lie back,' I said, directing him on the 'L' side of the couch that was empty. I was surprised neither of the guys wanted to go out to celebrate our fantastic win and their great individual performances but they seemed happy to stay in and hang out with a few drinks and pizza.

Tomás moved and stretched out, propping a cushion behind his head. The action game started opposite us with Nik and Cassie glued to the screen.

'It would be easier with your track pants off,' I said.

'Leave them on,' Nik demanded. 'If this gets too hot, you two are taking it to the bedroom.'

'You're sounding a little frustrated there Niklas,' Tomás tormented him.

'Shut up.'

'Mm, that's good Al...iss, so good,' Tomás groaned with exaggeration as I sat on his butt and started on his shoulders.

'That's it,' Nik groaned, 'I'm going to call a friend.'

'Is she a good German girl?' Tomás teased. 'Is her name Gertrud, Hildegard, Lieselotte?'

'I have two words for you *Tango*, World Cup,' Nik said and smirked.

'You may have won it last time, but remember South

America has won it more than Germany,' Tomás retorted. 'Ah that's so good, Al…is, so good.'

I turned around and began working on his legs and those thigh muscles, sigh, such a tough job but I was just the girl for it.

There was a knock on the door and no-one wanted to move to get it.

'Might be pizza,' Cassie said.

'Or Lucas and Mia,' I suggested.

'Come in,' Nik yelled out and the door opened. Lucas and Mia bounded in.

'For the love of God, you're doing that in public now?' Lucas grimaced, seeing me sitting on Tomás. I turned to give them both the look that said *you can talk.*

'Oh, you're both fully dressed, that's fine then,' Lucas said, coming around the end of the couch.

'Hello Mia and Luke,' Tomás said, in a voice that was groggy with relaxation and who knows what else.

After greetings, Mia dropped down next to Cassie while Lucas stuck their drinks in the fridge and grabbed a fresh round for everyone. I couldn't help but think as I looked at Cassie and Mia how strange it was that we had been friends for years at school and college and here we were with three hot Saints players and hanging together. I sighed with contentment.

'Where's Rick?' Mia asked Cassie.

Cassie cheered as she eliminated Nik in the game, and then turned to Mia. 'Get real, I like Rick, I'm not bringing him over here and scaring him off.'

'Well thanks for that,' Nik said.

She laughed. They enjoyed taunting each other.

'Call him, he should be here,' Tomás said. 'I wouldn't leave you by yourself with a single man like Kaiser in the apartment.'

'We know.' Nik shut him down. 'You've already pissed out your territory all over Alice's room. We get it.'

Tomás grinned.

'Want to turn over?' I asked him.

'Ah, probably not,' he said, keeping his eyes closed.

'Wasn't that any good?' I asked, shaking out my sore hands. I knew sports massage was a skill that I didn't have but I had a fair shot at it – okay, I enjoyed it as much as Tomás but every job has a silver lining.

'It's extremely hard for him to turn over at the moment, Alice,' Nik joked emphasizing the word, *hard*.

'Eww,' Cassie said and hit Nik. 'We all know that you don't have to voice it.'

'Well clearly Alice didn't know,' Nik said, looking at me.

'Oh,' I said getting it and feeling rather pleased.

'You are so sweet and naive, Al...iss,' Tomás said, smiling.

'I'm not naive, I just thought you were talking technique. It's hard to get it right.'

'It's hard, that's for sure,' Tomás said.

Cassie covered her ears. 'Okay, you two – Nik, Tomás – stop talking. Where's the pizza?'

'Call Rick.' Lucas nudged Cassie. 'We want to meet him.'

'Fine, but be nice to him you guys,' she said and rose to get her phone.

'Ask him to bring more beer,' Nik added.

'And a beer wench for the Kaiser,' Tomás added.

Cassie looked at me and rolled her eyes as she dialed the number. 'And you wonder why I don't ask him over.'

I rose to get off Tomás's butt where I had been perched for his back massage and as soon as I was off, he jumped up and picked me up, lifting me under my butt and pressing me against his chest, attempting to hide the bulge in his pants. I wrapped my legs around him and hung on.

'Got to show you something, Al...iss,' he said, and he strode with me towards my bedroom.

'Did it come from Buenos Aires?' I teased him.

'It's about to,' he said.

I heard Lucas laughing and Mia groaned. I really wanted to see what he had to show me.

Tomás flicked the door closed with his foot and rushed me to the bed. I reached over and turned on my stereo even though there was music playing in the living area, but just to mask any unexpected noises. While he pulled my jeans down I helped pull his clothes off – I know, I am so helpful. I opened my bedside drawer and pulled out a condom. 'I bought these anticipating you might use them.'

'Very thoughtful of you, gorgeous,' he said, taking it from me, opening the wrapper, and slipping it on as I watched with fascination.

Tomás was such an unselfish lover but tonight I just wanted to meet his needs. It would help relax him too after the highs of the day. He didn't need any encouragement and eased into me slowly, giving me time to adjust to him. I heard him exhale as he controlled himself to enter slowly; I suspect he wanted it fast and hard.

He rocked back and forward, his rock-hard stomach

hitting against me and the feeling that he was so deep inside me. His action seemed desperate for relief, more than he had been before – must be a post-game high.

'You feel so good my Al...iss, so good,' he hissed as one of his hands moved to my hip. His pace began to increase, steadily pushing into me, faster and faster he rode me. My body ached with pleasure and pain, tightness and tingles. He moved both hands onto my hips trying to keep me steady but he hit some sweet spot that made me arch with pleasure. I tried to muffle my cries; I didn't want anyone hearing my lovemaking to Tomás.

And soon Tomás came in a surge of power and energy, his powerful arms gripping me tightly. He made a noise that sounded half guttural and raw and I drank in his power and his recovery. But he didn't release me.

'We're not leaving this room until you come too,' he said in my ear.

I went to protest but he gently smacked my butt cheek which he still had good access to.

'Don't defy the teacher, Al...iss,' he said, pressing me hard against him and speaking close to my ear. He was still inside me as he stayed pressed to my body.

Then his hands worked their way around my body making me feel giddy. Thank God I was leaning against him, otherwise, I would have collapsed in an orgasmic heap.

And then he added a hint of pressure – building the pace, circling, faster. I came within seconds, gasping, trying to shut down my desire to scream his name.

He gripped my body and leaned forward, lowering us both on the bed. We lay naked, wrapped in each other.

'That was a good position,' I said, a little post-orgasmic drunk.

'So many to try... we may have to increase your homework,' Tomás teased.

I smiled with delight. Moments later a loud knock on the door had me reaching for the sheet but Tomás covered me.

'Pizza's here,' Cassie called without opening the door.

'Thanks,' I called back in a husky voice... my speech hadn't fully returned yet.

'Now Al...iss, try and keep your hands off me long enough to feed me; a man has to eat,' Tomás said. 'I need to keep my strength up.'

'Somehow, I don't think keeping it up is going to be a problem,' I teased him.

Five minutes later Lucas knocked on the door but didn't open it either; thank goodness everyone was well trained. 'Pizza is good,' he said, 'come on you two, surface for air or we'll all come in there and have a picnic with you.'

'They wouldn't, would they?' I asked.

We jumped up and pulled some clothes on. Tomás groaned as he dressed, his post-game injuries tender and his body stiffening on him.

'Are you okay?' I asked, stopping to watch him. 'Does the doctor or PT check you guys out before you go home?'

'It's just normal post-game,' he said and covered himself quickly.

'I'm sorry if my massage was too rough,' I said, having not realized he was sporting so many bumps and bruises.

He stopped and smiled at me. 'It was perfect. You have tender hands and a tender heart, Cookie.'

'I'm invested in that body,' I said and bit my lip as I ran my eyes over him. He was the most beautiful man I had ever seen or been with.

'Are you undressing me?' He faked a shocked look.

I giggled like a schoolgirl.

'We're not leaving this room if you keep that up,' Tomás warned me.

Nik called from right outside our door. 'Mm, pizza is so good there won't be any left soon.'

'Right, focus,' I said, 'you need to eat.' I caught myself in the mirror, I looked like a ruffled mess. At times like this, I wished I had the ensuite so I didn't have to go out in front of everyone to get to the bathroom.

'Leave it, I love that you look like you've just had sex.' Tomás ruffled up my hair again.

Lucas yelled from the living room. '*Tango*, can you teach Mia and me to do the tango?'

Tomás rolled his eyes and took my hand. He opened my bedroom door and we wandered into the kitchen where everyone was eating pizza.

'There's no meat on this pizza,' Lucas complained, opening one of the boxes.

'Because it's on all the other pizzas,' Mia said and steered him towards another box.

'So are you going to teach us all the tango, *Tango*?' Nik asked.

'No, fuck off, Kaiser,' Tomás said. He waved a diet cola at me and I nodded; he knew me so well already. He grabbed himself another beer.

'If you learned to dance, you might have a better chance of pulling a girl,' Lucas said to Nik.

'I do all right,' Nik said, defensively. 'Besides, I've met someone, she gave me an electric shock.' He glanced at me and I smiled, knowingly. How I would love Nik and Sasha to get together. I looked over at Tomás as he sparred with the boys. He took a long sip of his beer and I watched as he swallowed, followed the fluid as it made its way down the inside of his chest, traced his muscles and down to those sexy hips with his tempting... then I realized Tomás was watching me with his tongue in his cheek. Around us, our friends were bantering but we were locked in a gaze.

He smiled and took my breath away, again. He tipped his head slightly indicating I should follow him and for just a moment we slipped away. He took my hand and we exited to the cool of the balcony – it felt good after the heated passion of the bedroom.

'It's been a big week Al…iss,' he said and pulled me closer.

'And we're together now,' I said.

He gave me a slow kiss that tasted a little like beer and a lot like Tomás. 'Thank you,' he said as he pulled away.

'What for?' I asked.

'For waiting, for looking after me, for believing me, for not wanting anything from me, but me,' he said, sincerity and love shining in his deep brown eyes.

'You are more than enough,' I teased him, and narrowed my eyes, 'maybe too much sometimes.'

He smiled and shook his head at me.

'Thank you, Tomás, for not letting me go,' I said, meaning every word.

'I couldn't shake you… then I didn't want to lose you. Al…iss, I have to tell you something,' he started, and suddenly got very serious.

I frowned. I don't know if I really wanted anything but happy news now.

'I never did it… with her.'

I breathed in sharply. I hadn't asked this of him but the words were everything I wanted to hear.

'Tomás,' I whispered his name as I moved to hug him tight. I couldn't manage any other words.

'Tell me Al…iss,' he lowered his voice, 'when you look back, will you remember losing your virginity and how you lost it?'

I pulled away to look into his eyes. 'I'll remember, until my dying breath,' I promised him.

*****

THANK YOU for reading *Team Tomás*. I hope you loved Alice and the very sexy Tomás. Will they make it? Alex (the Russian) gives a hint in his story. Do you want to find out more about sassy Sasha and gorgeous Niklas? Then grab *Team Niklas* now on Amazon or Apple Books, and be prepared to fall in love.

Read on for a sneak peek… I hope you enjoy meeting more of the Saints' family.

Next in the Saints' series:

Read on and enjoy the first chapter of *Team Niklas...*

Team Niklas

Chapter 1

'Stop moving or I'll accidentally put it in the wrong place,' I ordered Nik. You would think a guy who had done military conscription at home in Berlin and stood at attention for long periods of time in all sorts of weather, could stand still for a few minutes.

'Sah-sha, is it even possible to put it in the wrong place?' he asked, with a raised eyebrow.

I couldn't help but smile – the way he said my name with his German accent always caught my attention; it started like sarsaparilla and finished like a dance.

Niklas Wagner, star midfielder for the national soccer team the Santa Ana Saints, had come to me for a suit adjustment – yep by day I was the media officer for the Saints, and by night I designed; it was my hobby-cum-passion. Nik was standing in front of me wearing only the black suit pants and the jacket, no shirt – I could see all those well-developed abdominal muscles just waiting to be touched and I wouldn't mind tracing those grooves with my tongue either, up and down, tight and tense.

Is it getting hot in here? Then I accidentally did what I had been threatening, jabbed him with a pin.

'Ouch,' he yelped and stepped back.

'See? What did I tell you? Stand at attention,' I barked.

He stiffened and stood straight… for about five seconds.

'I like the gym gear you're wearing, Sah-sha, did you make that?' he asked looking down on my fitted black gym pants and matching tank top. It was easier to do fittings in fitted gym gear, easier to get around the fabric and the client, if that makes sense.

I shook my head. 'I don't make gym gear yet. But I am going to do a gym workout when you leave,' I said, with a glance to my home gym in the corner of the room.

'We should work out together,' he said.

I laughed. 'Stand still and stop looking down; it makes the pants longer.'

'What? Why is the idea of working out together funny?' he asked, frowning.

'It's funny because I would lift a thimble compared to you and you'd give me a hard time.'

'Never,' he said. 'I respect any workout; I'd love to see you in action Sah-sha. We could put some music on, work up a sweat, you know? Okay, I have to stop thinking about that now,' he said and wiped a hand over his mouth.

Oh yes, he did indeed need to stop thinking about it. The bulge in his pants would change the line of them and the amount I had to take up.

'Should I readjust the measurements or assume when you

wear these pants, you won't be, um, quite as stiff?' I asked looking up from the floor at him, trying to get a reaction.

He grinned. 'It depends. Will you be coming to the Best and Fairest Awards with me?'

'I'll be there, working that night,' I said. 'So I'll leave the measurements as they are. Okay, you're done, get it off.'

He grinned again. I swear everything I said had a sexual connotation to this guy. He extended his hand like a gentleman and helped me off the floor. Phew, that was a rush, coming up past his bulge, then past the muscles in his bare chest and standing full height with my hand feeling so small in his. I think I just orgasmed. I looked away quickly.

'Thanks, you can let my hand go now,' I said, he did so slowly, running his fingers up my palm. Holy fuck.

I guess we had been flirting – if you could call it that – for a few weeks now and Nik was trying to get me to go out with him this weekend on our first official date. Tonight, however, the suit adjustment was business only. Maybe and it was a big maybe, on Friday night Niklas Wagner could take me out for dinner. Apart from deciding if I wanted to go out, I was considering whether to have sex with him before then and whether to order an entrée or save room for dessert. All tough decisions.

'C'mon Sarsh, aren't you going to help me take it off?' he said.

'So we're on nickname terms now?' I said and narrowed my eyes at him. 'Sasha, Sash-a,' I said, rolling it off my tongue. 'C'mon, practice.'

'Sarsh like sarsey?' he said.

'Never mind,' I said. 'You know the way to the change room.'

He looked a little dejected as I pointed him towards the guest room which I had set up for clients. It included hanging racks, mirrors, a sofa and a small en-suite bathroom.

'Look even Prada thinks you should help me,' he said, with a glance at my black Bombay cat who had moved closer to us and now sat watching Nik warily.

I smiled at Prada, such a handsome puss. 'Trust me, he's not giving you that look because he is on your side,' I warned Nik, 'he's deciding whether to jump on your head or not. He's not very social.'

'Oh,' Nik said and moved a step farther away from where Prada was perched near the window. 'This is a great place. Is that your bedroom up there?' His eyes looked at my lofty room.

'Yes, that's where I sleep and entertain my lovers,' I teased him and he laughed. 'Now get changed.' Even though he towered over me, I tried giving him a direct order and pointed to the guest room. Call it girl power... maybe not, he was still standing there frowning at me. Man, this guy was persistent; he was trying every trick in the How to Trap a Girl To Take Her on an Official Date book. I studied him. He was the biggest potential 'boyfriend' on my scene for some time, maybe because I had removed myself from the scene some time ago. And when I say big, I'm not just talking height from the sneak preview I'd had – you can get very close to the anatomy when you're pinning a client.

It would be very easy to fall for Niklas Wagner. He looked as though he was still in the military with his short blond back and sides, but the top was long enough to run my hands through. My hair was almost the same color, only messier – since I had decided to grow it again I hadn't bothered cutting it, so it was a mess of long lengths. Nik's haircut, along with his tan, set off his bright blue eyes and even though he was fluent in English, his German accent still made for a direct manner of speech. We were suited there too – I was always in trouble for being too direct. That's where the similarities ended – I was five-foot-eight to his six-foot-plus, and I was pale to his tan.

'What if I accidentally get stabbed by a pin when I take it off?' he asked, his lips curling in a smile. 'It could penetrate an artery and put me out of play. The coach would be very upset with you Sah-sha.' He put his hands in the pockets of his suit pants and rocked back on his heels. Sexy as all fuck.

'Niklas.' I tried not to smile, which didn't work, while I crossed my arms across my chest. That only served to bring his eyes to my chest. 'You managed to put that suit on all by yourself, taking it off is pretty much the same only in reverse. You can do it; I have full faith in you. Should I do a Saints' war cry for motivation?'

He looked vaguely interested in the idea, but that look changed to a different expression – one that said he wasn't quite beaten yet. His jaw locked with frustration as he planned his next move – I suspect he was a man used to getting his way with the women and trust me, since his arrival there was no shortage of women throwing themselves at him at the club and wherever the team socialized, from what I heard. I wouldn't know; being a groupie wasn't my thing.

He slipped the jacket off in front of me and strode off to the bedroom. I breathed out. I had won that round and enjoyed the spectacle of his muscles departing the room. Moments later he started up again.

'Sah-sha,' he called out from the guest room, 'I need your help.'

I shook my head. Men. I'll give him help in a moment. Ha, I sounded like my mother then.

'Coming,' I said. Yeah, he'd make something of that too I bet. I'd love to come by the hand or tongue of Nik; again with the sex thoughts. I really was too frustrated for my own good, but it was impossibly hard not to think about sex when you have a perfect specimen of manhood in your guest room.

I stalled him while I packed my sewing kit. I was just a little bit impressed that Nik wanted to get his suit adjusted because he had lost weight and didn't want to buy a new suit for a club award night. I liked the fact that he was on a contract worth more than this week's lottery draw, but he still wanted to get a suit adjusted rather than buy a new one, I hated waste too. When he mentioned he needed to find someone to do the adjustments, his housemate Alice – who happens to work with me at the Saints – told him I sew, wasn't that handy? Since they began flatting together, Alice had become the unofficial source of all Nik gossip, telling me all his movements even when I didn't want to know.

I had met Nik at the office of course before I played with his inside leg – a dressmaking term. You can't be a media officer for the Santa Ana Saints soccer team and not know the players or at least talk to them by telephone to organize media interviews. He had only joined the club late last year, but we had spoken on the phone heaps of times when I was setting up pre-publicity for his arrival – Germany's hottest recruit signed to the Saints, the Berlin wonder boy or 'wunderkind' if you translate it. Everyone wanted a piece of the 'Kaiser' and he was very obliging, doing all my telephone interview requests and there were heaps of them. His management team was really helpful with photos too, and as soon as he got off the plane, Shayne the Saints' football manager had Nik in the Saints' jersey and getting photos done before the poor guy even had time to unpack.

Nik cost the club a fortune, so I know he had a shitload of pressure on him to perform on-and-off the field for the club. Guys like Nik, the team's captain Lucas, goalkeeper Tomás and our forward The Russian had the pulling power to bring in memberships and ticket sales and to make the club big. Nik was definitely big. I wondered if he left someone behind in Berlin.

We finally met in the flesh for the first time when he came in to see Alice about a housemate position. He gave me an electric shock, way to make a first impression! Alice said it was an omen that we were suited and that we would always have a spark between us. Sounded like crap to me, but whatever, if it makes her happy to dream up this shit.

'Sah-sha? Are you coming in here?' Nik called again.

'Any minute now,' I answered, 'just cleaning up.'

'Can you make it quick?' he yelled back.

'Sure,' I said, slowing down. Man must think I'm an idiot. This reminded me of the next time I saw Nik in the flesh when I came off looking like the idiot… it was at a home game a few weekends back. Unfortunately, that didn't go well either. My job on game days is looking after the media and one of the journos from the daily paper wanted to talk with Nik before the game. Sometimes the coach allowed that. I chased down Shayne the football manager, who said Nik was getting iced and strapped so just go in and ask him. Unfortunately his groin was getting strapped when I walked in, so that's more evidence of how I know he's big all over. Yep, a fine import from Germany. Now on our third encounter, I'd stuck a pin in him, no wonder he was completely taken with me, what man could resist? Makes you wonder why he persisted; that guy must love a challenge.

'Sah-sha, seriously I need your help,' he called again, his voice a bit muffled this time. What the fuck, has he got caught in his zip or something? I smiled at his persistence, I love a man on a mission, and I headed to the guest room. Nik sat on the end of the sofa, the suit completely off and he was wearing a very nice pair of black fitted boxers. Blood poured from his nose and he cupped his face with one hand and used the other to keep himself upright on the bed. His tanned face had turned pale and his eyes were a little hazy.

'Holy fuck,' I said and ran to the adjoining bathroom. Thank God my towels were navy in color. So not important right now but later, I'd be pleased. I ran back to his side, spread one across his lap covering his prize bounty and gave him one to hold against his nose.

'Sit up straight and tip your head forward,' I said, and when he had done this, I pinched the soft part of his nose with my thumb and forefinger. I knew that first aid course

Aunty Sandra gave me for my birthday would come in handy – I love practical gifts.

'It's okay, I've got it,' he said with a muffled voice.

'Take over the pinch; I'll get an ice pack,' I said, removing my hand. I glanced into his eyes and they were not focusing on me.

To be continued...

Ally Adams is a journalist who lives in coastal Victoria, Australia, with her husband and furry friends. She is a literature major, romance reader and writer. Connect at:

Facebook: https://www.facebook.com/allyadamswriter
Website: https://www.allyadamsbooks.com/
Love letters: https://www.allyadamsbooks.com/loveletters/ (newsletter)

Acknowledgments

Special thanks to: the publishing team at Atlas Productions; Wild Hearts Creative; the wonderful Becky Strahl from InkEaters blog spot for all your support; to Julie from AToMR Promotions; Karen from Sparkle Book Tours; Kellie Sheridan from Patchwork Press Co-op; Goodreads for connecting writers and readers and those addicted to both; J'aimee Brooker from AusRomToday; Carole from The Romance Reviews; Debbie, Heather and team from ARRA (Australian Romance Readers' Association); and all the bloggers and readers who have supported me, Lucas and Mia, Tomás and Alice – thank you!

www.ingramcontent.com/pod-product-compliance
Lightning Source LLC
Chambersburg PA
CBHW031220120726
47905CB00002B/414